Count the Mountains

Count the Mountains

PAMELA LINDHOLM-LEVY

Aspen Eyes Press

Aspen Eyes Press, Portland

© 2015 by Pamela Lindholm-Levy

Editing and design by Indigo Editing & Publications

ISBN 978-0-692-56752-4

This story is dedicated to all those who have fought tuberculosis in their clinics and laboratories, especially my colleagues at National Jewish in Denver, as well as to all those patients who conquered tuberculosis and to the memory of all those who did not.

Denver

1

Denver moved in mud—over the ankles and up to the fetlocks. It threatened the sidewalk where Linnie Ann Adams waited with her skirt lifted to cross Fourteenth Street. On the other side, teamsters loading a flatbed wagon slowed their work to ogle a bit of forbidden leg, and if the sun had been lower in the sky, it would have silhouetted the rest. Linnie Ann wore no petticoat, only a shimmy, stays, and abbreviated pantalets under a thinning cotton dress. The missing undergarments had been torn into handkerchief-sized squares into which Peter Adams, her father, spat increasingly bloody and caseous phlegm. Linnie Ann was not squeamish, but she had a sense that these excretions should be burned rather than soaked off and the fabric rewashed.

Bodily fluids, insults, assaults, infection, effluents, and excreta did not bother her. Teaching school had exposed her to all of them and left her undisturbed, but this breakdown of consumptive lungs was different—and painful. Thus she was on her errand today, before the lovely, fluffy clouds in the west blew in another afternoon of thunder, lightning, and massive columns of rain. Only last week Cherry Creek had flooded; its dregs were on the street in front of her now.

She was so intent on her task that she did not realize what diversion she was providing as she waited for a path between the splat and splash of large hoofs, the slub-slubbing of mud from wagon wheels, and the spray from the dash of a careless rider. Finally, she found leeway and slogged through the manured slurry. The teamsters—one holding a box, another hoisting a chair onto

3

the wagon, a third and fourth leaning on a piano and not working at all—greeted her with whistles and invitations to come closer. She barely heard them over the butterflies in her stomach beating their wings in time with her heart. The object of her apprehension was just a few more steps away: a never-yet-visited drug store where she would casually walk in, casually ask for laudanum, pay with her closely watched money, and stroll casually out of the store, stopping first to smell some beautifully wrapped soaps as if she were trying to choose between the lavender tied with a thin purple cord and the rose wrapped in a doily and pink paper, as if she did it every day. That was the fear. If she did it every day, or too often at the same store, she would arouse suspicion. The druggist might suggest she see a doctor first, but there was no money for a doctor. There was hardly enough money for food and the firewood to cook it, and for laudanum. Opiates were easily bought in patent medicines, but she wanted good, pure laudanum, not some concoction made in a traveling medicine-show tent.

Peter had caught gold fever in Illinois, but he had not caught the confidence man who promised to meet him and Linnie Ann in Denver and take them to Central City, where the mine Peter had bought stock in was purportedly making millions. A month after their arrival in Denver, Peter, who had always had a delicate chest, began tiring and coughing. The boarding house owner asked them to leave. They bought a tent and supplies to live—no, rather to exist—in the temporary town across Cherry Creek. Peter's symptoms worsened. He promised Linnie Ann that his health would improve, as it always had, and that he had an even greater opportunity for recovery here in the high, dry, sunny altitude of Denver. That was what more and more arriving "lungers" hoped. He said he would find work or Linnie Ann might find a teaching job, and eventually they would go back to Illinois. They could have asked relatives to send money, but Peter said no. He could not admit to them he had been swindled. He did not want the relatives to sell the belongings stored in a cousin's attic, items that were to have been sent once she and Peter were settled: Barbara Adams's wedding china, family albums, a piano, books, quilts, and pillows.

Linnie Ann approached the shop door, squared her shoulders, and walked in. There was no one behind the counter, and there were no other shoppers. She relaxed a bit and enjoyed the familiarity of the smells, the bank of small beckoning drawers holding treasures of herbs and envelopes of crystals and chemicals. These were the kinds of things Uncle Asa let her bring to him when she was a girl and wanted to help in his store. She never told anyone that she had dreamed of being a druggist when she grew up, but she could not become a druggist, and so she became a teacher. She ran her fingers over the tall jars on the counter, then bent down to look at bottles in a glass case. When she stood up again, the druggist was watching her. The surprise unnerved her. In spite of her intention to be cool, her voice quavered when she asked for the laudanum.

"Is it for you?" he asked.

"No," she replied with what she hoped was a confident smile. She tried not to glance away from his gaze, which was not disapproving or questioning but simply interested.

He stepped from behind the counter and came toward her. He was not like Uncle Asa. He was closer to her own age. "Come over to the window. Hold still." He put his hands on either side of her head. She pulled away from this stranger's touch. Grown-ups didn't touch—unless, of course, they were courting, or they were your parents, and sometimes not even then.

"Please," he said, "just let me look a minute." He smiled, and she relaxed. He held her head again and examined her eyes: first the right, then the left. She and he were so nearly the same height, it was impossible to look anywhere but back into his eyes, which were a polished breccia of light brown with greenish inclusions. They were beautiful.

"OK," he said and took his hands away.

A voice came from the back of the store. "Your stuff's ready, Doc. Do you want to pack it, or..." Out strode a white-coated man. He chuckled. "Making a sale for me?"

"Probably," the doctor said. He took a step back and asked, "Who is it for, miss?"

"My father. I can't afford a doctor, but I don't want to buy just any old thing from the shelf."

"No problem. Doc here is bored," the druggist said. "You can be his project for the day."

"Go back to your bottles, Arthur," the doctor suggested. He turned to Linnie Ann again. "How did you know about laudanum? Tell me, please. No charge."

No one else had been sympathetic. In the boarding house and even more so in the camp, everyone had kept their distance in this knocked-together town that was only sixteen years old to her own twenty-four. In the face of Peter's having been duped by the mine promoter, she was suspicious of everyone. The doctor's manner softened her reserve just a bit, and she confided, "Consumption. His cough is very bad. He's changed so much just in the past several weeks. He asked me to get the laudanum. We both used to help my uncle in the drug store. He taught me how to fix just the right amount."

"Turn around." He was touching her again. She stiffened, but she nevertheless permitted his hands to stay on her shoulders. "Big deep breaths, now." He tapped her rib cage on both sides from top to bottom. "Good," he said when he was finished and turned her to face him. "No disrespect, miss, but let me…" Quickly he tapped somewhere between her shoulders and her breasts. "Most times it's right up here. I don't hear anything."

"I feel fine," she said.

"No fevers, no night sweats, no coughing?"

"No."

"And are you the only one taking care of him?"

"Yes."

"And you have this apprehension every time you need more medicine?"

She gave a deep sigh.

"Let's fix that," he said and walked to the counter.

The druggist, having witnessed the conversation, narrowed his eyes. "They always have a story," he hissed, "especially the pretty ones." "Cynic," the doctor whispered back. "Make this for her." He took a form from the counter. "I'm going to make it legal for you to buy more. You shouldn't have to go through this every time. What's the name?"

"Linn—oh. No. Peter Adams. Look, I really can't pay you."

"Where do you live?"

Linn had never heard of needing this detail before, but she thought perhaps some druggists were more scrupulous when selling narcotics. "Well, we don't really have an address. We had to move out of the boarding house when Dad got worse. We live in one of the tents across Cherry Creek."

The doctor shook his head and continued writing. He handed the paper to her.

"Dr. Blythe Walcott," she read.

"Yes, indeed," he replied.

"You've been so kind." She reached out and touched his arm. She had never done that to a stranger in her life. "Thank you so much."

"Glad to help," he said, raising his eyes from the place her hand had momentarily rested. "This place is my home away from home for a few more days. If you need anything, come back."

The druggist handed her the precious bottle, and she paid for it. She put the written order in her bag and patted it. "Thank you again, Dr. Walcott."

"You're welcome, Miss Adams," he said and watched her out the door.

Two mornings later, as she was putting the bedding out to sun, Linn saw someone wearing a wide-brimmed leather hat coming off the bridge across Cherry Creek. Too late she realized it was the doctor, Walcott. He had seen her before she could duck into the tent. She was mortified, even though she had admitted to him she lived here. She didn't want him to see the meanness of her situation: two

7

cots, Peter lying on one; a wooden chair; a couple of cooking pots and utensils; a few dishes; a water jug; a chamber pot. She had sold their luggage to someone moving on, and so their few remaining clothes were folded on the end of her cot. She used her winter coat as an extra blanket. She put the tent flaps down to conceal it all and watched him approach. She hated being thought of as a charity case. She wanted to tell him everything was fine and please don't waste your time. But everything was not fine, and that got the better of her pride. Perhaps if this doctor were just to take a look at Peter, perhaps he could reassure her that Peter had had a temporary relapse. Or perhaps he would tell her what she did not want to hear.

"How is your patient today?" Dr. Walcott asked.

"About the same," she answered.

"Do you keep him shut up like that all the time?" Walcott glanced at the tent.

"No. He used to sit outside, but now he doesn't walk, and I can't lift him." She felt she had to open the tent flaps now. Peter Adams lay motionless with his eyes closed. He was covered with a blanket. Another, folded small under a pillow, propped him up. Walcott's expression did not change, but he chewed barely perceptibly on his inner cheek. He walked into the tent, pulled Linn's cot closer to Peter, and sat down.

"Hello, Mr. Adams," he began. "I'm Dr. Blythe Walcott. I came to have a look at you. Your daughter tells me you haven't been up lately."

Adams did not respond.

"A bit chesty, she says."

There was still no reaction.

"I've got one of these newfangled things called a stethoscope. It lets me hear your breathing sounds. Maybe we can find out what's going on. If it's all right, I'll just fold back the bedclothes a little."

Adams mumbled, opened his eyes, and closed them again.

"So," Walcott told Adams, "I put one of these pieces in each ear and put this disc on your chest." He moved the disc up, down, and around on Peter's chest. "I can hear your heartbeat and your breath sounds."

Just then a rumble started in Peter's chest and became a rising cough, then an explosive one. At the first sound, Linn rushed to her cot, nearly pushed Walcott over, and in a split second had a square of newspaper over her father's mouth.

"Spit, Dad," she demanded. He did it listlessly. Linn took the soiled paper to the little fire outside the tent.

"I'm so sorry," she apologized to Walcott when she returned. "I couldn't help crashing into you."

"It's quite all right," he replied. "I should have acted more quickly myself. I'm interested in your newspaper handkerchiefs."

Linn reddened.

He was quick to say, "I wasn't making fun of you. You're quite inventive." He tried to look directly into her eyes, but she was biting her lip and looking beyond him to a place with a roof and a kitchen and a bedroom and real cloth handkerchiefs. She didn't stay there long. She was not a dreamer nor one for regrets, but she would have liked to be back home with two feet on the solid ground of Illinois rather than be walking a tightrope a mile high.

"Let's go outside," Walcott said. He bent down to Peter first, saying, "How's that laudanum treating you? Are you comfortable?" But Adams was still drifting. "I'm going to talk to Miss Adams now. I'll be back soon."

Linn and Walcott stood outside the tent, and Walcott brought out the stethoscope again. "I want to listen to you too. Auscultation isn't ideal. Big, deep breaths again." He started on her back. Linn saw a few of the tent people staring.

"Raise your arms," Walcott said. They stared even harder as he moved the stethoscope up her sides nearly into her armpits, then around front and dangerously close to her breasts. "Can't get more normal than that," he said when he had finished.

"I told you."

"You two have been sleeping in this tent together for how long?"

"Since April. Well, that's when we arrived in Denver. We had a room at first, but we had to leave when Dad started getting worse. They didn't want us there anymore. So we came over here, where there are some other people like us. There's no other place to go. There's no hospital that will take him—or them. Actually, there's hardly a hospital at all. It's just a house. So here we are."

"Well," he said. "You bear watching."

"I can't be going to a doctor. Do you think I'd be using newspaper handkerchiefs if I had any money?"

"No, and I think it's brilliant. And you're right to burn them. By the way, if you ever meet the editor of the *News*, don't tell him how you use his paper." He smiled at his little joke, and she couldn't help but return it. He cocked his head away from the tent and said, "Let's walk a little and talk about your father." They headed for the shade of the cottonwoods along Cherry Creek.

"I have to tell you straight out—he's very bad. He has no normal breath sounds. He tries to take in air, but there's no place for it to go. His lungs can't expand. Has he had any serious bleeding?"

"Oh, no," Linn said, dismayed.

"If he does, turn him onto his left side. Most likely it is coming from that side, and you don't want the blood running into his right airway. Turn his head over and down so gravity takes care of the flow, understand?" He positioned her head at the angle he wanted.

She had never considered this. She had been watching Peter fade away, never thinking the disease might take a violent turn.

"I don't want to frighten you, but if it happens, you want to be prepared."

Linn turned and searched his face. "He's not going to get better this time, is he?"

Walcott shook his head. "It would take a miracle. It's better for you to know the truth."

She bowed her head and stared at the still-damp earth that would turn to brick when it dried—earth Peter would lie under in this place that wasn't home, far from his ancestors in their groomed Midwestern cemeteries.

"I know it's better. I just didn't want to hear it, even though I…" She was trying not to cry, and it hurt her throat.

Walcott put a hand on her shoulder and said, "You don't have to hold it in. This is a good, quiet spot to let it go if you want to."

She walked away from him and leaned on one of the trees. She mourned for Peter, then for her mother, and then for her siblings, who had all died in infancy, and for home, which was no longer hers. When at last she was quiet, Walcott came over to her and put an arm around her shoulder. Grown-ups touching again, and it was all right.

He said, "You need more than a paper handkerchief," and gave her his.

She was embarrassed she had so lost control. She had been raised an only child in an already quiet household. "Don't start that," her parents had warned at the first sign of a tear. Here in this new setting—hot, close-quartered yet impersonal, noisy and busy, even menacing at times—she had been a rock. Now a stranger had shifted it just enough for the weight to change, for her to breathe a little, relax into her sorrow, and let it flow. But there was a new anxiety that gnawed at her center and almost made her lightheaded.

"I have to think what to do," she finally said.

"Are you ready to go back? There are some things you can do now."

They moved Peter out into the shade on the north side of the tent. Walcott said, "When the sun gets right overhead, have someone help you move the head of the cot back inside and leave the flaps open. If it looks like rain, get someone to help or just drag the cot in yourself. You're pretty strong, aren't you?"

Linn gave him a tight smile.

"Next, drench that soiled newspaper in bleach. That way, you won't have to keep up the fire. Burn it all at once after supper. It will be a stinky mess, but it will save you wood."

She shook her head and held up her palms. "No bleach."

"Bleach is cheap, and you dilute it. Also, if he spits or bleeds on anything, you can douse it. No matter what some so-called experts say, I believe consumption is contagious. And if it isn't, well, you haven't lost anything."

"Except the price of bleach," Linn said, thinking of her purse.

"Air out this tent all day, every day. Sleep with your head away from him and near the flap. You may get some more mosquito bites, but…"

"The least of my problems," she replied.

"If my supplies come in from St. Louis, I'm leaving town with tomorrow's transport. Mule train. If not, I can check back."

"Where are you going, if you don't mind my asking?"

"The town of 'Chrosite, actually Rhodochrosite, named for the pinkish-reddish semiprecious gem you can find up there. But the word was too much to say, so in no time it was abbreviated. The big thing is gold and silver strikes, and stamp mills—that is, ore-crushing mills. It's not as famous as some places, but it's growing."

"It must be blessedly cool there," Linn said, feeling the familiar heat building up even though it was only midmorning.

"Cool, but not a very lovely mining town. None are." He turned and pointed west. "Look at the mountains and count one, two, three ranges. I'm on the other side. The mountains are beautiful from here, aren't they? Majestic. That's my favorite." He pointed northwest. "Long's Peak. Its arms reach out for you. Do you see that? But you can't take in the whole range in one glance," he said, making an arc with his arm. "It's almost a physical assault on the eye. Do you feel that? But they beg to be looked at. Like one glass of whiskey not being enough." He laughed. "But you wouldn't know about that."

"I wouldn't mind knowing about it right now," she said.

"You'll be fine." He reached out to touch her but didn't. "Well, I'll be off now. All the best."

"Goodbye, and thank you again. I can never repay your kindness."

"Not expected," he said. He walked along the row of tents then turned toward the bridge and away from Linn's sight.

Walcott was back the next morning with a bottle of bleach and a stack of newspapers. Linn was surprised by the lift she felt when she saw him. She protested the bleach.

"You want me to take it back?" He turned and took a few steps away.

"No, it's just that, well, you keep doing things for us, and…"

"You keep needing things done. My supplies didn't arrive yesterday. I'm not a church-going man, and I needed something to do. Think of yourself as my diversion, my project, if it makes you feel better."

Linn dropped her head. "I so appreciate it."

He offered the newspapers with a bow. "Your handkerchief, ma'am, lifted from my hotel reading room."

She took them and hugged them to her chest. "Thank you for this as well. Before I tear them up, I'll look at the Wants. I don't have enough money to get us—well, me—back home."

"And where is that?"

"A town in Illinois. Normal. Have you heard of it? The flattest place on earth. Nothing like where you live."

"And what kind of work would you be looking for?"

"I can teach, but I don't want to commit to a whole year. I just want to make enough for train fare. I could be a baby nurse, care for old folks, work in a store, I suppose. Even so, I'll have to stay here until I have money to move into a boarding house. I won't like being alone in this place. People pretty much leave each other alone, especially when they hear bad coughing, but if that's gone from my tent, I will have to be careful."

"Don't let it add to your worries now. You could probably sell the tent and cots and things to someone else, and there you've got your room rent. Ever read Dickens? Mr. Micawber? 'Something will turn up.'"

"Yes, of course. Wasn't he an optimist. And I've read *A Tale of Two Cities*. It was heartbreaking, the scene in prison. Would someone really choose death just because he couldn't have the girl he loved?"

"You've never been devastated by love?" His tone was mocking, but he didn't smile.

"Not *that* much. Have you?"

"No. So. Let's move your father outside." Walcott listened to Adams's chest again then shook his head. "There's a sound there I didn't hear yesterday. If he can bear it, cut back the laudanum. It does depress breathing."

Linn nodded while she looked at the front pages of the several newspapers. They didn't look any different from papers she had already seen. There were no baby nurses, old folks' companions, or store clerks requested in the Wants. Wolfe Hall still advertised for a teacher, but for high school students. Besides the name of the place sounding sinister to her, she preferred teaching younger children. And she didn't want to commit to a whole school year.

Walcott stood a few feet from her, folded his stethoscope back into his pocket, and looked at the ground. "I wish I could do something more," he said finally.

"So do I," Linn said. "I mean, that I could do more." She caught his eye to reassure him she meant no criticism. Out here in the bright light, she didn't see the greenish flecks in his eyes and was disappointed.

"Well, I'll be off," he said, but he didn't move. "See you tomorrow. The freight wagons don't go my way on Mondays, but the train comes in from St. Louis, and perhaps so will my supplies."

"If you have time."

"I have nothing else," he said. He backed up, turned, waved, and walked away.

Peter Adams died that night as quietly as he had lived. Linn didn't know he'd passed until morning. She sat in her nightgown holding his cooling hand until she sensed body and spirit were truly gone. She was not religious. Her mother, Barbara, had left a close Amish community, more spiritually than proximally, to attend the college in Normal. In spite of their abandoning many of the old ways, her mother's parents had still railed against her marrying outside the community. The bishop pleaded. Some of the aunties, uncles, and cousins shunned her, but Peter, a Presbyterian, and Barbara came from large families. They knew neither would inherit land, and both wanted an education. Once established, Linn's parents failed to keep up a regular religious life. There was a bit of a whispering campaign against them, but it was quieted by their success at the college and in teaching positions. Peter became superintendent in a nearby town. After Linnie Ann was born, Barbara tutored at home in between birthing babies that lived for only a month or a year. Barbara wore down, and aunties forgave and came to help. Peter went back to teaching in Normal. Linn soothed herself with books and schoolwork. Barbara was buried alongside the babies in the ancestral plot in the country. Peter's recurrent chest condition was finally recognized for what it was.

Linn was at a loss now. She knew nothing about cemeteries in Denver and guessed there were no Amish here to have established one. The newspaper ads for undertakers listed caskets of rosewood, walnut, metal, and glass—so luxurious and so beyond her resources. She pulled on clothes and shoes to go for advice to the tent of a family that had recently had a death.

Linn arranged credit payments to an undertaker who did not advertise in the *Rocky Mountain News*. He carried Peter Adams's body to the funeral home in a cart just large enough for a simple pine casket, not walnut or rosewood. Peter would be buried the next day with only a small wooden slab showing hastily carved letters to mark his plot. The undertaker drove Linn back as far as the Cherry Creek bridge, and she walked to the tent reluctantly.

The pressure of Peter's care being relieved so suddenly left her empty as a spent balloon. There was no form to time now. It was all hers, and she had no use for it. She slipped inside the tent and curled up on her cot with one hand resting on Peter's. She flashed through remembrances of her life and tried to see how she had been brought to this place so unlike everything she had known. She mourned for the good flat land that had wrapped her in its steamy warmth instead of baking and desiccating her before blowing her away into drenching rain and hellish thunderstorms. She cried for family, for community, and for security. She wanted her mother. Barbara had not sought health a thousand miles from home nor been gulled by gold fever and a smooth-talking sharpie who touted a rainbow that began in Illinois and ended in the Territory of Colorado. Peter Adams lost his mooring chasing that rainbow, or was it the other way round: he had lost his mooring and latched onto the rainbow as a haven. Anger fought with guilt and in the process stopped her tears.

She had neither eaten nor drunk anything all day. From its pocket, she took the precious watch that had been her grandmother's, the watch she promised herself she would sell only if she were starving. It told her the time was well past noon. She rose, refreshed the water jug, and drank from it. She washed her red and tear-stained face. She pulled Peter's cot out of the tent into the sun and hung the blankets and pillow over an improvised clothesline. The sight brought tears again, so she moved them all around to the west side of the tent where she could not see them. She brought her own cot outside. The only other decision she felt capable of making was to start a fire and toast two pieces of bread cut from a shrinking loaf. She dressed one piece with thin slices of the little bit of cheese that remained. She sat down and ate it along with the second piece of toast while she stared into space and tried to rally. She startled when she realized there was a figure standing near her.

"I'm sorry to have frightened you," Walcott said. "I was here this morning, and I guessed the reason I didn't find anyone."

"Yes," she said. She didn't look up at him but continued to gaze unfocused.

"I'm so sorry. Would you rather I left you alone?" Walcott asked.

Linn shook her head. Walcott brought the wooden chair out of the tent, changed his mind about sitting down, and walked slowly to the bank of the creek to gaze at the mountains. Linn relaxed then, grateful he was letting her stay within herself until she was ready to come back out. There had been too many changes, none of her own making except that she had acceded to them. She tried one of her old habits, telling herself a bad situation was a bad dream and she would wake to reality. She could not fool herself, alone in this dismal campground bounded by a sleeping tiger of a creek and a stream they called a river. She looked west to the Rockies. She felt as if she were perched on one of the peaks, unable to understand how she got there or to see a way down. Thoughts swirled and exhausted her. Lack of thought frightened her. She lay down with her hat over her head and fell asleep. When she woke, Walcott was sitting in the chair watching the fire. There was a fresh pile of wood near it and a kettle of steaming water half on and half off the flames.

"I brought coffee," he said, producing a sack from a pocket. "I thought you might like some." He had her small drip coffee pot and two cups at the ready.

"You are so good to me, Doctor," she said. "I haven't had coffee for more than a month, and I do love it."

Walcott took the water reservoir off the coffee pot and set about measuring grounds into the metal basket. "Is that about right?" he asked, and Linn nodded. He put the reservoir on top of the basket, poured in the boiling water, and secured the lid. "Do we know each other well enough now that you would call me Blythe?"

"We don't really know each other very well," Linn said, "but I will. And you may call me Linn. Linnie Ann is for parents and teachers."

"Will you tell me what happened today, Linn?"

"I woke up this morning, and he had passed on. I don't know when. Sometime in the early hours, I think."

"And now?"

"Burial tomorrow. All tidy and over with. It needs to be that way, but it makes me sad. It's not how we had services at home."

"That's how the Jews do it. Burial the day after."

"Oh?" she said. "I don't know any." She drifted out of the conversation, imagining tomorrow and herself a lone mourner in a graveyard full of strangers. Blythe picked up the coffee pot, swayed it slightly to be sure all the water had dripped through, and poured a cup for each of them. Linn blew absentmindedly on the coffee. Her mother had ruled that blowing on soup and hot drinks showed "no fetching up," but rules didn't apply anymore. Linn blew on the hot coffee again. In her mother's house, blowing on hot liquids in cups or spoons was strictly forbidden. Chew with your mouth closed. Don't talk with food in your mouth. Don't lick your fingers; use your napkin. Break your bread into three or four pieces before buttering it. Don't reach. Take your spoon out of your soup. Yes, you may be excused.

I'm sorry, Mama, Linn thought. *I don't have napkins. I don't have soup bowls or spoons. We left all those things in Illinois. I didn't break my bread into pieces, and I am blowing on my coffee. The rules you taught don't apply here and aren't helpful here. I knew the rules un- til other rules got in the way, such as "a fool and his money are soon parted." Dad ignored that rule. He thought he could find health and wealth in the Colorado Territory, and he ended with neither. He left me sitting in a miserable encampment blowing on my coffee in front of a nice gentleman who will now take me for a low-class woman.* Linn smiled in spite of herself, and Walcott saw it.

"Is the coffee making you feel a little better?" he asked.

"Not the coffee itself, yet," she said. "It's just the recollection of my mother telling me what bad manners it is to blow on it. I hope you aren't shocked."

"When times go to hell, if you'll pardon me, a genteel upbring-ing can go with them."

"You aren't blowing on your coffee, so times must be good for you."

"Getting better, yes."

Linn looked at him, wondering whether he might have a grief of his own, but she had also been taught not to talk about those things or to ask about them of others. She hid her feelings and did not probe his.

"Sorry," Linn said, trying to brighten. "I sounded rude before.

I've never had a chance to meet anyone who wasn't, well, Midwestern Protestant. Even in Chicago everyone seemed the same."

"And you'll go back to that?" His tone was neutral.

"In a while, I suppose. You warned me to try to think ahead, but my mind is blank."

Blythe rested his forearms on his knees, the coffee cup clutched with both hands. He addressed the dwindling fire. "I apologize in advance for what I'm about to propose, because I don't want to rush you, and yet I must." He turned to look at her directly. "I can't promise Jews or Mohammedans, but how would you like to consider something out of the ordinary? Pretend you've looked in the Wants and found a listing saying, 'Doctor's assistant in mountain town.' Would you apply?"

Linn sat up straight and tightened her muscles as if she were physically pulling farther away from him. "You mean like a nurse? How could I do that? I'm not trained."

"You said you could be a baby nurse."

"That's different. That's not being on your feet twelve hours a day and living in a dormitory with a bunch of other women under the eye of a matron."

"What I have in mind is something different. Did you hear the mountain town part?" he said.

Linn finally met his eyes. They looked at each other in silence until his face took on a quizzical look, pushing her to speak as she grasped what he meant.

"With you? A doctor's assistant with you in your mountain town? I'm not qualified for that either," she said.

"Yes, you are. I will train you. Here's my problem. More and more men are showing up in 'Chrosite with families. Women and children usually don't present the emergencies I've been dealing with when I see miners, mill workers, and rowdies in general. Before I came down here, I signed a contract to start a clinic at one of the mills. I'll be there two days a week, so I need someone to stay in my clinic in 'Chrosite mainly for the women and children, plus the barroom-brawl type of injury. I can teach you that. Besides, this territory is going to become a state one of these days, and there will be papers and records to deal with."

"Where would I stay? How do I know you aren't just trying to entrap, you know, um…dance hall girls?"

"I don't think you meet them at the druggist's."

Linn took several sips of coffee in silence, trying to think of some other reason why this was a crazy scheme, but only one thing came to mind. "I don't have any mountain clothes."

"Easily remedied."

"I don't have money. And I owe the undertaker."

"I'll make you a loan, and you can pay me back with work. Sounds like indentured labor; I don't mean that."

"Well, what do you mean?" She didn't like the implications.

"We'll work out some arrangement at a boarding house. The one I have in mind is run by a widowed mother hen named Maudie Felten. She'll protect you from exploitation on my part." He chuckled.

Linn's thoughts whirled like dust devils in a barren field. It was all too ridiculous to go off with a man she'd met four days ago. Was he really looking for a helper? How could she ever work off his generosity? What would he expect in repayment, in spite of his protestations now? What future did she have in Denver? Home was familiar, but in truth it was a barren field as well. This was the kind of irrational thing her father had done when he had been frightened of the future. She had just been heaping mental scorn on such behavior.

"How much time do I have to decide?"

"Ten minutes." Blythe laughed. "No, not really, but I have to leave on Wednesday. Today is Monday, as you know."

"I can decide in ten minutes," Linn said.

'Chrosite

2

Before the journey to 'Chrosite began, Linn had sold the tent and her cooking equipment. She kept one cot and two blankets, which made a comfortable enough bed in the privacy of a small tent Blythe had found for her. He accompanied her to Peter's burial after asking whether she would like an arm to lean on. With the little money that remained after the undertaker's fee and on account with Blythe, she bought cotton and woolen fabric and wool yarn, as well as mattress ticking fabric for pinafores. She allowed herself one small extravagance: a red velveteen-covered blank book in which she would write notes on the things Blythe had promised to teach her.

Blythe had told the truth about 'Chrosite. Blythe had not told the truth about the road to 'Chrosite. To be honest, it was a sin of omission, since Linn had never asked. She had no concept of mountain roads. The way narrowed scarily from time to time along a stream that moved over rocks, eddied behind them, or rested in pools before rushing on again. The water charmed her and held her interest as no flatland stream ever had. After supper on the first night out, she found a flat rock to sit on beside the creek. She let the sound of the water wash away the discomfort of being alone in a lonely place with six strange men. Not that Blythe was a total stranger, but she had known him for only a week. They had rushed around Denver buying and selling in preparation for the trip to 'Chrosite. Blythe left her no time to reconsider her decision to go with him, and she had to admit the whole enterprise was a heady whirlwind. Now, tonight, she saw that the five drivers were so tired after unharnessing, feeding, and hobbling the mules, and preparing supper and cleaning up, they were ready to get into their bedrolls at sunset. Linn laughed at herself for self-absorbed thoughts that the men might be a threat.

The drivers were in a hurry and urged the mules to move fast on the flat portions of the road, but the going was slow up and out of Georgetown. Gid Brown, the driver Linn liked to ride with, pointed out the flowers and animals and their names. When Linn saw particularly beautiful wildflowers—columbine, gentian, aster, paintbrush, and tall pentstemon—Gid stopped and let her off the wagon to walk and investigate. She was enchanted by hummingbirds that flashed green and magenta in the bright light and drove each other off the pentstemon trumpets. Blythe scolded her when she fell behind. "You can take walks out of 'Chrosite and see the same thing. Hurry along." But she could not resist the sight of pikas, marmots, voles, shrews, bighorn sheep, white-tailed ptarmigan black and brown in summer, and the alpine plants: avens, sky pilots, bistorts, spring beauties.

On and on, higher and higher, Linn wished she were on foot the first time the mules and wagon approached a hairpin turn. In spite of timber on the steep downhill side of the road, a misstep would be irreparable: stop, swing, stop, back, step haw, stop, swing, and so on until they were in alignment again. The swaying made Linn queasy, and she asked to get down once again. The train traveled on and on uphill into sparse spruce and pine until they reached timberline. The understory thinned and shortened until only inch-high ground cover remained where bristlecone pine had thrived for millennia. The mule hitches navigated around rock outcroppings splotched with both gray-green and orange lichens. To their left, mountain range upon range drifted into the horizon. They were on top of the world when it fell away. Linn, riding with Gid, grabbed his arm to recapture her equilibrium.

"Here now, turn loose," he cried at Linn as he guided the mules away from the mountain view and brought them to the edge of a cliff—below which was nothing. Linn let go of his arm and dropped her head into her lap. She was afraid if she looked out into the great hole in the earth, she would tumble into it. It was more dizzying than trying to comprehend the vast night sky—then, at least, she had a grip on the earth. Here she felt suspended, perched, with nothing to hold her down.

"Let me off, please," she cried. The thought of staying on the driver's seat in the wide-open wagon in the wide-open space terrified her. She wanted her feet on the ground.

Blythe climbed down from another wagon and came up to her side of the driver's seat. "Get down. I'll help you." He lifted his arms toward her. But Linn had become frozen for fear of catching sight of the empty space on the other side of the wagon. He tugged at her skirt. "Come on now," he said. "We have to get a move on."

She turned her head toward him, gave him one hand, and jumped off the wagon frontways rather than backing down as she had been taught. This way her back was to the abyss.

"What is this?" she whispered. "I can't look at it."

"It's Horseshoe Basin," he said. "Ice scraped it out and left it for us."

"What are we going to do?"

"We're going down into it. What do you think?"

"I don't know," she said, sounding desperate. "I don't think I can go on." She hoped this was a bad dream and she was really back in Illinois, where the earth stayed firm front, back, and sideways, and did not disappear and take her breath with it. She walked past the end of Gid's wagon and back to the safe, flat alpine meadow, the summit of the road.

"Wait until the wagons pass," Blythe said. "We'll walk. First, though, consider your unique position in the world. This direction, from this spot, the water runs to the Pacific." He pointed west. "And this way"—he pointed the direction from which they had come—"it runs to the Atlantic."

She knew she should feel awed, as if she were straddling the Equator or the Arctic Circle, but she didn't. She wanted to go another direction. To the south a narrow alpine meadow sloped down to valley beyond valley and the mountainsides were blanketed with dark-green trees studded with pearls of lighter-green aspen. This side was something to marvel at. This half of the world was beautiful. The other side was a hell Blythe expected to draw her into. "Why doesn't the road go that way?" She pointed.

"First of all, there's not a road. Even if there were, to get to 'Chrosite from down in that valley, you'd have to go back up and over another range." He took her elbow to try to guide her back to the road. "You can't stay here."

"I'll wait for the return trip."

"You'll freeze—if the cougars don't eat you first."

"You didn't tell me it would be like this."

She reluctantly let him lead her to the precipice, bringing her closer to the wagon road that eased itself over the ridge and hugged the south side of the basin wall. She looked at the road, which had been hacked, drilled, and blasted into nearly a sheer face. If mule, man, or wagon slipped, there would be nothing to stop its tumbling to the bottom. Still, this south side of the horseshoe was the best of a bad lot. The toe was a cornice where the weight of a wagon or a snowshoe hare or a pinecone might collapse it. The north side showed a jagged face of rock and tenacious timber with above-ground roots writhing around rocks. If Linn had dared look to the bottom of the valley, she would have seen a spring-fed stream running through willow thickets toward the horseshoe heel in search of connections to the Blue River.

"Do we go all the way down there?" Linn waved into the valley but couldn't look at it.

"Of course. 'Chrosite is around the corner to the right," Blythe answered, pointing to the heel.

The wagons lumbered on. Linn and Blythe were alone on the top of the world. She wanted to stay there. He was becoming impatient.

"I can't walk that road. All I see is emptiness. It makes me dizzy." Her legs had turned to butter. One wobbly step, one fall, one plunge to the bottom.

In his best bedside manner he coaxed her, the frightened patient, along. He took a few steps onto the cliff-side road and told
her to follow him while looking either at his back or to the inside.

"But also keep a lookout at the road bed. You don't want to slip
on loose rock."

Linn made a throaty sound of protest at learning of yet one more
hazard. She was beginning to feel stupidly like a reluctant puppy,
and he was her increasingly impatient master.

"You can't stay here. Come on. No one has ever died up here.
Well, maybe if they just sat down and refused to move." He laughed,
turned his back on her, and began to walk away.

Linn took a few steps. "Wait," she cried, and he did until she
was close behind him. She concentrated on his back and glanced
down every few steps. The road had only a slight grade here, but
it naturally followed the soft undulations of the cliff face until the
first waterfall chute, where Linn balked again. The force of ten
thousand spring runoffs had carved a concave course down the
face, creating a curve too sharp for the road to trace. To bridge
it, the builders had secured split trees across the space by driving
railroad spikes through the wood and into the roadbed on each
end. As a precaution they had built a wooden curb on either side
of the bridge, but there was no railing. Linn's stomach turned over
to see that there would be thin air on not just one but both sides
of her. The combined force of fear and altitude left her breathless. Heat shot from her shoulders up her neck and into the back
of her head. It stayed there. She stopped short of the bridge and
turned her face to the rock face, hoping for some relief. In spite
of her panic, she was taken by the beautiful layers: reds, yellows,
grays, thin black lines, shiny facets. Somewhere behind them veins
of gold had been pushed up from the molten center of the earth,
surely by the devil himself. She considered the desperate drive to
find it in this blasted country. She had been the victim of gold
fever once, and yet now she was one again, here in its burning,
irrational, and foolish heart.

Blythe, on the other side of the bridge, turned and demanded, "Linn, for God's sake, just put one foot in front of the other and keep going."

Linn held her skirt higher and practically ran across. On the other side, she let out her held breath and tried to breathe as normally as the thin air let her.

"These rock layers," she said to him, "some of them don't look sealed together. Couldn't they just crumble apart and…"

"Sure," he said, "but so far they haven't."

She reached out a hand as if to calm the rocks. "Isn't there some easier way to get to 'Chrosite?" she persisted. "Isn't there a railroad somewhere?"

"One is coming over to Breckenridge, but this way is shorter, even in the winter."

"You mean the road we're on is used in the winter?" She was incredulous.

"Not too often. Depends on the weather. Imagine being up here in a white world, with the wind picking up little whirls of snow. I've seen avalanches. It's really quite exciting."

"I would be terrified."

"You will become accustomed to mountain living. It's a test most every day. You push yourself to see what you're made of." He was silent for a moment then said, "For instance, what would happen if you walked as close to the edge of the road as you could? How long could you keep your balance without tipping over?"

"Why would you even think that!" Her equilibrium shifted again. If he actually did it, was she supposed to grab his arm and pull him away? Was this a test?

"I think it. I can say it." He turned back to her and smiled. "But I won't do it."

He frightened her. What was she getting into with someone who talked like this? It was upsetting enough to be on a cliff on the Continental Divide with a stranger and going to a strange town. Did the thin air make people crazy? Would it happen to her? What

28

if she began imagining she could fly and jumped into the abyss? She halted and dropped her head but was afraid to close her eyes. She needed to calm herself, put Blythe's and her own fantasies out of her mind.

Though it was useless through her boots, she tried to make her toes grip the road on the gouged-out wall of Horseshoe Basin. This wound in the rock was not yet a decade old, but it was already home to tiny undemanding plants whose thready roots sought purchase in a vertical world. Their leaves were a matte gray-green. In the time it took Linn to reach out to one to see whether they were as soft as they looked, Blythe had disappeared around a bend and left her alone like an eagle chick in an aerie. But eagles are born and not made, and Linn was neither. The bend was not a sharp one; it couldn't be and carry a mule hitch and freight wagon. The road seemed to disappear in front of her, and she couldn't bear to look at it. There was only one security left, and that was to face the wall, touch it with arms stretched like eaglet wings, and sidestep until she sensed the road again. It was awkward but satisfying.

"Are you there? Are you coming?" Blythe sounded impatient again. "I'm right around the bend. I didn't want to come back and give you a scare."

"Thanks very much," Linn responded crossly. She faced forward again as the road became wholly visible. She dropped her arms before he saw her. Just as she thought she was back in control of herself, she saw another bridge down the way. Her insides turned over.

"How many bridges are there?" she croaked as she approached Blythe.

"Only two more."

Linn whimpered again. Thus she crossed the divide step by terrifying step and descended Florentine Pass back into the comforting embrace of timber. In and out of the forest, the road followed softer folds of the land, and on more substantial bridges it crossed several watercourses that were as much waterfall as stream.

Linn and Blythe came to flat ground along a creek at a tiny settlement with only a log house, a sawmill, and a tent. Its size was inversely proportional to the noise it made. Linn saw a sweet little millrace tearing along and pouring back into the parent stream. The millrace powered the sawmill, where a saw whined through log after log. One wagon crew had nearly finished unloading a fiercely large two-man timber saw and other supplies.

"*Välkommen*, Doc," a tall, dark-haired young man said with a big smile as he clapped Blythe on the shoulder. He had a long, strong jaw and eyes that sparkled. "You bring my stuff?" he asked, and Blythe nodded. The last wagon in the train was still unloading, while the others had gone on.

"First, I want you to meet Linnie Ann Adams," Blythe said. "I'm going to teach her to man the 'Chrosite clinic when I'm away. Linn, this is Victor Iversson. He's one of four brothers logging and running the mill."

Linn made a nod of new acquaintanceship.

Iversson laughed. "Not a man, Doc, a very pretty lady."

Blythe laughed as well while Linn stared at the ground. The two men looked into one of the crates for Iversson's medical supplies. Iversson had already opened another one full of round saw blades, each having different sized teeth.

"These things give me the willies," Blythe said.

"That seems strange for someone who, I imagine, has saws of his own," Linn replied.

"Mine aren't lethal. His are."

When Iversson was satisfied that every item on his list had arrived, Blythe and Linn climbed onto the wagon and waved goodbye. Blythe told her the Swedish brothers had named their hamlet—if it even deserved that title—something in Swedish that no one else could pronounce. The Americans just called it Little Sweden.

"Vic speaks the best English," Blythe said. "Gus, Pete, and Andrew work in the woods mostly and don't see other people much, but you'll meet them eventually. They have their share of accidents.

That's why Vic keeps some supplies around. He can bind up a wound or a broken bone, give a little sedative, and then get the patient to me—or me to him."

They were traveling across the floor of the basin now. Linn looked back to Florentine Pass. The road stood out along the south face like a cut on a battered cheek. Linn saw things from here that she had not seen on the trip down the pass. A wide swath of the base was covered by a talus field barely tolerating its angle of repose. To make its opinion known, it frequently lobbed rocks to the bottom. Linn saw that miners with the souls and skills of mountain sheep had staked their claims above Little Sweden. They had picked away at the surface, making a flat place to stand outside their tunnel, pitch a tent, and stack equipment and supplies. Linn was soon to learn about black powder, hammers and drills, falls, broken limbs, crushed fingers and hands, exposure, altitude sickness, and drunken celebrations of strikes, but from where she sat on this day, the whole enterprise of hard-rock mining looked impossible.

Blythe, sitting on a box in the bed of the wagon, played guide on this last part of the journey. He pointed out the junction of the Iverssons' Beaver Creek and the Florentine River, whose source sprang from the east end of Horseshoe Basin. The heel of the basin was wider than it appeared from the top of the pass. Beyond the heel a series of valleys fanned north and south of the wide, flat outwash. Great pounding sounds poured from the narrowest valley and flowed down on the wagon. Back in the valley, a trestle hugged one hillside and disappeared around a curve.

"That's the stamp mill and Xavier mine," Blythe told Linn, pointing to the nearest buildings. "The trestle goes to a tunnel."

"The Xavier men must go deaf," Linn observed.

"Just one of their problems," Blythe told her. "I'll share others with you as time goes on."

Another valley brought another stream to the Florentine River. This new valley and stream were quiet and pastoral. Farther upstream, log cabins clustered on the near bank. Sheep and cows grazed behind the houses. One wagon from their caravan turned up the willow-lined road.

"They're taking supplies to New Plymouth," Blythe explained. "Two married couples live up there. You'll meet the women soon enough. They're both expecting."

Linn closed her eyes. She had had enough of childbirth in her life. She dreaded it.

"At the end of that road, there's a trail to a waterfall and a hot springs. Really beautiful. The miners and mill workers take soaks in the pools. You can organize a ladies' day sometime," Blythe teased, and Linn blushed, though it did sound intriguing. She had never seen a hot spring. How did someone bathe in it? How could a group of ladies be so daring, with each one's waists and skirts, stays, pantalets, and petticoats all folded on the ground?

As the Florentine River bubbled on, the wagon road turned right and timber closed in on it. On the right-hand side of the road, a hill rose until it was a solid wall Blythe called Sugarloaf Mountain. It admitted no valleys, no streams. On an expanse between the fortress-like Sugarloaf and the shallow, rippling Florentine lay the town of Rhodochrosite, Colorado.

It was not a pretty town—not even an attractive town. It had self-assembled, one building necessarily forming next to another as space and function allowed. It was nothing like a Swiss mountain village illustrated in *Harper's Magazine*. There were no flower boxes in the windows, and there were few trees save the ones on top of Sugarloaf that the loggers couldn't reach. Linn would learn that the row of trees held off sunrise that much longer, keeping the mornings colder and darker. The chilly inhabitants could only curse the pair of founders who had bragged about a strike nearby, encouraged settlement, then decamped for lower, warmer panning on the Blue River. The main street paralleled the face of the Sugarloaf. In fact, it was the only street. At the other end of town, the road continued back into timber and followed the Florentine at a respectful distance as they both picked their way down to the wide-open valley of the

Blue River. In between lay the ragtag assortment of storefronts and houses, outhouses, horse corrals, and piles of gravel from failed and abandoned attempts to find nuggets in the river. Trash lay everywhere.

The wagon stopped in front of a small log house with a stand of aspen at one corner. "Here it is," Blythe said to Linn as they dismounted. "'Chrosite and"—waving at the little structure—"the clinic, the hospital, and my house all in one. You'll be in the white house we passed back there." He waved in the opposite direction. "Let's see what's going on in here."

An infant's wail poured out the door. "Doc Williams must be here," Blythe hollered back at Linn. "He said he'd come over from Breckenridge when he could."

Inside, Doc Williams was trying to get through a lineup of patients waiting on a bench that spanned the front wall. Four more patients sat on the chairs around a drop-leaf table. Linn tried to absorb the scene. Under a window were a large dry sink and a kettle-covered wooden drainboard. Cabinets lined the upper wall. An icebox stood beside a corner cupboard. The table and chairs sat near the stove, above which was a single shelf holding lanterns and pitchers. From the bottom of the shelf, on hooks, hung fire tools and a frying pan.

Stitched-together flour sacks served as the walls of two examination spaces, which were hardly private, as the corners of the sack panels did not meet and the so-called doors were rather short. Inside one cubicle Linn saw the legs of what must be a rudely made examination table; in the other it appeared there was just a chair and a small cabinet she imagined held instruments. Folded cots lay beyond the second cubicle. The rest of the room was hidden behind another flour-sack curtain. The teamster carried in supplies and stacked them in front of the icebox.

In the midst of this chaos, Blythe greeted each waiting patient and checked with Williams about the patients in the exam rooms. Blythe motioned to Linn and held out the squalling infant. "Take her outside for a little walk, will you?" The exhausted mother nodded her approval, and Linn took the baby out onto the small porch, but she was not consoled. Linn began walking up the street toward the cluster of buildings. People stared at her, and she smiled apologetically for being the stranger carrying the baby everyone knew. No one spoke. One of the other supply wagons was parked in front of a store, and when the driver came out, he grinned at her.

"That was quick work, Miss Adams," he said. Linn blushed and dropped her eyes. "Just my little joke, miss. No offense," he added.

Gid had tethered his team onto the back of another wagon. "It's been real nice knowing you, miss," he said over the hiccupping cries of the baby. "You be careful up here. A mining town's not the best place for a young lady. And don't let that doc take advantage of you." He winked, and Linn blushed again.

"I have no intention," she began, but he stopped her.

"I know," he said. "He's much admired in these parts. He's a good man, but some other people up here.... Well, I have a daughter, and I don't bring her along."

"Oh, dear." Linn couldn't think of what to say to that, so she turned the subject to Gid himself. "And you be careful up there." She waved in the direction of the pass. She thanked him for safe passage and apologized for upsetting him on the summit.

"It's never easy," he said and went back to his wagon and mules.

Linn continued up the street, talking quietly to the baby, whose sobs came at intervals now. She passed the grocery and dry goods store, which was being resupplied, the assay office, the newspaper office, and a saloon with the flamboyant sign reading *The Gem Stone*. The barber waved at her, and she nodded back. Here was a second saloon. At the end of these buildings were houses—some log, some clapboard, some single story, and some two story. Farther on was a tiny school. A gaggle of children played there on swings and teeter-totters. A couple of boys tossed a baseball. They all stopped and stared at Linn.

One of the little girls ran over, shouting, "That's our baby! Where are you going with our baby?" She tugged at the blanket wrapped around the infant. Linn knelt to the little girl's level.

"What's your baby's name?" Linn asked her.

"Mary Ann. Where are you going?"

"She was crying at the doctor's. The doctor asked me to take her for a walk."

The child was still suspicious.

"Do you want to come back with me and be with your mother?" Linn asked.

"Back to the doctor's?"

"Yes. Then you can be sure I'm not stealing your sister."

"I don't like the doctor's."

Linn smiled a sympathetic smile. "I'll tell your mother you're here. What's your name?"

"Flora."

"Well, Flora, you're the first friend I've made in 'Chrosite."

Flora looked from Linn to the baby and back. Then she scampered back to the other children without saying anything more.

The baby had fallen asleep in Linn's arms. Linn began retracing her steps to the clinic.

There's my new home, she mused as she walked past the white house. Would she have a big room? Or a small room taken up mostly by the bed? Would it be warm? The house had a quaint dormer window on the second floor. In this tacked-together town, the builder had taken the trouble to outline the peak in scrollwork and added the same pattern to the front-porch roof and railing. There were porch chairs waiting for summer afternoon loungers. 'Chrosite was sited for night owls. The sun stayed late in the west and came up late over the Sugarloaf. It would suit Linn's body clock perfectly. The summer morning sun in Denver had been her *bête noir,* as it penetrated pinholes in the tent fabric. There'd been nothing there to block the sun the second it hit the horizon, and even when she slept with her back to it, it had crept under her eyelids.

This will be perfect, she thought, not considering that the winter sun would be up after breakfast and she might not feel it on her face until she opened the door to the first patient.

A small figure appeared beside her and said, "I'm coming with you."

Linn held the baby in her left arm, and she and Flora walked hand in hand back to Doctor Walcott's.

After she had brought Mary Ann and Flora back to their mother, Daphne, Blythe put Linn to work placing certain supplies into the icebox and stacking others on the drainboard. He told her that because she didn't know where anything was at the clinic and wouldn't be of any more help, she should just take her valise and go over to meet Maudie Felten and get settled.

Maudie Felten had a beaky nose and flaring jaw. Her round eyeglasses only enhanced her owlish look. Her eyes became even rounder when Linn explained her situation. Her mouth became a little *o*, and then she invited Linn in. Good businesswomen did not leave clients standing on the doorstep. Maudie fed Linn early and sent her to bed in the room with the gingerbread dormer.

Next morning, Linn woke to disorientation. Her magnetic north was blocked. She didn't sense this was her room in Normal, with its striped and flowered wallpaper, maple dresser, and blue curtains over gauze sheers. It wasn't the boarding house in Denver or the tent. She would have felt that too. She searched her mind for her movements over the last few days and then remembered: the wagon train to 'Chrosite, the clinic, the town, Maudie. A mining town in the Colorado Rockies was going to be home now.

3

Blythe flooded Linn with information the very first morning. He was orderly and clear. She tried to make notes in the red-velvet-covered book she had splurged on in Denver, but she couldn't keep up. He sat her down with a cup of coffee from the big graniteware pot on the back of the stove. She would learn that water for the clinic always steamed in a big vessel in front.

"Whenever I'm up at my clinic at The Falls mine and mill, I want you to take appointments and write them in this book," he said. He placed it in front of her and pointed at a page. "It's ruled off in columns for date, time of day, and name. I left space for the nature of the visit, unless the patient won't say what it is. Usually I will have a fair idea. I know most of these people, but you're new, and you're a woman. They wouldn't want to tell you anything private. Explain who you are. Just make them comfortable. Smile and accommodate them. I know you can do that."

"I certainly hope so," she responded, thinking this was like taking roll at school.

"Mostly, though, people just drop in. Like yesterday. If anyone needs immediate help—an emergency, an injury—you can send someone from the livery stable to come for me. With time and training, you will be able to take care of more things than you can imagine—take calls out, for example. That's what I expect from you, and I know you can do it."

"If not, I will be sent packing back to Denver."

"Over the Florentine. Is it worth it?" He laughed, but she didn't.

"You said there was an easier way," Linn protested.

"No. I shall send you packing over the Florentine. Count on it."

"I'm concerned about the 'more things than you can imagine.'"

"We'll begin slowly and work up to them."

He showed her bottles, jars, and tins in the corner cupboard that were labeled in his flourished handwriting: soothing syrups; cough medicine light and heavy; syrup of ipecac; blue mass; calomel; teething relief; gargles and sprays for septic sore throat; fever abatements; jars of boiled, sterile water; tins of salves for sores or aching joints; jars of herbs and tea mixtures; jars of dried flowers; dropper bottles of oils; a large jar of sodium bicarbonate; tinctures of too many things to remember. He took down a bottle of soothing syrup and showed her the dosages, which were written on a label on the back.

"While I'm away, someone's baby or child will no doubt come here with a sore throat. You can give a dose measured in one of these spoons or glasses, or give a gargle or spray to an older child." On the shelves, she saw small, empty bottles the medicine could be decanted into for home-dosing. "Keep account of who gets what, when, and how much," he said, showing her a column in the book sitting in the cupboard. "Then go to the master book, here"—he opened a drawer—"find the patient's page, and record what transpired. I need it for bookkeeping, but this is so important if there is an epidemic. We'll have a path into it. And as I said that day in Denver, this territory is going to become a state pretty soon if Washington, DC, ever gets off its duff. Someone down there in the flatland is going to want to know how many cases of diphtheria and smallpox and all those other diseases we have up here. So get in the habit now. And by the way, you have had a smallpox vaccination, haven't you?"

Linn nodded and tapped her left arm. *The appointment book, the medicine book, the patient book*—she wrote this into her own book. *Doses on the back of bottles*, she noted.

He opened another cupboard. Inside were more jars and bottles and yet another book.

"These are the ingredients for the prepared medicines in the other cupboard, and this is the recipe book. Record each new batch you make. We'll do this together at first, but if you know how to cook, you'll know how to follow the directions. One warning, though: I keep ether in this cupboard, in the cans in the far corner. Never, never open one when I'm not here, and even when I am here, never, never open one when the stove is going. The ether fumes will reach the flames. The flames will travel the wave of fumes, and when they reach the can it will explode and create a raging fire."

"I never will," she promised.

"I don't want to scare you the first day, but I want you to know some emergency procedures." He looked straight into her eyes like a commanding officer. The excitement of the challenge rushed through her. At home in Illinois, such feelings were discouraged. One did not stand out in the family, or the town, or in a crowd. Girls did what was expected and worked at their tasks, not shirking or protesting. Girls learned to sew and cook and make life comfortable for others, especially their menfolk. Linn welcomed the chance to make life more comfortable for everyone who needed her here in 'Chrosite.

In teachers' college, the women students understood they should not aspire to becoming school principals—and especially not superintendents. Teaching school spun off a few years for most of the girls, but marriage was the real goal. Blythe had asked her once, as they ate a camp supper on the road to 'Chrosite, how she had escaped marriage so far, and she asked whether he equated it with prison.

"No," he said, "I meant that the boys in Normal must have had their eyes on you but you must not have laid yours on them."

"I grew up in town, but I saw how hard my aunts and uncles worked on the farm. I didn't want to be a farm wife. The doctors' sons left town to go to universities, the widowers always had a lot of children to look after, and I was aiming for a schoolroom-full instead. There were some nice young men at the teachers' college, but they were all busting to leave town. Some wanted to come west. Maybe I'll run into one of them someday."

"They'll have come looking for you."

She hadn't yet run into a classmate, but she felt the interest of a fellow boarder at Maudie's. The first week she saw his eyes flick between her and Blythe whenever Blythe happened to be eating supper there. She imagined the boarder was trying to judge whether there was some unspoken communication that would confirm that the rumors flying around town were true: Linn was Blythe's sister at best, or at worst, his mistress. The two of them rarely talked shop at the supper table, and when they did it was only about the clinic schedule or supplies. It was Blythe and Maudie who spoke to each other most personally.

Seemingly satisfied that Linn was a free woman, Myles Crenshaw asked her to go with him to church. 'Chrosite was on the circuit rider's schedule the next Sunday. Linn hadn't been in a church since her best friend was married in Normal the year before, and rarely before that. Her mother had never completely broken ties with the Amish, her family, but her father had walked away from the Calvinists when he was old enough to reject the idea of hellfire and brimstone and predestination. He had no objection to Linn's going to Sunday school with her young friends. He explained to her that it was just as well to learn Bible stories, seeing as how they were part of a cultural heritage, but she must understand that they were written long ago by people who hadn't been able to explain the workings of the world except in story and myth. "The world wasn't created in seven days, and Jesus was a person—a fine person who cared about his fellow man—but that was all. You are not going to any kind of hell, so don't let your friends or the Sunday school teacher tell you different. And no, I don't think it's a good idea for you to go with Susan to be baptized." When Linn saw her friend come up dripping from total immersion, she was so glad not to be doing it too.

She sat next to Myles in the schoolroom-cum-church and listened to the Old Testament reading and the gospel reading and stood for a few prayers. Her mind wandered during the sermon. It was gloomy, and the bright-blue sky made the world out the windows so much more compelling. Linn surprised herself with how much she loved the hymns, not religiously but as music. She could read music, and once she heard a tune, she could sing with confidence. She felt as if gravity no longer pertained, as if she could follow to the farthest reaches of her voice. When she hit a high note that no other woman there could reach, she smiled rather than shrank back from exposing herself to notice. After the social hour following the service, Myles commented that she had "quite a voice." She wasn't sure it was a compliment. She felt the eyes of some of the congregants while she stood beside Myles and sipped tea. He introduced her to the Reverend Cooper, who said he had always wanted a choir at 'Chrosite and she was just the one to lead it. Walking back to Maudie's for Sunday dinner, she wanted to ask Myles whether he was a real believer or a "congenital churchgoer," as her father called them, but she didn't know him that well.

Monday morning at the clinic, Blythe greeted her, saying, "I hope I'm not depriving you of a singing career."

"Goodness, news travels fast," she said.

"They think I'm a heathen, though not when they need a doctor," he said. "Thanks for upholding the respectability of the 'Chrosite medical practice."

"Not sure I did that. I liked the music, but not the rest of it. The readings, the stories—they're all right. But preaching! You have to sing to get yourself back up after being beat down as a sinner."

"That's what it's for. But don't take the rest to heart. First of all, you aren't a sinner, and you know it. And second, you are going to shine up here like the sun on fresh snow."

"You are much too much of an optimist."

"Let's see how you shine at this new task." He brought out a balance scale and a wooden box from a cupboard under the drainboard. He opened the box to expose a set of brass weights in a block of wood, each in its own fitted hole, from tiny and feather-light to heavy and awkward knobbed cylinders. He showed her how to pick up the small weights with a dainty forceps that reminded her of the one in her mother's sugar bowl. He cautioned her not to touch the weights with her bare fingers; rather, she should pick up the heavy ones with a piece of cloth. The weights caught her fancy because they were so perfect.

"They would make a wonderful little child's toy. Spill them out and let him put the weights back in the correct space."

"Don't ever, or you won't shine anymore."

"Well, maybe not in *your* eyes."

Myles escorted her to the Fireman's Ball. She had first declined his invitation on the grounds she had nothing to wear to a ball, but Maudie said nonsense. It wasn't that sort of ball. She could do something for Linn with the wool yardage brought from Denver, but nothing fancy because 'Chrosite was not a fancy town. The skirt would have to be all-purpose, for the winter was coming on fast.

Linn had no reservations about Myles himself. Over breakfasts and suppers, she had learned he was a mining engineer. He called himself itinerant because he consulted on prospect mines here and there rather than settling down to one successful project. He was from California, where his father had struck it rich at Sutter Creek. The senior Crenshaw knew when to quit, and he knew not to waste his treasure on Saturday nights. He sent his son to college, and his son headed for new gold and silver fields not with a pan or pickax but a diploma.

In the parlor after suppers, prompted by a casual question from Linn, he began her education in mining. She wasn't sure she wanted to know so much, but his enthusiasm caught her imagination and spurred a practical consideration: she should know something about mining if she was to take care of people when it went wrong. On walks, he talked of whims and headframes, shafts and drifts. During the ball he told her that he was awaiting shipment of a stronger cable for a cage counterweight.

"Cage," she said. "Sounds like something for wild animals."

"I've nearly talked the owners of a mine just this side of Webster Pass into getting a steam-powered hoist. The mine is getting too big for a horse-whim. Have you seen one? The horse can only provide so much horsepower."

He laughed at his little joke. Linn smiled and told him she hadn't been to Webster Pass. Myles continued on without noticing her cringe at the thought of another pass to negotiate. "The fellows are bringing up some good ore. They haven't gone very far yet, but they went so far as to give the place a name: the Lynx Paw. One of them swears he saw tracks in the snow."

Three of the four brothers from Little Sweden asked her to dance. She and Victor carried on more of a conversation than she would have expected. He taught her to say thank you in Swedish: *takk*. She said *takk* to Andrew and Peter and smiled at Gus, who was too shy to dance.

When she was back with Myles, he continued, "I wish I could take you down in a big mine sometime. Then you'd see what a hoist and a cage do together. But you know that the men think a woman underground portends bad luck."

At breakfast he sometimes drew diagrams for her. Most of the details gave her chills. Drill steels and hammers and black powder, the bread and butter of mining, sounded like tools of disaster. He coveted the air-compressor rock drills he had seen in his catalogs. The concept went over her head, which was already filled with solutions, ointments, and the sterilizing of instruments. Blythe believed in the germ theory. He promised to show her some bacteria in his microscope. Myles laid plans for men who used large tools to blow the earth to rubble and dust. She was learning to work with tiny instruments that had to be spotless. Myles waved off any discussion of Linn's work. He blanched at the thought of blood, in spite of having seen mine accidents aplenty.

Maudie's clientele came and went, but several boarders seemed to have put down roots in 'Chrosite. One was the newspaper publisher's widowed mother, who surprisingly thrived at high altitude. Blythe thought she would live to a hundred, and when Linn learned to listen to her heart and lungs, she thought the same. Mother Mason walked or snowshoed every day, and made desserts—chocolate, when she could get it—for the boarders. Mr. Stratton hid behind newspapers most of the time he was in the common area of the boarding house. He received the *New York Times* and the *Rocky Mountain News* by mail and seemed to absorb both as if their contents were not only current but vital to him. He picked up the weekly *Rhodochrosite Record* and read all four pages intently.

Myles and Linn began a running score of gin rummy games. She taught him two of her favorite games of solitaire, and sometimes Maudie and Mama Mason joined in playing poker for matchsticks. Mama played the piano for sing-alongs. She loaned Linn novels and helped sew the pinafores she needed to wear in the clinic. When Blythe ate supper at the boarding house, he never stayed to socialize.

The Colorado autumn lingered long that year. Whole hillsides of aspen shimmered gold in the sunlight. Linn felt their round, black eyes under black eyebrows on their smooth, white trunks were watching out for her. Both Blythe and Maudie warned her not to be hoodwinked by bright sun in the bluest of blue skies. The sun would take its warmth with it, they said, as it sank behind the mountains down the valley to the west. Blythe took Linn with him on calls into the valleys and up to mines so she could learn the land. She met stockmen and their wives. She met miners from everywhere: Cornwall, Wales, Germany, and Austria and its satellites. There were weathered forty-niners looking for just one more strike or at least a steady wage at a mill. Adventurers, unsettled war veterans, confidence men, and gullible, soft-handed newcomers crowded into the area's slopes and valleys.

Blythe convinced Linn to sew up a split riding skirt for herself. She had never been much of a horsewoman, but she found riding astride drew her more and more to being outdoors. As she and Blythe got to know each other better, Linn felt the freedom to ask him about his life before 'Chrosite.

"My parents—well, really my father—sent me to Edinburgh to study."

"Your mother didn't want it?"

"I was her only child. She and I were Northern sympathizers in the state of Virginia, but at least I could get out. She was trapped by convention and marriage."

"Did your father go to war?"

"Yes, he did. As a physician. He expected me to be one as well."

"Did you want to? Did you like Edinburgh and Scotland? I wish I could go there someday."

"I had a first-rate education. They're so far ahead of us. Anyone in America can hang out a doctor's shingle. Even if you're motivated to go to school, they don't teach much here. For example, they don't teach that the phenol spray I use prevents infection. They don't teach anything about the medical problems of women. They're medieval. You can work out a play on words with that, if you'd like.

"You've probably never heard of Joseph Lister. He's a British surgeon, and one of my heroes. He had a passion for preventing wound infections, which can be horrible. He was working in Edinburgh when I was a student, and I volunteered as a clerk during some of his studies. I kept records of which wounds were treated with or without phenol-treated sutures and dressings, which was his best candidate chemical. It soon became clear that during his earlier work in Glasgow, his methods and his dressings resulted in clean wounds. He wrote up the results and tried to convince the rest of the world to follow his advice. Some of his colleagues didn't believe him, but he was right. He convinced many of them to adopt his treatment."

"That's what you use now? The phenol spray in that atomizer that looks like a perfume sprayer, and the phenol dressings? You brought them back to America?"

"But try to get most American doctors to believe. You'll see, if another doctor comes into these parts. It's a hopeless cause. I spent some time in Germany and France. They're ahead of us as well."

"Why didn't you stay there, then?"

"I ask myself that. It seemed like time to come home. Not strictly home, not Charlottesville, Virginia. I couldn't have stayed in the East at all. I guess the untamed West appealed. I hope it is beginning to appeal to you."

"I like it now that I'm beginning to feel settled. I didn't so much in Denver. I was frightened there most of the time. And can I admit I'm frightened of some of the things you expect of me? Not making syrups and such, but having to touch, push, pull, say 'open wide'."

"Everyone is at first, but that's what the patients expect. How else can you find what's wrong? Now here's what you should really be frightened of: winter. And it's coming soon."

When it did come on, Blythe lectured Linn again on the dangers of winter: how a blue sky clouded up and floated, spit, blew, and blasted snow everywhere and especially blasted it into the unprepared face and down the neck and up the coat sleeves. It could fill up the wrists of gloves. He bought Linn a pair of arctics, the most horrid things she had ever put on her feet, and told her never to go anywhere in the winter without them. Or gloves. Or a hat. Or a scarf to tie around her face. He continued to take her out on calls whenever she was free. He wanted to demonstrate that his warnings about winter were real.

Myles and Linn snowshoed to the mining hamlet of Joseph and Mary and had a stand-up picnic in its small park. Linn was disappointed how little mind Myles paid to the bird life, the snowshoe hare tracks, or a line of elk crashing through the trees. Blythe had already shown her the gray jays, the mountain chickadees, and the brown-capped rosy-finches that came to lower altitude in the winter, but Myles's goal seemed to be just getting through the day's outing.

"It's an outing," he said. "An outing is about getting out and doing something."

Full steam ahead, she thought. *He is rather like one of his coveted drills.* He purposely led them home past a production plant to show her what a successful mine was made of. She appreciated the complexity of the workflow as Myles led her along. They watched the blacksmith repair a heavy chain and sharpen drill steels. She looked at every step and every piece of equipment as potentially harmful, if not downright deadly. What if cables snapped? What if black powder exploded prematurely? How often did a steel driver's eye and hammer misalign and crush his hand? How careful were the men who dumped pay rock from the ore cars into the ore bins? How aware were the men who maneuvered the ore bin loads onto wagons going to the railway terminus down the valley? Where did the blacksmith dispose of his spent coals? What if they blew into the wooden sheds that were everywhere? Did the hoist cabling ever catch anyone's coat and pull him into it?

She asked Blythe about all these hazards and how often he had to treat badly injured men. As a consequence, Linn's knowledge, under Blythe's training, overfilled her little red book. She purchased some colored pencils and a sheaf of loose paper that she organized to her own satisfaction. She had never liked cooking, but she liked making cough syrups and ointments and phenol sprays. She learned how to differentiate healing wounds from infected wounds and what to do about it.

"Soon I'll teach you to stitch those up in the first place."

"On a real person?"

"No, not at first."

"On what, then?"

"I have to find one first."

Linn and Myles carried on the most circumspect of courtships. He gave her short kisses, leaving her no time to respond. She wasn't sure it was even a courtship, and she didn't have time to dwell on the

47

direction—or lack of one—it was taking. There was no question of whether they would ever climb the stairs together at the end of an evening. He held her hand at dances and scowled when other men asked her to dance more than once. There were so few young women. She always took turns with the Iversson brothers, and once, when Vic claimed her several times, she saw that Myles was working his way into a pet.

I really must speak to him about being a baby, she thought as she took Vic's hand for one more dance.

Blythe took her to her first labor and birth; at least, it was the first at which she was expected to help. Most times women helped each other, but this woman was expecting her first baby, and she was too young and slight. Blythe came prepared for trouble. Linn proved a steely assistant, but when the baby arrived stillborn, she turned ashen. She soothed the sixteen-year-old mother's bewilderment and sorrow and then left the house with an aching throat and hot eyes. She hadn't counted on this being so much like home, like Mother's yellow babies, some living for a few days, maybe a month, some dead at birth. She fought down her own emotion until she and Blythe were out on the road in the livery cart. She moaned and dropped her head in her lap. She saw her brothers and sisters dressed in white and laid to rest in the country cemetery. She could not stop the memories of those tiny bodies and the one being mourned by his parents today, especially by a mother who might grow thinner and weaker with each successive loss, as Linn's own mother had.

"I wish it were as easy as telling you that you'll need to get accustomed to things like this," Blythe said.

"It's not that entirely," she said, her words muffled by her coat.

"What else?"

"Mother. My mother."

"Had a stillborn baby?"

"They all died."

He stopped the horse and put his hand on her back. "We have empathy for our patients. We wish bad things didn't happen to them or that we could fix the bad things. Right now you're seeing the past in the present. It's all right to cry now, but tell yourself that each incident is a thing to itself. It's part of learning."

Linn sat up and tried to dry her face. Her eyes felt puffy and hot. Her nose was stuffed, and her throat hurt. "I'm sorry to be such a mess."

"You aren't such a mess." He pretended to inspect her. "You've learned that your memory and the present are two different things and the trick is to keep them separate."

Blythe showed Linn many, many stitches on the many, many patients who had cuts, knife wounds, split scalps, and run-ins with saws. For the latter he took her to the sawmill to stitch up Vic after he pushed a piece of ill-aligned timber into a running saw. It bucked into his upper arm and left a jagged cut. Blythe joked that he should let Linn practice on Vic, who would almost certainly have agreed to have her clean, white hands on his skin, except that he needed that arm to heal fast and right. So Linn just watched the fine, even sutures build up a ladder on Vic's arm. She sprayed the stitched wound with the antiseptic and dressed it.

"When you bring a load in at the end of the week, come into the clinic, and we'll take a look at that. Come earlier or send a message if it starts looking red and streaky."

"What's 'streaky'?" Vic asked.

"Lines." Blythe drew a line with the used needle. "Red. *Rat. Rat* lines."

"*Ja*, OK." Vic nodded. "If Miss Linn will be there."

Linn learned to stitch wounds. She learned that if she were called to look at a chronic sore, she could begin treatment using bread or cheese mold on the lesion. She learned to make plaster casts and set simple fractures. She learned about life upstairs at the Gem Stone,

Opal Faye's establishment, where doses of calomel did their best to kill infections. In spite of precautions, a girl would try herbs or chemicals or a sharp object to get herself "out of trouble." Blythe had a standard lecture for the girl after he had stilled the uncontrolled contractions or the hemorrhage. Linn shuddered after they left the first time.

"Life isn't all lace curtains, nice books, and whatever else you've been accustomed to. Try not to judge. We don't know what brought these women to the life. Give up modesty, because you and I have to discuss these things without it."

"Trying very hard," she replied.

"Trying hard about everything. I knew you would."

Blythe and Linn continued to discuss everything as she learned and grew.

—*I've asked everyone who comes into the clinic whether they've had a smallpox vaccination, as you told me.*

—*And looked for a scar.*

—*Yes, and that new man at the newspaper claimed he'd had one as a schoolchild but it didn't take, and he wouldn't submit to another. Will you press him, please?*

—*I'll press him to write up a piece about the importance of vaccination.*

—*I must ask you again…*

—*I know. To keep the medicines in the order in which I found them.*

—*It drives me crazy not to find something where I expect it to be.*

—*Sorry. It's been a busy few days.*

—*Don't be sorry. Just don't do it.*

—*I had to go down in the Horseshoe mine yesterday.*

—*What is it like?*

—*Claustrophobic. Dusty. I don't like being underground.*

—*What happened? Were there bad injuries?*

—*An ore car in the number-two drift got loose, knocked a young fellow down, and broke a couple of ribs. The other men didn't have* much to bind him except the shirts off their backs, so they called me over from my Falls clinic to wrap him up. We had to get him upright into the cage and hold him that way up to the top. We carried him back to the bunkhouse on a cot.

—I've learned some things about mining as well as medicine. I didn't have to ask for definitions.

—Nice to have a professional engineer teaching you.

—He said they wouldn't allow a woman into a mine. What if you're far away and they need someone?

—You don't know enough yet to take care of most of the disasters that happen down there. When you do, well, that's another story.

—Couple of men in The Falls bunkhouse got into it. I had to extract some teeth. Bloody mess.

—I won't be expected to do that ever, will I? I don't think I could.

—There are lots of things you might not think you could do until you have to.

—Daphne Hunt stopped by. She's "that way" again, as she says it, and probably will have the baby in mid-August. She is not happy. In fact, she's distraught. I didn't know what to tell her. That "every baby is a blessing" speech didn't seem like the right thing. I told her to come back when you were here.

—I can give her something to prevent it in the future, but I'll be damned if I'll get rid of it now.

—She didn't want that. Will you show me the preventive? Can I tell women about it? Isn't it against the law to have it?

—It's illegal to send those things through the mail. No one said anything about wagon and rail.

—Close the door quick. I've got three kids in here wrapped in blankets and thawing out. They almost drowned today. They thought it would be great sport to raft the Florentine.

—In spring runoff? Are they crazy?

—*They nailed some boards together and sailed down about a quarter of a mile before they hit a submerged rock and were thrown into the water. It's a miracle they got out.*
—*And their clothes are drying over the stove, I see.*

—*When you go out on calls—and I do trust you to do that now—try to discourage granny recipes for treatment. I'm sure you've heard them.*
—*Cow manure on snakebite.*
—*On anything! Luckily there aren't very many cows around here.*
—*Horseshoe under the bed to ease toothache, assafetida bag around the neck, weed ash tea. Back home they used to say that passing a horse collar three times over a child's head would save him from childhood diseases.*
—*Hate to say that's as good as anything else.*
—*So discouraging.*
—*I told you about bread and cheese mold, didn't I? It sounds like granny medicine, but most times it works. Maybe someday we'll know why.*

—*Molly Harwood had her baby yesterday. Everything must have gone all right. They didn't call me in.*
—*I need to teach you more about what to do when the delivery doesn't go right.*

—*I'm taking about ten days to go to Cheyenne to meet Dr. Lister.*
—*Ten days! You can't leave me alone!*
—*Williams will come over again. He'll be here and at The Falls.*
—*And will he let me, a mere woman, do the things I do?*
—*I told him you're invaluable. Don't worry.*
—*You told me Dr. Lister worked in Edinburgh. What is he doing in Cheyenne?*
—*Coming through on the train. He's been in San Francisco and is on his way to Chicago and on back east for a medical congress in Philadelphia in September. I can't pass up the opportunity, as time-consuming as it's going to be to get there.*

—*I've been here a year.*
—*And learned well.*
—*Will you teach me to treat compound fractures?*
—*You can't begin on a human.*
—*Is this another "I have to find one first"?*

Winter had disappeared into mud season. In June, spring run-off had flowed and overflowed. In the mines and in the mills, men worked long hours to make up for winter. When Blythe returned from Cheyenne, he was energized by the reunion with his teacher and idol. He was away from the clinic more than ever, and Linn was there more hours every day. With school finished for the year, the children played and explored and had more accidents that needed ice or stitching, or at least a stern warning as to next time. Some evenings Linn was called out or back to the clinic. Some days Maudie kept a plate warm for her, and sometimes Myles brought a tray and kept her company while she ate. He told her that as much as he enjoyed his work in 'Chrosite, he missed California, especially the ocean.

"Is there mining along the ocean?" she asked him. He laughed and said no but then told her about tin and copper mining in Cornwall, where the tunnels and drifts stretched beneath the sea. You could hear it down there in the mines.

Linn was scrupulous in keeping up the medicines, the record books, and the patient notes. On the evening of her year-and-a-week anniversary since arriving in 'Chrosite, she was exhausted and didn't go home for supper. She had been called that morning out to one of the farms for what had been such an easy delivery, she wondered why none of the neighbors had been called instead. She had cleaned and dressed a dog bite. The family insisted the dog could not possibly be rabid. He was their pet. He rarely strayed from home and was never aggressive, and there had been no rabid wild animals around. Linn insisted in turn they keep the never-aggressive dog confined and watched for at least a week.

It appeared that everyone in town had at least one ailment that afternoon and either showed up at the clinic or wanted her to come out. When the clinic finally cleared, she began replenishing medicines and sterilizing supplies. She groaned at a knock, but it was Myles with a supper tray. He sat with her at the table, and they made small talk until another knock set her on edge. It was only Fred Carlisle to pick up Myles for the men's choir practice for the statehood celebration on Sunday.

The supper's warmth and the glow of the stove made her drowsy. She looked at her watch and saw that she could afford a catnap before she finished the day's record keeping. She pushed the flour sack curtain aside, climbed onto the foot of Blythe's bed, and pulled a quilt over herself. She was asleep in an instant. She woke slowly to rustling, clinking dishes, and the scrape of a chair.

"Bloody hell," Blythe swore. "What's going on? Linn?"

Before she could get up, Blythe pulled back the flour sack divider and held the lantern over her. She was blinded by the flame and couldn't see his face, but his voice was rough.

"What has been going on here?" he demanded while she tried to get out from under the quilt clinging to her skirt and stockings.

"Get up. Get off my bed. I won't have you entertaining Myles in my bed."

"What?" She shook her head. "What do you mean? I was only napping."

He turned to the other room and picked up Myles's coat from the back of the kitchen chair. He shook it at her. "And this? Supper? What else?"

"So much to do today. I was tired." She finally stood up.

He flipped open the medicine cupboard. He looked at the patients' book. "You have time for supper and God knows what else, and you haven't finished your work."

"I told you…"

He opened and shut other cupboards. He looked at the instrument baskets. "Pin up your hair and finish your work."

"Take back your accusation that I would 'entertain.' You told me not to be modest, so why don't you just accuse me of going to bed with Myles? Because if that's what it looks like to you, you haven't bothered to know me at all."

"No, I won't. And apparently I don't know you at all."

"I can't work this way."

"You don't have to."

"Then I've worked off my debt."

"More than."

"How much do you owe me?"

"Train fare, at least."

"So I won't have to go over the Florentine."

"Unless you want to."

She made a snorting, snuffling sound that wasn't pretty. She was embarrassed. She held out her hand. "Train fare."

He felt in his pockets and came out empty-handed.

"Monday morning, then," she huffed.

"Sure," he said.

"I'll finish my work."

"Don't bother."

"I'd rather. At least I won't have that on my conscience," she said, happy to see his face turn from anger to uncertainty. They stared at each other. He took two steps back.

"Bank the fire before you leave. I'm going to bed."

"Would you like me to change the linen?" She turned her back to him, sat down at the table, and began to log the day's patients. Eventually she heard the bedsprings. She kept working.

4

THE CELEBRATION OF COLORADO'S STATEHOOD BEGAN WITH A church service at the bandstand. Father McKenna revised his normal circuit pattern to be able to join the Reverend Cooper in offering prayers for the new state's future. They gave thanks for its beauty and riches and fine people. Each sermonized on hope rather than sin, and after everyone said amen, Editor Mason read the short version of the Declaration of Independence, the long version having been read only six weeks earlier on the Fourth of July, when the schoolchildren had been given the grievances against King George III to recite: "He has caused…"

The mayor read the preamble to the US Constitution and worked his speech around it. Coloradans were now officially part of "we the people," with all the rights of citizenship. Linn wished to raise her hand to point out that well over half the audience was barred because of age, sex, or nationality from exercising the most obvious right: the vote.

The parade began. The fire brigade, the lodge band, horses and riders, decorated horses and wagons, and schoolchildren showed off to their fellow Coloradans. There were games for the children, horseshoe pitching, a baseball game, and free coffee for all. Tom Shipman set up a scene in front of bunting and took pictures. Chet Marshall gave rides to the children on his best-natured horse. After picnic lunches were put away, the town council members gave speeches as people drifted around the bandstand. The speeches echoed the pride of statehood and the glory of Colorado's future. The listeners looked forward to November when they would be able to vote out the rascals in Washington and elect their first congressmen.

Another baseball game started. Linn took her turn at the booth selling raffle tickets for a quilt. She saw Blythe for the first time that day, playing catcher on one of the teams.

You get hit by a foul ball and hurt your hands, and who gets to do the extra work then? she thought. Then she remembered it was no longer her responsibility, though it seemed to be her worry. Myles was an outfielder on the opposing team.

The sound of the drilling contest rang out. Linn found it hypnotic and alarming at the same time. To think this went on in the mines day after day after day, not in bright sunlight as now but in dim stopes where a mis-strike—whether single jacking or double jacking—could cause a bruise or a break or jammed fingers, or the drill steel might cut into a hand or arm or shoulder. The men inhaled the dense dust, and chips flew into skin and eyes.

The August sun was warm. Children went home for naps, and women went home for cooking and baking. Blythe disappeared when the game was over. Raffle tickets were no longer selling well. Linn put her head down and tried not to think about leaving 'Chrosite, but there was nothing else for it. She would not speak to Blythe. She would never marry Myles, not that he had asked her, and when he kissed her she felt no spark whatever. The teacher's position was taken. She could go back to Normal, live with cousins for a while, teach school, and look for a suitable match: the man with five children, her flirtatious second cousin, a railroad man who would be away from home at odd hours, or worse yet—or maybe better yet—a traveling salesman who would be away from home most of the time.

'Chrosite took a year out of her life. It could be an adventure story to tell her grandchildren: Grandma went to the gold fields and came back rich—in experience. Grandma made a trip over the Florentine, can you feature that? If Grandma had stayed in 'Chrosite, you children wouldn't have been born. Or would you?

People began wandering back to the festivities, and the women arranged tables, made more coffee, and picked hot potatoes out of the coals in preparation for lifting the roasted pigs. Food baskets appeared not only with families but also with men who were sharing tents or cabins and men living in mine bunkhouses. Cutlery and plates came out, and as they were set on tablecloths or newspapers, few matched. Food to share was spread on one of the tables while Linn sliced bread that Teddy Spence had spent all morning baking in his shop. Like a Pied Piper, Jimmy Crocker fiddled people into line to fill their plates, and he continued to play while they waited. The roast pigs fell apart into great striations that were taken up cat quick.

Maudie brought a basket for her boarders, and their group sat down together, with Linn and Myles sitting shoulder to shoulder on a bench. Eating made Linn feel better than she had all day. Myles brought her seconds of fried chicken, potatoes, coffee, and a lovely piece from the large cake that symbolized the rectangle of Colorado with a big red C in the center, a star for Denver, which had been named the capital, and a star for 'Chrosite sitting in some frosting mountains. Linn devoured her food; Blythe was nowhere to be seen.

Children ran to play again. The full-bellied adults continued to sit. The men smoked and talked about statehood and voting, and mines good and bad, new and old. The women talked of babies and wanting things they'd had back home, for of course no one was a native. They complained of the price of cotton fabric and the quality of wool the sheepmen were producing down on the Blue. The Cornish Cousin Jacks and the Welsh men's choirs took turns singing a cappella. The band tuned up for dancing, and the women cleaned up.

Surprisingly, the frequenters of the Gem Stone stayed around. Opal Faye's girls danced with each other at first, then in a spirit never to be seen again, gamblers danced with other men's wives, storekeepers danced with prostitutes, miners danced with each other or with wives or with young daughters watched carefully by their parents. A councilman danced with Maudie, and Linn danced with Myles through a reel and several waltzes. Linn begged off the next, and Myles wandered off to smoke.

Vic Iversson claimed a dance. "I watched you today," he said. "You look sad."

"I'm going to leave," she told him. "I had a row—an argument—with Doc. He was rude, and I'm leaving."

"Pete and me, we'll have a talk with him."

"He told me he doesn't want me here anymore, and I agreed."

"So you marry Myles, no?"

"Oh, no, Vic. He's a nice fellow, but no."

"I would ask you myself."

Linn had never mastered the polite refusals she'd read in Jane Austen, but Vic's didn't sound like a real proposal.

"I don't have enough money," he admitted.

And you have too many brothers, and I don't want to live in a tent in Little Sweden, Linn thought. *But you are a sweet man.*

"You come to me if you need anything, all right?" There was such sincerity in his voice Linn agreed. She was touched at his kindness.

Vic handed her off to Peter, who gave her to Andrew, but Gus was still too shy to dance with anyone and was a wallflower. The band played until ten, and dancers with energy left were invited to the Gem Stone. Linn and Myles danced the last and started for home.

"Vic seems very fond of you," he complained.

"He's the lion whose paw I healed," Linn told him. She tried to keep her irritation with him out of her voice. She had had enough of his nonsense but was too tired to tell him so. She allowed him to kiss her, and she went up to bed.

A commotion downstairs woke Linn. Her alarm clock said two thirty, and Maudie was at her door telling her Floyd Hunt was there as Doc's messenger. Daph appeared to be having twins. Doc needed her; bring everything on this list. Linn couldn't refuse.

Once she'd dressed, she found the grumbling Floyd in the front hall. She tried a light tone with him: a new baby—two new babies. Congratulations. He would not have it.

"Don't need no more kids, and now Doc says there's gonna be two. Come on; let's get this stuff." He thrust the list at her. He drove and she walked to the clinic. Linn gathered into a basket gauze, flannel sheets, clean cloths, iodine, cotton rolls, and nursing bottles. Silently, she climbed into the cart, and they started off. She asked him about the baby. He said it was another damn girl.

"And the second? Has it been born, or…"

"No, and I hope it's a false alarm." He was so gruff, Linn didn't speak the rest of the way to the house. She barely waited for the cart to stop before she was out over the back and into the house without knocking. The children directed her to their parents' room.

"Linn, thank God," Blythe said without looking at her. He was holding a small bundle in his left arm and with his right held bloody cotton between Daph Hunt's legs. Linn thrust the basket toward him and pulled out more cotton. Another baby lay on Daph's chest, but Daph was, if not in shock, exhausted. The room was overly warm. Blythe was sweating; Linn took off her coat.

"Take off all the rest of whatever you're wearing on top. Strip to the waist. Quick."

"What?" she exclaimed. She couldn't grasp what he meant.

He barked, "Do it. Now. These babies need warmth. You. No modesty, remember?" He turned and skewered her eyes with his. "This baby needs a warm body. Daph is in no shape at all."

Linn turned away from him and began on her buttons. The waist came off. She loosened her skirt and pulled her chemise out and over her head then refastened her skirt. She had been in too much of a hurry for stays. She covered her bare breasts with her arms and turned back to him. He abandoned Daph for the moment, took a flannel sheet from the basket, and handed it to Linn, telling her to fold it the long way and wrap it around herself. She turned her back to him again. She turned around again when she was done, now tense and flustered.

"Please. I'm not interested in your body. This is serious. Hold the sheet aside."

As she did, head bowed, he unwrapped the newborn and placed it over her chest and one breast, turning its head against her shoulder. A baby boy. Blythe wrapped the sheet around her and under her arms to secure the infant and tuck in the end. Blythe stepped to Daph and plucked up the other infant, the girl.

"Hold onto him," Blythe told her. She supported the boy while Blythe unwrapped the sheet. He placed the infant girl over Linn's other breast and turned the tiny head toward her brother. He rewrapped the sheet then placed over the head of each newborn a knit hat that had belonged to the other children as babies.

"Sit down, stand up, do whatever you want to, just keep these babies warm. Daph isn't capable. I just pray her milk comes in. We'll fix diapers later."

Linn sat down on a wooden chair at some distance from the overwrought stove. She felt sweat move between her breasts and onto her stomach. Blythe had only slightly cleaned the babies. *I'm going to be a fine mess,* she thought. She looked down at the little faces and knew she couldn't leave 'Chrosite now. She felt their bodies with her hands. The girl was substantially smaller than her brother, and he was small for a full-term newborn. He slept; the girl's blue-gray eyes were open, and her tiny mouth and tongue worked. Fearing an outbreak of wailing hunger, Linn washed her hands and let the girl mouth a fingertip. She petted the cheek as one would a kitten.

You can't help it that your father is such an ass, Linn thought, and the devil she spoke of poked his head in to find out that he had only one "damn girl" and another boy to bully and set to work about the place. He grunted and shut the door. Linn made the sound of disgust in her throat.

"Yes, indeed," Blythe replied.

As the night moved on, Linn tried to catnap in the chair, which was quite a precarious seat. She got up and paced the room until Blythe told her gruffly to settle down. She propped herself on the bed next to Daph, whose bleeding had almost stopped and who was deeply asleep. Linn slept fitfully until a desperate infant cry awoke her. Blythe, slumped in the wooden chair, woke slowly, and Daph startled and raised an arm that fell back.

"Baby?" she asked.

"Right here," Linn answered, grasping Daph's hand and bringing it to the babies.

"Two." There was such sadness in Daph's voice that Linn turned to see whether Daph's face matched her tone or whether it was borne of exhaustion. Daph's look might have been one of loss. In Linn's family, babies often did lead to loss. She was always secretly relieved when aunts' and cousins' babies thrived, all the while feeling her mother's forced gladness for them. So now, Daph's expression troubled Linn. Was it because these babies were frighteningly fragile or because they existed at all?

Blythe came alert and told Daph he wanted her to try to nurse the crying baby, the girl. Linn sat up and unwrapped the sheet. Blythe folded the baby into a flannel blanket, took her to Daph, and nestled her under the covers and against her mother's breast. The baby rubbed her tiny nose against the breast then found the nipple, but in no time she was crying again, then sucking again, then crying in hunger and frustration. The baby boy woke and began to whimper. Blythe began preparing nursing bottles.

"Try the other side. It might be fuller. Linn, help her."

The baby began the same process: nosing, seeking, finding, crying out. Linn tried to placate the boy with a fingertip, but he sensed it was a fraud.

With the girl back and wrapped against her, Linn held one nursing bottle and Blythe the other. Whether they stood or sat, it was awkward. His hands were against her skin and his face close to hers. Because he was no longer charged with anger, she softened and was suffused with a glow she had never experienced before. She looked at Blythe, and they grinned at each other.

"You might have left town and missed this," he said.

"I'll never forget it."

"I hope you'll remember me but forget what an ass I am."

"Unlikely."

"It's been killing me that I said those things."

"I can't exactly leave now, it appears."

"Good."

When the babies were placated, Linn sat down on the bed again and rested against pillows. Blythe placed a pillow on the top of a chair back, straddled the chair backward, and rested his head on the pillow. Linn woke to morning light and the sound of pouring water.

"Let's get you and those babies cleaned up," Blythe said.

She struggled up and went to the little wood-fired room heater. Water was steaming. A bucket of cold water sat on the floor, and a small empty basin sat on a small table.

"I'm going to take one at a time in a warm towel, bathe it quickly, and wrap it against me, with your help. Then the other. You can clean yourself and take some time to do whatever else you need to do."

He began unbuttoning his shirt, fingers moving down the placket slowly as she watched. He freed his shirt and undershirt from inside his pants, pulled the shirt over his head, and tossed it onto the chair. He slipped the undershirt over his head and tossed it on the chair as well. Linn had seen the bare skin of men, women, and children in the year she had been with Blythe, but nothing prepared her for his. His eyes caught hers and seemed to say, *Who is looking at whom now?*

Linn unwrapped enough to free the baby girl. Blythe placed a warm towel around her back and sides and plucked her away. Linn looked down at her own skin to see streaks of blood. She decided not to care anymore. No modesty.

Blythe rebundled the baby, placed her against his chest, and exchanged the towel for the same kind of wrapping Linn had. He took the boy in another warm towel, and they repeated the process. She turned away from Blythe, dropped the wrap altogether, and washed herself in fresh water.

For three weeks Linn stayed bound to the babies except for diapering, feeding, and her own few needs. Daph's milk did begin to flow. Blythe stopped in as often as he could to give Linn some time away. *Now I understand why the polite word for childbirth is confinement,* she thought. She took walks to breathe fresh air, see the aspen leaves turn from green to gold, and hear birds telling each other it was time to gather and leave.

I guess that won't be me after all, she thought.

She spoke to Myles several times through the front door. *Saving him from embarrassment,* she told herself.

The heat in Daph's room was lowered, and Linn wore a flannel blanket shawl. Flora rinsed out the diapers that her elder brothers boiled and laundered. Flora always brought the clean, folded laundry in to Linn, but her ulterior motive was to spend time with her mother. Linn allowed it. The little girl made no demands and was gentle with the babies. Daph tottered around the house after the second week. The children kept the fires up, and they and Floyd attempted to cook. Floyd Hunt had been sleeping in a bedroll in the main room. Sometimes Linn heard noises in the night. Flora's face turned inward at the same time Floyd appeared defiant and threw aggressive looks at everyone in the house. Daph pressed her lips together and said little. She was still exhausted, but then so was Linn, for if one baby slept the other was hungry or wet and woke the other.

One evening Linn heard Floyd speak roughly to Daph and the words "in my own bed." She didn't hear Daph's reply, but that night when Daph came to bed, Linn, sitting up against the pillows, heard her sigh deeply after she put on a gown and crawled under the covers. Linn sensed she was crying. With her free hand, she stroked Daph's back. "I know you're very tired. The babies will be fine. Don't worry."

Daph turned over and faced Linn. "It's not these babies I'm worried about. It's the next and the next. I just can't anymore."

Linn had never in her life discussed intimate women's problems with anyone except Blythe, and then only in strictly clinical terms.

And so Linn felt it was not improper for her to pass along her knowledge to Daph.

"There are certain things you can do to prevent it. If you want something, Doc can get it."

"Oh, no, I couldn't, Floyd would…" Daph began but then sighed again.

"Floyd would never know. There are silly laws, the Comstock Laws, but Doc has ways. And Daph, it's something only you know about and you take care of, and the man never knows."

"Is that what you do?" she whispered.

"I do?" She was flummoxed.

"I know you're going around with Myles, but honestly, everyone in town thinks you and Doc, are—or at least were—well, you know."

Linn had to stop herself from protesting too much, not wanting to be caught out in her thoughts that the warmth and intimacy she had built with Blythe the past weeks led exactly there.

"Doc and I are not lovers," she said. She surprised herself in using that word. She wasn't even sure where the word lay on the courting-to-bedding spectrum. She wondered, given the past few weeks, whether she and Blythe had moved toward it.

"People won't talk about personal problems," he had told her. "But you must listen closely to what they're saying or not saying and try to prize out the truth. Talk honestly. That's the only way to heal, or patch up, or shine a light on darkness, especially when it has to do with—how should I say it—things below the waist. And that's a term I'll never use again with you, because if you're going to do this work, there will be no modesty."

Linn had dropped her eyes.

"Just so," he accused. "Just like that. I don't want modesty. That's my rule. There is a line between honesty and prurient interest. You have to keep that in mind as well. Modesty, honesty. They don't quite rhyme, but you get the idea."

When the Hunts' front door closed behind her and Blythe, Linn wanted to run in circles and kick up her heels like a horse turned out to pasture, not to celebrate her release from the babies so much as from the crushing atmosphere of the house. The sun on her face and the deep drafts of cold, fresh air were ordinary pleasures, now so sweet and celebrated. They began walking toward 'Chrosite while Blythe led the horse he had ridden to the house to collect and bring back his supplies.

"Thank God I'm out of there. Thank you." She smiled at Blythe when she said it. "I'm so, so, so happy to be freed from that prison."

"You're a heroine for having done it," he replied. "There may be a parade in your honor."

"Don't be silly. Anyone would have done the same," she said, but the praise gave her joy.

"No, I mean it. Those babies would probably have died. You were their savior." Blythe stopped and turned toward her. He put a hand on each of her shoulders and met her eyes. "Believe me, you were magnificent."

One of his hands moved across her back as they walked on, and he stayed with his arm around her, like the team they were.

"I heard that Myles visited a few times," he said.

"People will talk," Linn replied.

"And is there something to talk about?"

"How could there possibly be now?" She turned to look at him. His tone had been light, but there was something else in his voice.

"What do you mean? You're still going to leave 'Chrosite?"

"Why do you care about Myles?"

He turned to face her but didn't take his arm away. Their eyes caught, then he looked down. She had never seen him so serious.

"If you were another man's wife, I couldn't bear to see you, work with you, teach you"—and here he raised his eyes to hers—"and then watch you leave me and go to him."

"Whose wife should I be, then?" she whispered.

It was not a Myles kiss. It was confident, breathtaking, and endless except for a moment when he said, "Mine," and found her lips again.

In the clinic there were so many more kisses when the instruments were on the boil, and while the linens soaked, and after they checked the afternoon clinic schedule. When they sat across from each other, eating the toasted cheese sandwiches he had made while she wrapped the instruments and put them on to steam, he reached across the table and stroked her free hand and her wrist. He brought her hand to his mouth and kissed the tip of each finger. He traced the line of her jaw and her lips.

Blythe was not the only man besides Myles she had kissed, but the others had kissed her minding only their own pleasure. They had never done what Blythe did: coax out her sensuality with words and touch. There were two or three young men at the college who had given her the same chaste pecks that Myles did. When she was teaching, the music instructor from the college came to her school twice a week to instruct the children in band and singing. She was vulnerable. She missed her mother and craved attention. He was ready to give it. When she saw him in Normal one day with a woman and child, that was the end of that. She had a brief episode with a widower with five children. Once or twice a week, he stopped by when school was over for the day. He was attractive and hid his desperation poorly. She knew she should not allow kisses because, as she suspected, he thought they were a basis for marriage. She quickly put an end to it. With these other men, kisses had been pleasant enough, but now she knew what real kisses were. She had to know something else.

"I want to be sure that you've thought through marrying me. That seeing me half undressed didn't go to your head."

"Well of course it did." He smiled wickedly. "And you've seen me. I felt something change right then."

Linn smiled. "All that touching."

"And," he said through the last bite of bread crust, "I didn't have to see you half undressed to..."

"What?" She wanted to hear.

"Love you." His hands made a pleading gesture.

"Truly?"

"Now and always. Before now. It was when I looked into your eyes to see whether you were a laudanum addict." He laughed and explained how he'd put that feeling away as well as the even stronger one he felt the night she fell asleep on his bed. "I just wanted to lie down beside you and hold you. And we would end up under the covers, and I would say, 'Marry me tomorrow.' I was angry at myself for being too much of a coward to suggest it. Still, I knew you would be insulted, and that made me angry at you for not being soft and yielding. I wanted you so much, and I had to hide it."

She hadn't forgotten that night, and she wanted to understand it. "You loved me, you were angry with me and with yourself, and you were willing to send me away? That's hard to understand. What happened to your favorite word, *honesty*?"

"When I met Dr. Lister again, I remembered what a wonderful wife he has. She helped him with his studies. They're devoted. It reinforced what I so wanted with you, but I was afraid to be honest. And I was going to beg you to forgive me for that night. I didn't expect it to happen over the heads of two newborns."

"I don't recall that you actually did. Beg me now."

Linn's happiness saw her through the afternoon's rush of patients. When the last one was out the door and she began to tidy up the clinic again, a cloud of fatigue settled over her. She wanted supper and craved her own bed. Blythe came up behind her, circled her waist with his arms, and kissed the back of her neck. She leaned back on him to rest. He didn't take it that way and became more ardent. She turned in his arms and put her hand up to his mouth.

"I'm exhausted," she said. "I need to go home to have supper and sleep."

"Stay with me," he said and nuzzled the hollow of her neck.

"Can't."

"It's all right. Marry me tomorrow."

Linn extracted herself from his arms and headed for the door. "I have to wash. I have to have supper. I'm so tired."

Blythe reached the door before her. "You can have me for supper," he said softly with a smile and turned his back to the door to block it.

Linn put her hands to his face and stroked one cheek. "It's too soon. Do you understand?"

"Marry me tomorrow anyway," he said while he took one of her hands in his and kissed it. He stepped away from the door.

5

LINN CLUTCHED GID BROWN'S ARM, BUT HE WOULD NOT LET her get off the wagon. The mules were fast-trotting along the Florentine when the lead team pricked up their ears. They slowed and then crow-hopped dangerously near the edge of the road, finally halting just before it turned into a talus field. The wagon jolted and bucked. Linn screamed to be let off and woke herself up.

She lay awake living and reliving the dream until its anxieties grew too large for her single bed. She arose and walked the room to calm herself. She leaned on the sash and looked out at a late-night 'Chrosite that was awake as well. She knew she could not be a married woman and keep doing the work she had learned to love. Rather, the work would be different. Her hands were rough now. When they were fissured and bleeding and the nails ragged, when she had dark circles under her eyes, when she woke at night to feed a newborn, would Blythe Walcott love her then?

Next morning, Myles waited for her at the bottom of the stairway on the way to breakfast. "Are you all right?" he asked her.

She was not only conflicted about Blythe, she didn't know what, when, or how to tell Myles about her pending marriage to the doctor. Now was certainly not the time.

"Yes, I'm fine, just reliving a twisted version of my trip over the Florentine."

"Doesn't everyone?" he said. He put an arm around her and propelled her into the dining room.

In her kitchen after breakfast, Maudie plunged right in with a statement to Linn, not a question. "Something's bothering you."

"I dreamed I was up on the pass in an out-of-control wagon," Linn admitted.

"What isn't in control in your life?" Maudie demanded. "Dreams mean something. It's about Doc, isn't it? Is he bothering you? Is he making advances you don't want?"

Linn sank into a chair and looked up at Maudie, childlike. "He asked me to marry him. I said yes. Now I don't know."

"Why don't you know? He's a wonderful man, but then, if you don't love him…"

"I do. I do, I do. I fell in love with him over the heads of the twins, if you can imagine. But I'm afraid. Everything has happened so fast. We spent only a few hours together after I said I'd marry him. He swept me off my feet. He's too persuasive. He captured my mind so I could see only him."

"Fiddlesticks," Maudie said. "You've been in love with him since I don't know when."

"I loved my work first. He made me love both him and it, and now I'm thinking I love the work better. I don't want to be a wife." Linn couldn't help but pour her feelings out to Maudie, who had been a wife and had then gone on to make her own way in the world.

"I can certainly understand that."

"But how can I back out now that I've agreed? He'll be crushed. He won't want to see me anymore, and I'll have to leave him and the work I love. I've put myself in a bind."

"You shed your sweet, agreeable, obedient-girl skin and grow a tougher one, and you talk to him. There's a compromise in there somewhere. Think of all you've learned in the past year. You can learn this as well."

"Change overnight? Really overnight? He'll be home tomorrow. "

"I had to. 'Course, I was in shock. Plus, I was angry. More than that, even. "

"About what? Do you mind telling?"

"I was mostly angry that I couldn't confront my unmentionable husband because he was dead."

"You found out something terrible?"

"Dying in a mining accident was bad enough, with us barely making ends meet. A week later a young woman came to see me. She said Walter had been saving up to take her away, and she wanted the money. Saving up, indeed. It turns out he had been high-grading—or at least that's what would account for the stash of nuggets I found under the floor of our cabin after I told her to get off my property."

"What happened after that?"

"I could have taken it to the current partners in the mine, but I didn't know but what he had been in cahoots with one of them too. I left Russell Gulch, took the gold to Denver, cashed in, and had this house built to my plan: the six bedrooms, the dining room large enough for the table I ordered up from Denver, the sitting room for guests, my own private apartment, and the kitchen I never had in a miner's cabin."

"Do you ever think you should have given the gold back?"

"Never. Who should get it? By the way, when are you going to tell Myles?"

Linn sighed. "If I tell him I'm marrying Doc but then don't because Doc won't do it my way, and then when I have to tell Myles I'm leaving town, will he think I'm fishing for a proposal from him?"

"You wouldn't marry Myles."

"Can a mining engineer afford housekeepers?"

"And you would do what? Have a nanny for your babies and go into competition with the man you love?"

"Oh, Maudie," she cried as she began pacing the kitchen.

"Prepare yourself. Think of what you want to say. Write it down and don't waver."

"Hmm," Linn said. "I'll try."

At the clinic she refilled medicines, touching the bottles and jars lovingly as if for the last time. She couldn't stay in 'Chrosite unmarried, so where might she go and what might she do? She didn't see how she could marry and keep up her work, instead becoming a wifely drudge to a dynamic, appealing man who would hire a new assistant and fall in love with her next. Linn lived with anxiety all day. Only two patients came in, and their minor problems did not take her mind off her own. She would have liked being called out, but no one needed her. She made an unnecessary visit to check on the twins just to think of something outside herself.

After supper Myles asked, "Want to take a walk or play cards?" She begged off with the need to get a good night's sleep.

She hadn't accomplished Maudie's recommended metamorphosis soon enough not to be back on the Florentine as she slept that night. Gid gave her the reins while he drew out a can of chewing tobacco. Newspapers blew and tumbled across the road. The mules were backing, backing, and she couldn't see where.

She couldn't go back to sleep. Maudie's advice flew about the room while Linn tried to catch it and make it her own, but she felt as if she was swiping at it with a net full of holes. *I have to tell him. How?* she thought, starting and stopping opening lines and conversations.

In the clinic the second morning, though, after she checked tonics and gargles and antiseptics, she sat putting together the list of supplies for what were likely the last wagons in from Denver before the snows came. She continued a list in her mind: *Let me count the ways I do not love thee,* she said to herself as she looked around the room, for it was just one room divided by a cloth wall and the patient cubicles. *I would be back in a tent, almost. I do not love thee enough to exchange washing and mending your shirts, cooking your food, tending your fires, and most of all having your babies for what I have accomplished here as a single woman and what I have yet to be.*

How could she explain so Blythe would understand? She loved him, and she loved how much he loved her. Who would not be swept away by his ardor, his admiration, his seriousness, and his playfulness? They hadn't even properly courted. Heads together and touching bare skin keeping twins alive was not a common court-ship, nor was anything else that had sealed their bond. He had not made one advance until he kissed her. *And didn't I ask for that?* she admitted. *When he took his shirt off, he caressed those buttons. He knew I would watch.*

All morning, through patients and medicine and equipment, she tried to suppress dread. She made up her mind that after dinner, or even here in the clinic after supper, she would write her thoughts and have them firmly in place when she next saw Blythe. She would come in early tomorrow morning, and before any kisses were al-lowed, they would sit down with coffee and she would tell him.

When all was quiet, with the equipment washed and on the boil, the room swept, and the records completed, she sat down to think and write.

> *Don't want to become a housewife*
> *Don't want to wash, mend, and iron*
> *Don't want to cook—breakfast OK*
> *Babies*
> *How can I marry and do all plus learn more medicine*

Pounding on the front door brought her running. Merle Chandler supported a young man, almost a boy, who was bleeding down his shirtfront.

"Fix this bastard—oops, sorry, miss—up, will you please?" Merle said as they entered. "Someone went after him with a broken whiskey glass."

Linn unbuttoned the man's shirt and looked at the wound. It was deep and jagged in his pectoral muscle.

"Is he sober?" Linn asked. "You'll have to stay here with me if he's drunk."

"Naw, he's not drunk," Merle said, settling the poor bastard in a chair. "He'd just walked in, him and his big mouth."

"That doesn't mean..." Linn began.

Merle stooped and put his nose up to the bleeding man's mouth, then poked at his face. "Tobacco," he reported.

"A chaw?" Linn asked. "I can't be sticking needles in him and giving him morphine if he's got a chaw in his mouth. He's apt to choke on it."

"So take it out," Merle suggested. "You're the doctor. He's your patient."

"You men take up nasty habits and then expect women to clean them up." Linn's anxieties made her jump on Merle and his attitude.

Merle winked. "Not such a bad way to relax. You ought to try it." He was halfway out the door.

"I will not take chaw out of this man's mouth!"

"Oh for God's sake." Merle spat, turned around, walked back, stuck his index finger into the man's cheek, and extracted a wad of tobacco, which he tossed to the ground outside.

The patient absorbed all this without a word and was quiet even when Linn began gathering needles, scissors, sutures, and morphine. She asked him his name. He gave it. She ordered him to hold still and began her treatment. She was so absorbed in the work that she hardly saw Blythe come in. He quietly came over to watch her stitching.

"Perfect," he said, then walked away to take off his coat.

Linn finished her work, put a carbolic dressing on the wound, and told the patient how much it cost and to come back in two days. She demanded he go straight home, not drink alcohol, and go to sleep. She closed the door behind him and turned to find Blythe standing by the stove with her paper in his hand.

"'Breakfast OK,'" he read, smiling. "Am I to starve the rest of the day?"

"Oh," Linn cried, going toward him and trying to snatch the paper. "'No washing, no mending.'"

She was caught, and her organized thoughts evaporated.

"Do you just expect to sit around on a cushion all day?" He was laughing now.

"No. Don't. I meant it to be serious. Please. Let's talk it over."

"About babies? Is that a do or don't? If it's a do…" He tried to put his arms around her, but she ducked away.

"Everything has happened too fast. If we marry, I'll have to give up everything I've learned and been doing here." She swept an arm to include the clinic. "I can't do that. I just can't. Do you understand at all?" She appealed to him with soft eyes and an edge in her voice.

He looked thoughtful. "No more joking," he promised. "Tell me more."

"No," she said. "You tell me what you think a wife is. What do you want? What am I?"

"Someone to love and go through life with. It sounds so simple. You're making it complicated." He turned and gave up her list to the fire.

"But it is complicated. It's real. Think of what women do. You probably never noticed. You probably had slaves, for all I know."

He whirled on her. "Absolutely not."

"Well then, servants at least." She was not cowed. "They're easy to get in a settled town. But up here the women do all their own work. They wash, mend, clean, buy the food, and spend hours cooking it and cleaning up after. Did you look at my whole list?" Her voice was sharp. She wanted his attention.

"Listen to me," she demanded, thinking clearly now. "I don't want to do that. I want to clean up blood and stitch up wounds and make medicine for children with the croup. You created a monster—one who loves you and doesn't know what to do about it."

"You didn't need a list, honey. I knew we had to have a talk. I wish I hadn't had to go up to The Falls before we could."

"I had bad dreams."

"I don't want you to have bad dreams; I just want to love you and make you happy." He reached for her, but she held up her hands to stop him getting any closer.

"I want more." But she smiled when she said it.

"Let's sit down and calmly find out what it is."

"I just told you."

"You want to stitch up wounds while you're thinking about maybe making breakfast."

"Oh." She let out a breath streaming with disgust. "Don't tease me, and don't patronize me. Are you going to do everything here and at the mill while I turn into a Daphne with a little one at my skirts, a baby at the breast, and another one coming? Carrying wood, splitting kindling, toting kerosene. Will you build me a bigger house? Shall I go on?"

"Well! I have created a monster. But one I love and can't do without as a wife and a partner. And we do need a bigger house." Linn let him put his arms around her as he spoke. "Then how can we arrange things?"

"We have to have a bedroom wall instead of flour sacks. Is there money to add on a room and move the clinic there so we can have some privacy?"

"Let's ask Maudie if she would cook for us. Louie can do all our laundry. He can mend. We'll find someone to do heavy work as it comes along."

"Is there money for all that?"

"We'll be more strict about patients paying."

"Another thing. No babies, Blythe. Not for a while, at any rate."

"No babies if you marry me tomorrow."

She married him ten days later. She had had the least Jane Austen–like conversation with Myles the evening after she and Blythe had sealed their marriage agreement with a lingering kiss. She asked Myles to stay in the common room of the boarding house after the other boarders had gone to their bedrooms and Maudie had retired to her suite.

"So the rumors are true after all," he said.

"Apparently, they were all over town. If you believed them, why did you keep asking me to dances and other things?" Linn bristled.

He shrugged. "A man needs a companion. And really, a lot of our companionship was right in this room. Quite proper, don't you agree?" He walked to the window and flicked absently at the curtains.

"Yes, quite," she agreed.

"So now it's my turn to tell you something. I'm married. My wife stayed in California. When I said I thought about going back, it was because of her."

Linn kept her voice as low as she possibly could with the anger she felt. "You're married? Taking me to dances and holding my hand and kissing me?" she hissed.

"Not very serious kisses, you'll admit."

"Well, I'll agree to that. But still, *married*? How could you?" After all, what if he weren't? How angry would he be if he thought she went places with him because she seriously cared?

"She and I have had our differences and thought some time apart would be good. It's not so scandalous this way, my working in Colorado."

Linn felt she had walked into someone's private life and didn't know how to back away gracefully. They stared at each other.

"Well," she said finally, "I hope you can find a way back together."

"Thanks," he said. "I hope you and the doc have a happy life."

"Then you and I can still be…"

"Card partners."

"Exactly," she said.

He kissed her cheek and went upstairs.

Maudie helped her make a new skirt to wear with her high-necked white shirtwaist.

They found a dark-blue fabric, black being too funereal and white impractical.

"Even if you are a virgin," Maudie observed.

"How do you know that?" Linn felt her cheeks flush, but she looked Maudie in the eye.

"I wasn't sure at first."

"Sounds like everyone in town wasn't sure." Linn told Maudie about her first meeting with Blythe in Denver and the fear she herself had had of his intentions. "But I had almost no choice, the way he laid out my future."

"He made that up. He wanted you even then," Maudie said.

"He told me that, yes."

"Now, Linn, this isn't my business, but I'm older and you don't have a mother to confide in. Do you know what you're getting into in marriage? Do you love him as much as he says he loves you?"

Linn had never confided anything personal to anyone until the morning after her first bad dream. She kept in mind that Maudie's marriage had been difficult. But Maudie was her best friend and someone she trusted, so she said, "I do love him, a hundred ways, and I admire him for all he has accomplished and for what he has taught me. I more or less understand what I'm getting into in marriage. He promised I could keep on with my work. I took your advice, and we talked it out. I do know where babies come from."

They laughed together. "Men," Maudie said, "can be, well, demanding in other ways, if you get my drift."

"I guess I'll find out."

"Just come to me. I'll get after him."

"I've no doubt you will. Maudie, you seem to know him quite well. Does he ever talk about his family?"

"I used to ask him, but he always turned it in another direction."

"Same with me. Virginia, Edinburgh. There's quite a lot before, during, and after."

"Some people are just that way."

They sewed quietly for a while, then Linn gathered her courage and said, "Maudie, I'm not going to have children right away. Maybe not for a long time. Please don't ask me about it, all right?"

"I wouldn't dream of it. I must tell you, though, I sometimes miss not having any. You're the best daughter I could wish for. You're all grown up. No diapers, no teething, not too much trouble."

The wedding was in the park. Everyone brought food and drink, and the Walcotts were toasted and teased by much of the town. Somewhere Blythe had found a wedding band, though there was no proper jewelry store in 'Chrosite. Everyone clapped and cheered when Blythe slipped it on Linn's finger and kissed her. The hammered gold facets flashed in the warm autumn sunlight when Linn raised her hand to look at it. The sun lingered down the Florentine River, and when the last of the feast had been eaten, Linn and Blythe were escorted home. When they extinguished their lamp sometime later, a shocking racket broke out under their bedroom window: buckets banging together, pans being beaten with wooden spoons, a trumpet, whistles, whoops. Linn clung to the covers. Blythe cursed. Even his relighting the lamp did not quiet the din. From the window, Linn and Blythe laughed but shouted for the crowd to go away, provoking even more noise.

"Let's wait them out. They'll go away. It's getting cold outside," Blythe said.

Then someone pounded on the front door.

He bounded up again. "Goddamn it," he shouted toward the door. "That's going too far." He threw open the door and found Artie Benson holding his mule closely behind him.

"Doc," he croaked, "Up at Santa Croce, Johnny Place crushed his leg. Somehow it slipped between the cage and the shaft and flesh is sheared off. Bone's stickin' out. Please, won't you come now?"

Blythe frowned and dismissed this emergency as another wedding-night prank.

"Honest to God, Doc," he pleaded. "I'm sure sorry. You seem to be having a party here"—he gestured to the side of the house—"but Place, he's hurt bad, bone stickin' out and everything. Honest to God, Doc."

The revelers were floating up to the porch. They swore to God they hadn't put Benson up to this. Blythe looked from one to another, believed them, and went for his equipment.

"What can I do?" he appealed to Linn, then kissed her and left for the mine. And so for the second time, she slept on Blythe's bed alone

Linn and Blythe consummated their marriage the afternoon of the third day. Blythe had set Place's tibia, stitched up the torn tissue, and slept at the Santa Croce bunkhouse for what was left of the night. The next day was a clinic day at The Falls, and Blythe was not finished until suppertime. The weather had changed by then, and it became prudent for him to sleep there. When he reached home under a clear blue sky and on top of the first snow of the season, he opened the door to find Linn mixing a gargle for the five Keller children, who looked solemn and feverish sitting in a row on the bench. The pregnant Deborah Gunn, who was waiting behind the curtain, was convinced she had marked her baby by seeing a half-dead, trapped rat watching her with hateful, beady eyes.

"Tell her it's just superstition," Linn whispered to Blythe as she turned the medicine bottle back and forth. "She doesn't believe me that the baby won't have a rat face."

George Merry was there to have his ears lavaged. "And don't try to clean them yourself with cotton on a stick next time," Linn admonished. "Just come on in, and we'll fix you up. You probably couldn't even hear the racket you set up the other night."

He grinned at her. The last time she had seen him, he was running a stick up and down a washboard under her window. Linn forced the warm water into his ears, and it came out with floating wax fragments into a metal dish.

"Sit there a minute," Linn told him when she was finished. "You might be dizzy."

"Nah, I'll be all right," he said, rising from the chair. "I'm going to leave you two alone now." He winked at Linn.

Deborah reluctantly left with an uneven gait through the slush. Blythe put the shut sign on the front door.

"Let's start over," he said, holding out his arms.

"But it's afternoon."

"Doesn't matter," he said.

Blythe was nearly asleep when he rolled onto his side. He managed "I love you" and was out before he heard Linn say the same. She fought the impulse that she ought to be up doing things. She thought she would feel changed, but she didn't. This first experience had not been earth-shattering, painful, ecstatic, or degrading. She was still the same woman, but she enjoyed the novelty of being skin to skin with a man she knew well yet in some ways hardly at all. She caressed the skin she had wanted to touch the morning after the twins were born. She relived his fingers slowly unbuttoning his shirt. She ran her fingers up and down his exposed arm, his neck, his face. He was dead asleep and did not stir. She was not good at imagining the future. Perhaps it would be exactly like the past, except she would go to bed and wake up with Doc instead of climbing stairs to her own little room. She would take care of patients. He would teach her more and more about medicine and about love. For now she was warm. She slept.

When she awoke it was dark outside, and she was chilly. She moved close to his warmth. He gathered her up again. She thought of what Maudie had said; was this "demanding"? He was kind, gentle, and oh so intent.

Afterward he said, "I'm a selfish bastard getting too far ahead of you, and you're missing the best part. I'll have to help you with that."

If he had plunged his hand between her legs, she would have been repulsed and reluctant, but his approach was so subtle, so leisurely, into hollows, over and around soft mounds, across flat places and into creases, that when he reached his goal, she was there waiting for him.

6

"We have an ideal marriage," Linn told Maudie one evening when they were washing the supper dishes at the boarding house. "We aren't together every day getting in each other's way. We're happy to see each other after."

"Hmm," Maudie said, then she smiled. "I'm no one to talk about marriage. He does have his ways. Just keep loving him."

"We're so busy I lose track of time, but I haven't been out of the 'Chrosite area since I arrived here. I'm going to see whether he won't take me down to Denver for a little holiday. Or at least to Twin Lakes, or maybe Leadville. I hear it's quite the place."

"I hear Denver's getting to be quite the place, even though they still haven't paved the streets."

"There's a new doctor in Breckenridge. We could ask him to come over for a few days."

"And another thing I hear—that doctor is too sharp for his own good. Some people don't like him."

"Sharp?" Linn asked. "You mean intelligent, or do you mean can't be trusted?"

"I haven't heard he's a bad doctor, but he's pretty liberal with his criticism of others."

"Of Blythe? Do you know?"

"Not Blythe directly, if you catch what I mean."

"Of me?"

"That's what I've heard."

"I'm not exactly performing surgery."

"You have stepped outside expectations. Just be careful."

Blythe read journals avidly. 'Chrosite was not so godforsaken that he couldn't receive European medical journals. He knew enough French and German to understand them, especially the technical terms, if not exactly the sentence structure. He had a passion for keeping up. He recognized names of some of the writers and researchers and explained to Linn how he knew them and what work he had done with them or had known about. Sometimes he was inspired to try new methods and treatments. Linn absorbed everything. The more she learned, the more she wanted.

Linn had already read, at Blythe's insistence, his basic medical text. She had never seen the inside of a body, and so it was difficult to imagine real muscle, blood, and bone from drawings in the anatomy book he suggested she tackle next. She had been aware of messy human remains brought above ground after one devastating black powder explosion. Blythe intercepted her as she had arrived in the aftermath with bags of supplies.

"You can stay over there, or you can come closer," he told her. "Coming closer will make you stronger. You can decide."

Linn closed the clinic late. She had been out in the morning to several households in which children had the usual spring infections. It seemed that chicken pox had attacked every child who hadn't already had it. Linn had had to beg temporary homes for a couple of infants whose big brothers and sisters were down with it. Another few children had mumps. So far neither type of measles had appeared, and she was grateful. There was little but palliative care for these diseases. "I know you told me that spontaneous generation is a myth, but where do these spring outbreaks spring from?" Linn asked Blythe. He only shrugged and said he wished he knew.

By the time the last patient left the clinic, with a bottle of castor oil for any and all intestinal distress, Linn's back hurt, and she felt heavy in her lower abdomen, a symptom of her infrequent monthlies.

Before she could begin looking for the pads and cloths, she sensed warm dampness between her legs, then a flow, then a rush before she collapsed from pain. Black spots danced before her eyes, and she gave in to them.

She woke to a voice from far away repeating, "No, no." Then it was Blythe's voice a little closer saying over and over, "Not again." He was bending over her whispering, "My darling girl, please, please." She opened her eyes and saw that his face was strained and full of fear.

"Thank God," he said. He rolled her onto her back and began to remove her bloody shoes and stockings. He brought a towel, put it on a chair, and propped up her feet. He knelt beside her, took her pulse, and told her to lie still while he cleaned up.

She whispered, "Was it a miscarriage? It's never been like this before."

"I don't know, but I'll look for any trace."

"We were being so careful."

"Yes, we were, and I'll be careful now. Just rest if you can on this hard floor." He rose to his feet and went for water and rags.

"Sorry to make such a mess," she said while he was on his knees cleaning.

"I'm just happy you are all right."

"What did you mean, 'not again'?"

"Oh, I've seen too much of this, done on purpose or not."

"You don't think I..."

"Of course not, my love. Never. Please. Don't talk, just rest."

Linn struggled to help him take her dress and undergarments off. She tried to get up, but he insisted she lie still with a blanket to warm her. He kept working until the floor was clean. He began to sponge up her legs, and she protested again.

"It's not right for you to clean me up like this," she said.

"This part of you isn't exactly a mystery to me."

"No, but let's retain what mystery we can."

Linn always awakened when Blythe came in after a late call. He was cold no matter the time of year. Even summer nights around

'Chrosite were rarely warm. After he got into bed, she wrapped her arms and legs around him and rubbed his back and shoulders. No matter how late or how tired, once he was warm, Blythe always said, "You saved my life." At first Linn protested, but he meant it in every way, he told her. "I don't mean I thought about ending it all. It's just that I was too busy trying to fill up my life with work, but I was lonely at the same time. Now, on the way home, I know I'm coming home to you."

One night when they had been lost in each other, Blythe asked, "Are you back down to earth? I want to tell you something if you are."

"Mmmm," she replied slowly.

"I think this is the glue that holds two people together. It gets us over the rough patches. It's a sort of amnesia or a dose of warm, sticky morphine."

"Sounds like you're speaking from experience. Am I not your first passion?"

"Just something I've thought about, wondering why some couples are more content than others."

"And what rough patches? Aren't we perfect?"

"So far, honey, so far."

Sometimes she practiced alchemy and changed his ice into fire. Sometimes he fell right asleep. Some nights he slept restlessly as if in troubled dreams. Many times they lay together and talked about the week, the day, the patients.

—I'm worried about a couple of men who've been working at the mercury retort at Brimful. I've told the supers to tighten up the tubing and make the men use gloves and masks. Workers are expendable to the managers, it seems, but the men are just as bad in their way. They think they'll look like sissies.

—Tell them they'll end up in that new hospital being built in Pueblo.

—Jesus Christ almighty!

—What? Why are you waving the newspaper like that?

—*Garfield died. Those ignorant bastards mucked around with his gunshot wound and infected it. Those high and mighty doctors were taking care of the president—the president, for God's sake! And they didn't believe in anything new, anything lifesaving, anything scientific.*

—*Let me read the story.*

—*It won't tell the truth.*

—*I checked on Rebekah and Royce this morning. It's been one thing after another at the Hunts' with the twins and Mary Ann. Flora has had all those diseases already, so she's nursing them, and Daphne is in her usual fog.*

—*Bess Evans had another sick headache. She locked herself in her bedroom, and the children went all helter-skelter. One came in for some laudanum, but I told him no, I'd come to the house, but she wouldn't let me in, she was that mad at me. I would have given her a tight bandage, like I read about in one of your books, but she screamed at me to go away.*

—*Three drops would be all right next time. Sometimes I think just a big dose of whiskey would produce the same effect. Or maybe chloral hydrate, but I've never seen a patient with sick headaches before her. I'd better write to someone down in Denver for advice.*

—*To the medical school? You said they just taught the old ways.*

—*The university is starting a new one. I sense there's going to be an effort toward improvement.*

—*The Falls men are complaining about mice and rats in the bunkhouse now the weather's turned.*

—*I think something has moved in under our house.*

—*Someone took a cat up there, but it just went back home.*

—*Chet has some half-grown barn kittens. He'd be happy to give them away. Maybe we should take one too.*

—*I put guaiacum on the order. I want to try that new test for blood, using it with turpentine.*

89

—You've been reading the journals.
—When you aren't here at night.

—I sent some of the older mill hands and miners up to the hot springs for their arthritis and rheumatism. Former cavalry, carpenters, blacksmiths. Too much wear on the body.
—Remember how scared I was to take off all my clothes the first time we went there?
—Now you're a real nature girl.

—Benny Percy was in yesterday while you were at The Falls. His face is healing up, finally.
—You know, that's the only sutured wound we've had that's become infected, and I think that was because Benny wouldn't leave it alone. He kept picking at it.
—His mother promised to watch him, but...
—Flaxseed poultice with carbolic spray, and now he has a nasty scar. Jim Bridger said arrow wounds always healed in the mountains.
—But this wasn't an arrow wound! Who's Jim Bridger?

—A cable splice gave way at the Carmarthen this afternoon, and I spent the rest of the day and half the evening over there. The frayed ends whipped all over. There's no shaft house, so it was a loose cannon. One end tore into the side of the blacksmith shop and scared the men working in there half to death. Then it flew up, then down into a man who was running every which way trying to avoid it. It looked like he took a hundred lashes—clothes all torn and cloth stuck into the bloody lines on his back, arms, and bottom. I lost count of the stitches. He wasn't the only one who was hit.
—Did the cage drop? Did you have to go down?
—Luckily the cage was already down in the pit.
—Luckily in some ways, but how can the men get out?
—They can go along one of the adits to ladders to the rail tunnel and out.

90

—All the older kids went out sledding and snowshoeing the other day, and some came home with frostbitten fingers.

—They don't feel the cold, and then they really don't feel the cold.

—A couple of men are working a patch upstream from Joseph and Mary. I don't like the looks of them, and I don't like their attitude. If you're called up that way, take the upper track and avoid the creek.

—They'll have to leave come winter.

—They aren't the only shady characters around these days. I want you to have some extra protection. By the time you fished that little pistol out of your bag, God knows what could happen.

—I had the little children on a dandelion hunt this afternoon after school. We had cookies afterwards. Those kids in Camp Seventy-Six probably didn't have a decent meal all winter, and I'm worried about scurvy. I've brewed some dandelion tea to take to their poor mother tomorrow.

—We ran out of dried apples early. Let's order up extra in the fall.

—I'm going to send that young New Yorker down to Denver to a specialist. He hasn't worked long enough to have miner's con. Maybe it's actual tuberculosis.

—I finally finished Koch's paper the other day. Do you think everyone believes him? It's a very big breakthrough.

—Didn't I tell you years ago tuberculosis was passed from person to person? The patients will have to be isolated at home.

—Who will make them?

—That's the problem.

—I expected you last night, but Chet stopped over and told me about the accident. Who's hurt? What happened?

—The new stuff—dynamite. Some men don't know how to handle it. There was a premature explosion in drift number six. Rocks flying, dust and dirt everywhere. A broken cheekbone. Someone else was hit in the head and knocked out. I had to wash out some eyes.

91

—*There was no cave-in, though?*
—*Thank God.*

—*Oscar Wilde lectured in Leadville. I wish we could have been there. And they say he went down in the Matchless and had a drift named after him.*
—*And created a sensation, no doubt.*

—*I know we couldn't have been gone at the same time. You could use some time for yourself sometimes. Think about it.*
—*I have my own way of taking time, and maybe you do too. On rides back from calls or The Falls, I frequently find a place just to contemplate the views or the movement of a stream or sit quietly on the horse and watch elk and deer.*
—*I've never told you that I do things like that too. I thought I might be wasting time.*
—*No, no. We both need to waste that kind of time as an antidote to the death and destruction we see around us.*

—*Dr. Anderson's been criticizing me again. He says I don't have any training and that the Sprague eldest son didn't really have tick fever at all, even though I know and their mother knows I took ticks out of all the children. And they'd been out hunting and crashing though the underbrush looking for elk up on Webster Pass. It all fits. And he said I was wrong to give them quinine.*
—*Anderson is a vulture. Won't he be surprised when you come back with a diploma.*
—*Come back? From where? What do you mean?*
—*You could go down to Boulder to medical school.*
—*They'd never have a woman.*
—*Think about it.*
—*I'd rather have a baby.*

There was no baby—not then, not later. Most of the time, Linn and Blythe were too busy to regret it. He brought home a half-tamed puppy that attached himself to Linn immediately. She had to teach the puppy that he did not need to protect her when she and Blythe were in bed but not asleep. When times were quiet in the clinic, he lay down in a place where he could watch her. When she went out, he followed her, and as he grew larger he set to barking when strangers approached. He learned to stay a respectful distance from horses' hooves when she was riding out. He made her feel safe. His shaggy gold-and-white coat attracted snow, mud, and dust. She named him Argonaut.

There was a new silver strike in a remote valley west of Joseph and Mary. Myles came back from Leadville to manage it, and the railroad spur from Breckenridge brought men headed for their chance at riches. 'Chrosite was booming again for a while. The outfitters cashed in. The doctors saw more results of amateur and careless mining. A regular rotation set up between The Falls mill and promising but quickly abandoned workings in the new strike area, which was rugged and high. Linn and Blythe saw cases of altitude sickness, for which they prescribed rest and, though it was rarely followed, advice to leave town. They treated slips and falls and pronounced dead one eager young prospector who had aspired toward wealth but was defeated because he did not have the agility of the mountain sheep that ruled the world in which he was only a pretender.

7

Two adventuring Cornishmen had drilled, blasted, and dug the St. Agnes mine out of the side of a hanging valley above Marmot Creek. They built an oversized stovepipe chute to send the ore straight down, but it clogged with dirt and snow. They built a trough, but it was slow and needed prodding. When they sold the St. Agnes to Henry Spangler, he expanded the mine in the once-pristine hanging valley. He built a rail trestle to carry ore cars from Upper St. Agnes to the mill he built close to the main road that led to the railhead. He drilled, blasted, and dug a tunnel into a hillside near the mill, hoping to catch a vein of gold from above and to eventually drill, blast, and dig a shaft from one tunnel to the other. To carry out his scheme, he needed more workers, and to that end he built a bunkhouse near the lower tunnel and the trestle. His medical department sat in one corner of the shaft house, and the miners tended to each others' problems unless they were serious enough to call out Doc Walcott.

Henry and his managers rarely thought the injuries from hastily burrowed tunnels through rotten rock, skimpy shoring with cheap lumber, and questionable fuse cord were that serious.

The morning the bunkhouse stove exploded, some men were eating breakfast, some had gone directly to bed after working the night shift, and some were doing not much of anything. The first victims were killed by flying metal pieces of the stove. The stovepipe hung precariously askew. Flaming wood and red-hot coals burst through the room and landed on men and bedding. Fire roared into the rafters. The thin wire supporting the stovepipe melted away, and it fell onto the stairway. The men sleeping on the second floor saw their escape route in flames. Built too close to the trestle, the bunkhouse served as a torch to ignite it. Some of the workers had escaped with minor injuries and run to alert the mill hands, who had been deafened to the explosion by the thunder of the stamps. When help arrived at the bunkhouse, everyone could hear screams from men inside. Some of the trapped men smashed windows in an attempt to escape, but that only supplied more air to feed the fire inside. Some jumped from the second floor while their backs were on fire. Some were able to run out through the flames, but they were not unburned. When the roof collapsed, none of the men still trapped inside survived. All the men with burns threw themselves or were led onto the snow. Some of the mill hands chopped a hole through Marmot Creek ice and started a bucket brigade.

One of the mill managers galloped into 'Chrosite to find Blythe, then went on to have Chet Marshall hitch a fast horse and small wagon. But Blythe was at The Falls, and Linn only guessed at what she needed as she collected supplies. She and Blythe had never discussed serious burns. They had never had to treat any but minor ones in all those years. Usually they lubricated the skin liberally and dressed it lightly in order not to rip new skin when it was safe to uncover the wound. How was she to grease a whole body? Once Blythe had mentioned using honey and sugar on burns. She sent the driver to general store to buy as much as they had. The only thing she was sure she needed was morphine, and she took the whole supply. She sent the messenger on to The Falls to tell Blythe to come right away.

"We piled snow on 'em," the messenger had said when he arrived at her door. "Better to freeze than burn up. They were in so much pain."

She felt an uncharacteristic panic rising while the horse and wagon tore along the road to St. Agnes. She wanted to turn and run when she saw the men in the snow. One was clearly about to die and still screaming. She would have given him morphine, but she didn't know where to touch him. He screamed louder when she began to cut off a partially burned boot. When she found a vein in his foot, she gave him the drug, and hoped it eased his death. She gave it to all who had visible veins. Some men were blistered red; some were black.

The fire flared on the trestle, but at least it was moving away from the mill, blown by the west wind up the valley. The fire on the upper trestle had ignited trees on the steep mountainside. The needleless, dry lower branches provided tinder to move the flames farther up and out. The higher the trestle, the more timbers burned and fell. When the upper trestle collapsed, sparks flew everywhere, and blazing timbers ignited a shed and pile of lumber. Mill hands ran to them and threw snow on the blaze to little effect. The miners at Upper St. Agnes had no egress except the trestle. They were isolated but not burned.

Linn created a clean-enough corner of the shaft house as a hospital, but she left the most badly burned men in the snow. Those who could tolerate being touched at all were lifted, screaming in spite of the drug, out of the snow onto a litter. Linn drizzled mineral oil onto each man, not daring to touch his agonized skin. She let honey run onto burned patches of the least-affected men, men she thought had a chance to recover. The faces were the worst, because she probably knew some of these men, but not now. She placed a sheet over each of the dead and wondered how awful it was going to be when she had to remove it. She wondered whether or not to use phenol spray; she feared creating more pain. She moved from man to man murmuring encouragement for her sake as well as theirs. The only real treatment she could give was to stitch the cuts on the men who had climbed out the windows. The last man to do so had bad burns that had cauterized the cuts on his legs. She prayed Blythe would come.

He arrived about two hours later. He did not dismount, but only stopped the horse and stared up at the trestle and the trees, which were still burning and throwing off sparks. The air smelled of burning: flesh, wood, and pitch.

Linn ran to him. She tugged at his coat as if to pull him off the horse and make him pay attention. He kept staring at the fire, mesmerized. "Help me. Get down and help them," she almost sobbed. She took hold of the horse's bridle. Blythe slapped her hand away hard, and she was so shocked she let go. She clasped his pants leg. She screamed, "I don't know what else to do."

"Nothing. Give them morphine." He turned the horse and pressed it away into a canter.

In disbelief, Linn watched until he disappeared around a bend in the road. Nothing but morphine. And so she did what he said.

Linn returned home days later, defeated, dirty, and nearly out of supplies. Twelve of the men had died as their body fluids seeped out of their skinless bodies onto the hard floor or into the snow. All the men who had been left in the snow died before sundown that first day. With no way to bury any of them, she and Henry Spangler agreed that the dead should be packed in snow for the time being. The men who would probably live and needed constant care were handed off to homes that would take them. Maudie's clientele was low, and she agreed to take a man who could walk but not use one arm or hand.

Chet drove Linn home with Argo in the back of the wagon. He helped her carry her stained and filthy sheets and her empty baskets to the door. She entered a cold and silent house. Blythe never let the stove burn out. She fired it up and set water on to heat before she did anything else. When she went into the bedroom to change out of her filthy clothing, she startled to see a body in the bed. She called Blythe's name, but there was no response. She bent over him, thinking the unthinkable. How else to explain the condition of the house? She saw him breathing, and she spoke his name, close now. He was unshaven, and he opened the most hollow eyes she had ever seen. There was no expression in the light-brown eyes with the green inclusions.

"What's wrong? Are you ill?" She stroked the covers over his shoulder.

"No." He closed his eyes.

"What happened? What's the matter?"

"Nothing. Leave me alone." He turned his back to her and pulled the covers up close around his head. She went to her side of the bed where she could see his face again. She sat on the edge and stroked him again.

"Well, something must be wrong. Tell me." She tried to find his hands to hold. He pulled away and turned again. She continued to sit on the bed while she massaged his back.

"Don't," he mumbled and moved his shoulder away from her hands.

Her concern for him flew out the window. The man had ridden away from her panicked need; the man had let their home turn into an icehouse when she needed warmth and solace. She leaned over and hissed, "What is the matter with you? How could you leave me up at St. Agnes like that? It was horrible. You could have done more for them than I was able to. You let those men down." She went on scalding him. She had never spoken to anyone this way, but she had never been abandoned in the midst of horror. His silence ignited a fire she had never felt before, and she could not damp it. "It's freezing in here. How could you let the stove go out? Haven't there been any patients? What have you been doing?" She placed her hand on the blankets and shook him. "Get up and help me. This time. Get up, for God's sake. You can't do this. You can't just abandon me with dying patients. Answer me." She shook him again, then pounded on his back harder and harder. Argo began barking and running from one side of the bed to the other. Linn had never reprimanded the dog the way she did now, with a screech that sent him hiding under the table in the kitchen.

"Blythe," she cried out in anger, frustration, and exhaustion. He didn't answer. She didn't know what to do except keep attacking.

He turned over and looked at her with eyes that frightened her. "I have no answers. Leave me alone." He lay back down and covered his head.

Blythe alternately hid from the world and went about his work. Linn begged him to help her understand, but the more she probed, the less responsive he was and the more he slept—or seemed to. When she offered her body, he mumbled excuses. When she became angry, he stayed away from home. When he returned he mutely went to bed. She spent many evenings alone, reading, searching Blythe's books for answers to puzzling symptoms, mindlessly playing solitaire, keeping up the books and supplies because Blythe didn't. She saw less of Maudie and felt even more lonely because of it.

Linn had been to the Hunts' every day and twice overnight for a week and a half. Flora, Mary Ann, Rebekah, and Royce all had had septic sore throats. The older boys escaped the infection—probably, Linn thought, because their father kept them at work outdoors twelve hours a day cutting, hauling, and delivering wood.

Flora, Mary Ann, and Royce improved, but Rebekah languished even after her throat lost its angry redness and she said she could bear to swallow. Linn felt helpless.

"Where have you been?" Blythe asked when she got into bed late one night.

She was exhausted, and worry made her snappish now. Before it had provided for conversation between them.

"Where do you *imagine* I've been?"

He turned over, surprising her. She had become so accustomed to his back.

"You're frozen," he said.

She resisted when he tried to pull her close. He simply moved his own body until she had no more space to retreat. Wrapped in his arms, feeling safe for the first time in months, she couldn't stop tears from wetting her face as well as his. He tried to dry both of them with the hem of the sheet.

"Help me," she said. "Help me with Rebekah."

"Isn't she getting better?"

He hadn't been involved with any of the Hunt children's illness, but uncannily he knew that Linn had been seeing them.

"She's failing, fading."

He knew immediately. "Rheumatic fever."

"I'm so afraid. I'm afraid it's an omen."

"You've never believed in such things."

"It's about us. How we were when she was born, and how we are now. If she dies. If we keep on this way." She said these things in a whisper: signs, omens, secrets of her heart she couldn't say aloud. "We'll be…"

"No," he said. "Never. No matter what happens, we're Linn and Blythe forever and ever. As long as we both shall live, as the man said." He held her tighter. "I'm feeling better. I want to get out of the black hole I've been in. I know it's hard for you to understand, but I'm trying."

"How can I if I don't even know what it's about?"

"Let me be. Let me work it out. I'm close; I feel that. This is a rough patch."

"The kind you told me would happen, and that was cured by this?" She began pulling up both their nightgowns.

"You remembered," he said.

The rough patches were not gotten through after that night or any other. Knot after knot, little by little, Linn loosened the ties that bound her so tightly to Blythe Walcott she had forgotten she was separate. She had given him everything—in life, love, and work—and she had to begin to take it back.

Conversation came apart first, like a child's wooden puzzle swept to the floor in pieces that no longer even touched. Day by day they had shared their patients' ills and health, the weather, the gossip, the newspapers, the journals. Now Blythe came in, said hello, or not, and went to bed. When Linn stopped him long enough to ask a question, he referred her to a textbook or article, never saying more than that, never probing for more information about her concerns. She froze when patients were right there in the clinic and he said nothing—no greeting, no interest—but went straight into the bedroom. She had not pulled away enough not to feel responsible for his behavior and bad manners. He stopped coming to supper at Maudie's. Cooperation ceased after conversation. Not only did Blythe not tell her when he took supplies and medicines, he left her to wash, sterilize, compound, mix, dilute, and bottle. She asked him to do his share. He said he would but didn't. He had asked her to let him be, but she couldn't. She cajoled. She blamed and shamed. She accused. She couldn't stop herself, because she was so afraid.

She never spoke to him of Rebekah again. She searched the books and journals to confirm that Rebekah had rheumatic fever. *Maybe it is spotted fever. No. She'd had the septic throat. No, she hadn't had the rash. She totters around and then spends days in bed, exhausted. She's eight years old and she should be outdoors playing with the other children and helping her mother.* Linn visited as often as she could. She read to Rebekah and tried to further her reading. She played card games to teach her some arithmetic. Flora borrowed readers from school and worked with Rebekah. Rebekah did not die, but she was never the same little girl.

Linn hurried home from the livery stable on a clear and starry night that was beautiful but so cold she thought her lungs would freeze with every breath. Orion hung in the winter sky in his own configuration of worlds. Linn had left Argo at home to save his paws from this extraordinary weather turn. As she reached her porch with her head down and face buried in a scarf, she nearly tripped over Floyd Hunt sitting on the step.

"Is it Rebekah?" she asked, heart in mouth.

"No." He rose and stepped up, towering over her. "It's about me and you."

She was alarmed by the heat in his voice. "I don't understand," she said, taking two steps backward. He stepped down, and she felt she had to stand up to him, whatever this was about.

He fumbled in a pocket and brought out the device she and Doc had given Daph years earlier. He shook it in her face, and this made her back up again but only to take a deep breath and try not to explode.

"This is not between you and me," Linn said. "It's between me and Doc and Daph. You have nothing to do with it."

"Hell I don't. It's in the way of my natural rights."

"What?" She had never heard such nonsense, but she kept herself from scoffing or laughing. It would just enflame him further.

"My rights are between me and my wife, and she can't have this." He threw the materials to the ground and stomped.

"More children might kill her or damage her so much that she couldn't take care of the ones she already has. She asked for help."

"She can't be talking to anyone about her and me. It's not decent. This thing"—he stomped again—"isn't decent."

"It's what she wanted, and you have no right to stop her."

"Hell I don't. She won't be down here to ask for it again. I made sure of that. And you stay away from my kids and my house."

"I need to keep seeing Rebekah at least." She hated bargaining with this man or pleading.

"And if I see you"—he grasped her forearms in his rough hands—"you may be sorry. And nothing gets in the way of me and Daph, understand?" She tried to twist away, but he pulled her against his body. "Some dark night, sometime coming home like this, nothing might get in the way of you and me. Your droopy ol' husband prob'ly can't do the job."

She was able to raise one foot just enough to be able to kick his shin. He laughed and let her go. "You're pretty tough, aren't you, Mrs. Doc."

She knew any stream of insults would only make him laugh again. She had to settle for "You're disgusting."

8

Ephriam Taylor came for Linn in the middle of a late April morning.

"Emmy's having a real hard time," he said. "Please come and help her."

Emmy Taylor was a big round woman with a round face and round hips. Linn thought the baby ought to slide out like a pat of butter, same as there was no stopping talk coming out of Emmy's mouth. Emmy and Eph already had a three-year-old. He had come into the world with just the neighbors' help. Too bad Emmy wouldn't do it that way this time. Linn changed into her divided skirt, packed a bag of supplies, and mounted the horse behind Eph. Argo followed in his exploratory way, over snow banks and through mud and the hazards of winter snow and spring rain.

They could hear Emmy before they reached the farmhouse. She yelled, she groaned. The little boy jumped up from the front porch and ran to his father, who brushed him off with a quick pat on the head. Linn went into the bedroom and found Emmy on her feet, pacing. The neighbor girl who helped with milking and butter making stood by helplessly.

"Time you got here," Emmy said. "Let's get this over with. I didn't want another baby in the first place." She grasped the footboard of the bed and moaned.

"Can't your mother come?" Linn asked the girl.

"She's sick, and I was already here, but I don't know what to do."

"Go back to your work then, or go on home," Linn said.

Linn tried to get Emmy to lie down, but she resisted. "It hurts worse that way. My back. Oh, God." She went into another spasm.

"Emmy, listen," Linn insisted. "I need to examine you. If your pains are this close together, the baby will be coming soon. Lie down, now. I can't help you like this." Linn began to help her undress. Emmy's underclothes were soaked.

"When did this happen?" Linn asked, holding Emmy's pantalets before her eyes.

"Right after I got up this morning. I had to fix breakfast, I had to wash up, I had work to do. No one helps me around here. I don't have time for this baby. It's making me hurt too bad." Emmy went on mumbling complaints, but she did lie down before another contraction arched her body. Linn scrubbed up in the basin Eph had brought. Emmy screamed again. Almost before Linn got back to her, the baby girl came. *A pat of butter, indeed,* Linn thought. She cleaned Emmy, then she cleaned the baby and gave her to her mother.

"Humph," Emmy said. "Well, at least I'll have some help around here. Someday."

Linn saw that Emmy cuddled the baby before she unwrapped the blanket and looked her over. She handed her back to Linn.

"Too tired," she said and went right to sleep.

Linn and Eph got the baby settled and the little boy fed. Linn stayed at the house awhile longer. Emmy and the baby continued to sleep. Eph shrugged, apologized, and offered Linn either a borrowed horse or snowshoes. The few warm days earlier in the week had melted big patches of snow on the road. She chose the horse, noted heavy clouds in the west, and started home with Argo beside her. The horse seemed to remember that Linn was the extra weight he had carried in the morning, and he made her pay. He tried to veer off the road toward anything that looked edible. He shied at the squirrel Argo chased up a tree. She tried to encourage him to walk on faster or even trot. She took off one of her gloves and smacked him on the hip to little effect. Through a clearing Linn saw blue-black clouds, and just then she felt the first raindrops that turned quickly into a shower, then a deluge. She and the horse heard thunder, and he used it as an excuse to crow-hop and try to turn around for home. She could cut off a mile by taking the old trail that passed the abandoned Florida Pearl mine. She turned into it as a wind picked up. The trail turned west and became a wind tunnel. She put her head down against rain that blew into her face. Thunder echoed again around the high peaks of the valley while the rain increased. Linn chastised herself for not being prepared for this weather. She worried that she dwelt too far within the depths of Blythe's behavior to carry on a rational everyday life. After nine springs in the mountains, she still forgot that a beautiful morning could become a deadly afternoon and that rain could be even worse than snow. A yard-wide stream of melted snow and rain ran across the trail, and the horse would not cross it. Linn kicked him forward, and so he bolted on and up one of the steep portions of the trail that made travelers avoid it. Halfway up he stopped dead. Argo bounded on and off the trail, snuffing up evidence of other creatures that had passed by. He set up a nonstop bark and ran toward a boulder that was thirty feet uphill off the trail. He stopped beside it and began to bark even more loudly, looking back at Linn, then at the boulder, as if she should see that he had found something unusual.

She called him to come. He ran behind the boulder. He and a cougar jumped straight up at the same time. Linn screamed. The horse jumped sideways. This time Linn could not keep her seat. She fell off and crashed on the rock-strewn trail, but she kept hold of her medical bag. Her purse, which she had hung over the saddle horn, went flying in the opposite direction and landed in a mud patch. The pistol she always carried was in that purse, far out of reach, and how could she aim, at any rate, with such cold hands at a moving target? The horse wheeled and galloped off in the direction of home. Argo and the lion faced off. Argo seemed to have the better of it, feinting one way then the other as if this were a game, while the lion backed up and looked puzzled. They were both back behind the rock when Argo whined long and loud. The lion screamed and sprinted up the hill and away into the trees. Argo did not come out. Linn was frantic as she struggled toward the boulder through patches of old crusty snow, her skirt becoming even more damp and heavy. Argo kept whining. She found him down, lying in the depression the struggle had made under the two animals, but he was paddling with his left leg to pull himself up. The snow was bloody around him, and smudges dotted the line the lion had taken. She examined Argo's wounds. A flap of skin hung from behind his ear, along his neck, and down across his shoulder—a tear at least ten inches long. The claw had missed the big vessel in his neck, but it had dug into the shoulder muscle, and blood welled into the slash. She talked to him and told him to lie still, but he struggled to his feet and stood on three legs on the uneven footing of the snow patch, disturbed needle litter, and small rocks. Mud caked his right side, where he must have rolled in the fight. Linn told him to stay while she retrieved her medical bag and purse. With chilled and shaky hands, she pulled packing and a roll of gauze from the bag, pulled the skin back up against his body, and wrapped the wound to save it from exposure.

Argo limped back to the trail. They made slow progress up the hill, where at the top a large stand of budding aspen left them even more exposed to the rain and wind. Hundreds of eyes stared unmoving and unmoved. They frightened her now instead of watching over her as before. Linn's hair was soaked and falling onto her shoulders. Her wool coat became heavy and began to leak into her dress. With her hands in her coat pockets, her gait, slow as it was, felt awkward and off balance in her heavy arctics as she tried to avoid rocks on the trail. They stymied Argo, so Linn picked him up and around them.

Dark crept over the eastern sky, and light was fading from the west. In the dusk she passed the abandoned workings of the Florida Pearl and considered taking shelter in the lift house, but she wouldn't dry in there in the cold, and Argo needed help before infection worked deeper into his tissues, which were already coated with dirt, fragments of scat, and dead meat. She talked herself down from panic and trudged on. If she kept moving, she reasoned, she would not freeze to death. No, she reminded herself, that was not necessarily true. She couldn't feel her fingers. She didn't know how long Argo could walk in the cold and wet, even in his shaggy coat.

Argo fell. A chill, almost like a seizure, shook Linn's whole body and chattered her teeth. Dizzying thoughts took over her mind even as Argo lay at her feet whimpering.

Blythe won't be home. How can I suture Argo with hands so cold? Her mind began churning on Blythe's absences, his silences, his retreat to bed, his response when she told him how afraid she was when she didn't know where he was, when she needed to ask him questions about treatment.

"I'm going to kill someone someday," she'd said.

"No, you aren't. You can do everything."

When she began to tell him all the things she in fact could not do, and he should know it, he had walked out of the house and didn't return for two days.

Don't stop, don't stop, she told herself. She bent over Argo. His eyes were closed, but she felt his breath and that deep in his hair he was warm enough. *I could go into the lift house and use Argo as a blanket. Do I have matches? No. Keep going.*

Put one foot in front of the other and keep walking.

Linn lifted Argo to his feet, but he could no longer walk on three legs. She hadn't carried him since he was six months old, but now there was no other way to get him help. She would rather have carried him over her left shoulder, as most women hold a baby, but his injury was on his right side, and she didn't want it to be pressed against her and made worse. It was even more difficult to anticipate the large rocks on the trail. They sent her to the left or right, zigzagging and losing momentum. Finally she reached a wider road. Instinct told her to turn right. She listened for a wagon or a horse, but all she heard was the grinding of windblown tree limbs against each other. The sound irritated her almost beyond endurance. She screamed, "Stop it!" and only succeeded in frightening Argo. She laid him down several times when she felt a shaking chill about to overtake her. Each time she felt more lightheaded than the last when she bent down to regain him. She was on edge against more cougars, but her hands were too cold to hold the gun. In fact, she could hardly feel them at all.

The world was in deep darkness now. She recognized that she had reached the main road from Brimful to 'Chrosite. Two miles to home. The road was deserted. She almost cried, and she kept going. Her soggy coat felt so heavy she wanted to throw it off. She became frustrated, angry, and irrational. She wanted to sit down in the road and scream again. Or give up. It was difficult to bend to the task and shiver at the same time. A snow mist started up in the nighttime cold and closed off any faint visibility of the way ahead. The mud patches told her where the road lay. Flakes swirled in ghostly and disorienting shapes. Her nose was an icicle. She imagined hearing footfalls, and time and time again had to damp down her hopes. But now they were real. A lantern and then a horseman appeared out of the gloom.

Some dark night, sometime coming home like this.

She was afraid to call out, and she was afraid not to. Her voice came out as a croak.

"Who's there?" the voice was suspicious. He said it again farther off and then close beside her. "Oh my God. Doctor Linn."

Adam Smits jumped off his horse and clasped her shoulders. She couldn't remember how she knew this man. But it was not Floyd Hunt, and that was all that mattered. She whispered out that Argo was hurt, to please be careful with him. Smits kept saying oh my God and telling her how wet and cold she was. She could barely move her lips enough to say, "Get home." She could not even manage "please."

She put Argo down. Smits boosted her onto his horse. She was too cold to sit up straight. She couldn't find the stirrups, and he said not to bother. He took her coat off and put his around her shoulders. He picked Argo up, and they walked into town.

The house was dark and the door locked. Linn's heart and spirits, so low already, curled into a ball in her depths. Her tears were frozen with the rest of her. Her mind saw Argo die, but she saw that his eyes were bright when Smits placed him on the porch. She told Smits how to unlock the door. He carried her off the horse and into the house, where she leaned on the table while he went back for Argo and the lantern. She heard a sound coming from the bedroom, but there was no light, and she knew she couldn't hold a match.

"What's all this?" Blythe said when Smits tried and failed to be quiet bringing in the dog.

"It's your wife, goddamn it. She's half froze and her dog is hurt while you're standing there in your drawers. Get some more light in here. Put on some clothes, and do what you're supposed to do instead of moping around all the time like some sick cow."

Blythe struck a match into the lamp and in the light stared at Linn, who was sobbing great gulps of air and unable speak, and then at Smits, who was scowling and holding Argo with his blood-soaked dressing. Blythe seemed paralyzed. Smits lowered Argo to the floor, knocking into the table and upsetting a coffee cup and candlesticks. The noise brought some life into Blythe's eyes. Smits threw wood from the box into the stove. He took his coat from Linn.

"Get this woman's clothes off. Get her feet into some warm water," he shouted as he pulled a basin from a nail on the wall and tested the tank, which was luckily still warm on the stove. He dipped the basin into it. He helped Linn out of her arctics, placed the basin on the floor, and set it at her feet. He helped her sit down, and when he placed one of her feet, stockings and all, in the water, she flinched and tried to draw it away. She was seared. But Smits said no, it wasn't boiling water, it only felt that way, and placed her other foot in. Blythe moved toward her and reached out a hand.

"That's right, you worthless bastard. You fix her up now, or the whole town will be after your sorry ass. Or worse." He fixed Blythe with an eye, backed out of the house, and slammed the door.

The old Blythe took over. He began to unbutton her dress. She croaked out, "Argo first."

"Argo what? You need help."

"No. Argo now." She pulled the words from some deep place. "He's hurt. A cougar. He needs cleaning and stitching. I'll take care of myself." She tried and failed at the buttons.

"Let me, quickly." He brought a blanket. He helped her out of the waist and skirt and stripped off her petticoat. "You should give up stays," he said while he struggled with the hooks.

She almost laughed but couldn't manage it. He put her into a flannel nightgown, wrapped her in the blanket, and sat her down again. He rewarmed the water and brought another basin for her hands.

"Argo," she demanded.

"I'm not a dog doctor. I'm concerned about you."

"Argo saved my life." Why pretend anymore? She gathered up the strength to speak the truth. "*He* takes care of me. *He* loves me, and if you don't help him, I will leave and never...and if you hadn't been here, we might both have died, because my hands are so cold..." She wouldn't let him hold them. She shook them away. They were wet, and she splashed him and herself. She could feel herself losing control because Blythe just sat there beside her.

"Clean him up. Stitch him up." One of the chill seizures was coming on, and she had to make herself clear. Her voice rose in spite of its waver. "Give him just the right amount of anaesthesia. I'll know. I swear I'll never forgive you. I'll leave, I'll..."

She held his eyes for so long—those light-brown eyes with the beautiful green flecks—that blue fire in hers was the only warmth about her.

"Do it now," she said. "I can't help him, and you can. And that's what you're supposed to do."

Blythe spent more than an hour clipping, cleaning, shaving, anaesthetizing, stitching, spraying, and bandaging. Linn looked to him from time to time. She sank into her own world now that Argo was being cared for. She relived the rain, the rocks, the foolish horse, the cougar. Over and over she played Argo's fight with the cougar. She couldn't let it go. Sometimes the cougar was a full-grown male. Sometimes he was an emancipated youngster. Sometimes the story ended with Argo dead. Sometimes the cougar came after her as well. Sometimes she whimpered as Argo had, and Blythe soothed her by saying that everything was all right now.

When he was finished, he asked Linn whether she was able to stand over Argo while he looked for something. He returned from the rag bag with the shirt from a discarded set of long johns. He pulled the sleeves over Argo's front legs, carefully put Argo's head through the neck opening, and pulled the shirt over the dog's body. He buttoned up the placket and opened his hands upward as if to present her newly dressed pet to Linn.

"I couldn't think of anything else to try to keep him from licking or biting the wounds."

"I wish we could have a photograph."

Blythe used a sheet to make a pad on the floor. Linn felt strong enough to help lift Argo onto it. He was still asleep but breathing steadily.

"He's going to heal if he behaves himself. Now let's take care of you." He steered her into the bedroom, took off the blanket and nightgown, and put her to bed. He stripped off all his clothes, lay down beside her, and gathered her against his warm skin with her back cupped into him.

"This is the best thing for hypothermia. Skin on skin. We would have done this immediately if not for Argo. Now, tell me what happened."

Linn thought she was telling the true story, but she might still have been floating through jumbled versions. Maybe even the past few years had not been true after all. She kept drifting to sleep, and Blythe woke her with the admonition not to. He kept her talking.

"How do you feel now?" he said after a while.

"Warm," she said. She hadn't meant her voice to be so low and breathy. It aroused Blythe. This is how they had always been. With them, this was the truth. She moved to take him, and after a long time, after it was over, he talked and talked. He told her how much he loved her, how he couldn't do without her, that he had been off the rails but now was back on. The moment she came in the door this evening, he knew how it would be from then on: the old Blythe and the happy Linn. When she asked him again, for what seemed like the hundredth time, what had gone wrong, was it her fault, how could she help him, he said not to worry about that anymore. They would begin again and be happy.

When she woke in the morning, he was gone.

Argo healed, but Linn did not. Blythe's warmth, love, and promises were like the snow in spring, and she became the defiant wildflower that thrust up through it and watched it flow away. She and he saw less of each other because he stayed away longer. When he came home, she was more upset than when he was gone. They hardly spoke. He had spurts of energy and interest. At least she had not heard that he failed to keep up his clinic duties at The Falls. When there was a crisis and he was at home, he rose to it, but she was obliged to take on all the responsibility for supplies, appointments, riding out on calls, payments, and the banking. When he asked for money, she gave it grudgingly. When he was in their bed, she got into her side silently and more resigned these days than angry. At least he provided warmth, whether he cared to or not. She hired Flora to help her with the simple tasks after school and in the summers. Flora sometimes asked to spend the night with Linn, and Linn let her. Linn never made calls to the Hunts' and learned through Flora that the children, except Rebekah, seemed to be thriving. At least their father's temper hadn't resulted in the need for medical attention. Flora reported that Rebekah remained quiet, tired, and obedient. Her spark of life was steady but dim. Linn worried about Flora and her faraway expression. She seemed like a different child away from home.

"Doctor Linn," Flora said one day, "Miss Beard is making me teach the first- and second-grade children. She says it's because

I'm bright enough and can catch up with the older group in my spare time. I don't have any spare time. You know what it's like at my house."

"Have your parents talked with Miss Beard about it?"

"Mama doesn't have time or doesn't care, and Papa certainly wouldn't care. I'm afraid to say anything to him."

"I'm awfully busy too, but let's see whether we can make time for some lessons here. And if I see Miss Beard, I'll try to find out whether they need another real teacher."

Linn mined her past to create lessons for Flora, and the girl eagerly undertook each assignment. They spent the rare slow afternoon on fractions and decimals and why they were the same, moving on to what elementary algebra Linn had ever known. She set Flora to reading the books she had loved and instructive articles in *Harper's*. She borrowed *Little Women* from Mother Mason and made Flora dissect the personalities of the March girls. They read *Tom Sawyer* and listed the ways it could have been set in 'Chrosite. Flora already knew the states and their capitals, and so Linn made her learn by heart all the countries of the world and their capitals, a challenge for Linn, who tried to affix them in her own memory as she rode out to calls.

Linn still tried to visit Maudie in the mornings, but days might go by before she had time to sit in Maudie's kitchen and relax with a cup of coffee and a piece of toast and jam. They never spoke about Blythe, until one morning Maudie reached out for Linn's hand and held it.

"I want to tell you something, because I think it is important. I don't want to hurt you, but I must." She nodded for Maudie to go on. "They say—don't ask me who they are—that Blythe is, well, spending time with one of Opal Faye's girls."

The breath went out of Linn at the same time she felt she might vomit. She gripped Maudie's hand harder. "No, that can't be. He wouldn't."

"He is."

"How can you be sure?"

"Somehow a lot of people know."

"He wouldn't be that blatant. That's not like him."

"Nothing is like him these days."

Linn chewed this over and knew she must swallow it. She had seen people looking at her. In pity, scorn, revenge for being the woman she was? She closed her eyes to make the images go away. If only she could find Blythe on a good day and confront him, even though confrontation drove him away. The consequences could be no worse than her life was now.

"I'll have to talk to him," she said and looked at Maudie.

"You'd best. And I'm sorry to be the bearer of bad tales, but you need to know for several reasons."

"Not likely I'll catch anything. I know you don't want to know this, but that's how we are now."

"You can tell me anything you want to."

"I know, and I don't hold it against you that you told me." They smiled at each other.

"If you want to kill him, I'll help you."

"I'll let you know."

9

LINN HAD RIDDEN OUT ON CAP, ALWAYS HER FAVORITE HORSE, WITH Argo at her side, to check on the burns two brothers had suffered in their own secret Fourth of July fireworks display. Their mother invited her to stay for supper. Linn accepted because she had not seen the knowing expression on the woman's face, as she sometimes did from some in the community. She took this excuse to delay going home and to talk with someone about something besides their symptoms. She enjoyed learning about the woman's garden and the elk that had to be kept out of it, grocery shortages, and the latest news. She felt like a real woman on a real visit in real life. She helped with the supper dishes before she and Argo started back to 'Chrosite on this warm, long-light summer evening.

At the stable, Chet was busy, and so she untacked Cap and set him to his own supper. Argo sniffed about for cats. She stayed at the stable because the horses relaxed her as they ate their drawn-out evening meal. Cap chewed rhythmically the bites of hay he nosed out of the bottom of his manger.

"Why do you do that?" Linn asked him. "Isn't it just as good on top?" She pulled a mane comb out of the jumble of grooming tools, climbed onto a wooden box, and began to untangle Cap's mane, which if left to itself tended to fall into dreadlocks. Simple and mindless, this work was soothing to Linn, who always liked working with her hands. The anxiety of her nearly sole responsibility for Blythe's medical practice receded for the moment. Cap radiated warmth, and his chewing was hypnotic.

She was half finished combing when Blythe strolled into the stable as if he had not been away five days. He did not say hello, but his arm swept the scene.

"Munching herbivores, the faithful dog, the watchful cats, the saintly mother—I can almost see the halo. We're missing the babe. And the sheep. I shall be a lost lamb wandering in."

"A black sheep," Linn said, keeping on with her task and not looking at him.

Blythe picked out a brush and began grooming the opposite side of the horse. They worked in silence. Linn assumed he had been drinking. She hated the sarcasm it brought on. She wouldn't, couldn't, talk to him now about her problems: questions about a difficult pregnancy up in Brimful; supplies to be sent up from Denver; if he had collected any money; did he want another *Harper's* subscription; and would he please, please, for the tenth time asking, fix the hook for one of the lanterns hanging in the clinic.

Blythe finished brushing the left side of the horse and came around to the right just as Linn pulled the ribbon from her own hair and was about to braid it into Cap's mane. When she shook out her hair, Blythe looked up at her, put his arms around her hips, and whispered, "Holy Linnie Ann. Mother of none. Pray for us sinners." He buried his face in her bodice and ran his hands up her sides.

Linn didn't understand the allusion but sensed again sarcasm, and she replied in kind while she pulled away from him. "I would if I thought anyone was listening. And keep away from me."

"I'm sorry I've been keeping away from you. That's what I'd like to talk about."

"You're sorry? That's not what I was told. I was told you have someone to keep you company. Don't touch me." She stepped back as far as the box let her.

"Where did you hear that?"

"Apparently it's all over town. You disgust me." She stepped down from the box and carried it out of Cap's stall. She returned for the grooming tools without speaking. Blythe watched her.

"Did Maudie tell you that?"

"What difference does it make?"

"I don't go to bed with her."

"I don't care what you do with her." She tossed a comb into the pile and rushed out of the stable and home.

She didn't expect him to follow, but he did. The first thing he said was, "You don't mean that."

"I do. Yes, I do," she said absently. She was trying to write in the patient register, but she couldn't focus on the lines and names. He walked to her, took the book from her hands, set it down, and sat in the chair across the table from her. She didn't look at him. "You told me at the beginning of this sorry change in our lives to leave you alone. That's what I want now." She rose, but he moved fast and stood behind her. He wrapped his arms around her shoulders.

"Will you listen to me for a little bit? I've been up at The Falls," Blythe said. "I know you won't believe me, but I've been sober all the time I've been away. I've been working like a demon. There was a raft of injuries one day—cave in—minor, luckily—at Kings and Queens and some sore throats in the bunkhouse. God, I thought if it was diphtheria, we're a goner. And then that woman up in Little Sweden had her baby. Don't know whether she's married to Vic or not, but at any rate they're a family now. She was as big as a house, and that's why Andrew called for me. They thought it might be twins."

"I'm not doing that again." Linn couldn't stop herself from being drawn into the conversation.

"Well, I wouldn't have to be ashamed to look at your breasts this time." He ran one hand up and down her neck.

"Don't do that." She tried to pull away from his embrace, but he held her fast. "Don't touch me after you've been with…"

"I told you, I don't go to bed with her."

"Then why?" She didn't want to be in the conversation or for her tone to be so searching, but it came out all the same.

"I don't know," he said with one side of his face against her hair. "I've been thinking so hard about what's wrong, and now I feel so much better about everything. You know that I've said I felt like a train off the track, and if I could just get back on everything would be better—normal. I feel I've been on the track the past few days. Don't give up on me. Please. I love you so, and I need you." She struggled to turn in his arms and face him. He reached a hand up and caressed her cheek with his fingertips. "Linn, do you love me?"

"I don't know," she whispered.

He pushed his body hard against her. A warm yielding swept over her. It had been too long, and she was too susceptible. She pushed back, wanting him in spite of herself.

"Let's start over," he said.

Let's start over.

"I'll always love you. Love me again." He outlined her lips with a fingertip and kissed them.

I shouldn't do this, she thought. But she did. His shirt begged to be unbuttoned. His belt buckle was never undone so readily. Her divided skirt fell around her feet. The hooks of her bodice came apart. Linn and Blythe had always undressed modestly and put on nightclothes before reaching for each other under the covers. Now, the surrender of each piece of clothing made them whisper and laugh. In this unusually warm mountain summer, no covers were needed until well into a night of touch and words and touching again. Finally they slept, sated in body, drugged with love, buoyed on promises neither would keep.

Linn woke to a pounding on the front door. Blythe was gone, but she was too fuzzy-minded to dwell on it. She never slept this late. She put on her robe and went to the door. It was Opal Faye. Linn wondered whether a purveyor of sex could sense that she herself was under its influence.

"Doc here?" Opal Faye asked.

Linn shook her head.

"Girl needs help. Will you come?"

"What kind of help exactly?" She didn't think an abortion required this urgency, unless it were botched. "Did she try…?"

"No. Guy beat her and cut her up."

Linn began to come to life. "Is she bleeding? Is she conscious?"

"She'll live."

"Give me ten minutes. Get some ice on the bruises."

Opal Faye nodded and turned to leave. "Ten," she reinforced.

Linn rushed around finding her own ice bags, sutures, needles. Then she tidied herself up, glowing but suppressing the warmth of last night as she sponged off its remnants, trying not to think where Blythe might be. She dressed and left for Opal Faye's.

Opal Faye led Linn upstairs and down the corridor with striped wallpaper and painted doors. Behind the red door a young woman sat naked and slumped on the edge of a rumpled bed, its sheets blotched with blood. Her face was tear-stained and also blotched. Her left arm dangled uselessly.

"For God's sake, Opal Faye," Linn snapped. "Couldn't you at least have covered her?"

Opal Faye shrugged and then pulled the bloody top sheet up over the girl's uninjured shoulder.

"What's your name, honey?"

"Yvonne," Opal Faye said.

"Well, Yvonne," Linn said, "I'll try not to hurt you, but I have to see what this is all about." Linn looked her over, gently touching her upper back and arm. The girl flinched each time. "Oh God," Linn said to Opal Faye, "her shoulder is popped out. I don't know whether I can fix that by myself." She cursed Blythe for a liar and every other sin. "Can you send someone out to try to find Doc?"

Linn could have strangled Opal Faye for the look she gave her before she walked away. She left the red door open, mirroring the red on Linn's and Yvonne's side of the room. Linn began to examine the girl's other injuries. Her lip was split. She had bruises on her neck and on the useless arm, and a rising knot on one hip. Linn filled two ice bags and told the girl to hold one against her neck. The other Linn rested against the hip. There was a long cut above one breast, and blood had smeared everywhere then dried. When Linn cleaned it away, the girl cringed.

"I'm going to give you something for the pain, and when it takes effect, I'll fix you up. Let's leave your shoulder until last. I need Doc to help me."

The girl nodded, and Linn injected morphine. After the girl relaxed, Linn helped her lie down then stitched up the wounds. When there was nothing left to do but the shoulder, Linn felt she couldn't wait any longer for Blythe or she would have to inject more morphine. She carefully sat the girl up again and knelt behind her on the bed. She had seen this done but had never done it herself. Blythe was slick as a whistle at it. Damn him. Could no one find him? Linn pressed on Yvonne's back to get anatomical bearings. The girl made mewing sounds.

"Hang on," Linn said and at the same time seized the arm, pressed hard on the shoulder blade, strained, pushed, and rotated.

The girl screamed, and Linn collapsed onto the dirty sheets. She was too triumphant to care. The girl moved her arm normally.

Opal Faye came running, fire in her eye. "What are you doing?" she shouted.

"What am I doing?" Linn was incredulous. "Where were you when someone did this damage I'm cleaning up now?" She stared Opal Faye down. "Get some more ice," she demanded. She found a clean sheet, wrapped Yvonne in it, and sat with her for a while. "Do you know how to keep yourself from becoming pregnant?" Yvonne nodded. "Wouldn't you like to get out of this life?"

"Can't."

"Why not? After what just happened?"

"Yeah. Usually it's not this bad. I'd rather do something else, sure."

"You can. Think what you want, maybe not here, but somewhere. Back home. Denver."

"I owe Opal Faye."

"How can you owe her? You work for her."

Yvonne shook her head. "You don't understand, and I'm too tired to talk now."

Linn stopped questioning and continued to sit with her. She stroked her arm and shoulder, and refilled the bags after Opal Faye brought more ice. Still Blythe did not come. In spite of the blow of his disappearance after what they had shared last night, the memory washed heat over her and sent her nerves tingling.

At last she heard footsteps on the stairs, and his voice. She went into the hall.

"Oh, Blythe, thank God you've..." The breath and blood went out of her. There was no precedent for finding one's husband with a prostitute. It was not a pearl of wisdom she had been handed from her mother. Fainting would have been a blessing, but the steel rod of pride supported her as she stood in that hall. Blythe dropped his arm from around the girl's waist. Linn recognized her as Clara, a girl they had helped after a self-induced abortion. Linn's eyes might have burned them both to cinders, but the girl wisely slipped away from Blythe and went inside the room with the blue door. Blythe did not meet Linn's gaze but only looked past her. His face was troubled.

I will not become hysterical in a whorehouse, Linn told herself as the standoff continued.

Finally Blythe spoke, and his voice was unnatural. "Opal Faye says you've treated Yvonne."

"Yes," Linn said in a strictly professional tone. "Please have a look at her."

Blythe followed her into the room. He examined the stitches and the bruises.

"I had to pop her shoulder back in," Linn said, touching it.

"My God, you did it alone?"

"You weren't here, were you." If her words were knives, he too would be bleeding.

"Then you've done everything you can do." Their eyes caught for a split second, then he turned and walked out of the room and down the hall. Linn heard a door open and close. A blue door.

"Yes," she said. "I have."

Denver

10

For a second day, Linnie Ann Adams Walcott lay dry-eyed and catatonic on the hotel bed in Denver. Where her ribs met her breastbone—a place she had never seen inside a body—a whole hell roiled. Sometimes an emery wheel or one of Vic's saws turned and turned in that space, shearing her into a hollow drum, ribboning her lungs, and leaving her breath ragged. Waves of palsy struck her clenched fingers. Worst of all, the relentlessly churning creature inside her stole her thoughts and brought them to an album, the pages of which would not stop turning: the fire, Blythe in bed, freezing with Argo, falling into Blythe's arms only days ago, the scene at Opal Faye's. Of this last there was picture after picture, the pages moving slowly, and Linn dragging her eyes across every detail. Yvonne. The girl. Blythe standing in the hall. *You've done everything you can do.* The blue door. The girl. The blue door closing.

After the blue door closed, Linn had found Opal Faye and demanded payment.

"Put it on Doc's account," Opal Faye told her.

"Doc did not treat Yvonne. I did, and I want to be paid."

Opal Faye smiled a knowing smile that Linn wanted to slap.

"You know who hurt Yvonne," Linn said.

"These things happen."

"It was a crime. Go to George and report it."

"No."

"If you won't pay me, I'll go myself."

Linn had to watch more moving pictures in that bed in Denver: taking Opal Faye's filthy money, going to the sheriff anyway, going to the bank, going home, packing a small bag, taking off her beautiful ring that sparked in the sun and leaving it on the table, leashing Argo and getting them a ride to the station.

She held herself together all the way to Denver. The force of her will got her a hotel room, albeit reluctantly on the part of the desk clerk. She could hear him thinking, *Tsk! A woman alone.* She spirited Argo up the stairs to her room and left it only to spirit him out and back for walks, to find something for him to eat, and to have coffee herself in the morning. She lay on the bed. After they tortured her enough, she forced all the pictures into a box in her mind and locked it.

Denver had changed, but in her mind her place in it had not, and she wondered why she was not there. She belonged in the encampment across Cherry Creek. She knew where to pump water and collect firewood, which tent rows to avoid, who was friendly and whose eyes roved over her checking for anything of value including, perhaps, herself. She had learned how to function there. Every day she had stood and scanned the Front Range: Pike's Peak, Mount Rosalie, Long's Peak. What had made their unbroken majesty? What lay behind them? She found out and must never remember. She was the struggling plant hanging on now to a horizontal rather than vertical world.

On the third morning, Linn bought a *Rocky Mountain News* and saw a Want she had the credentials to apply for. She wrote a letter on hotel paper, and posted it. Then she and Argo walked all the way to the prospective employer, Maimonides Mountain Hospital for Consumptives, on the eastern edge of town. She walked all around the grounds and past the main hospital building, a massive three-story brick rectangle with sunporches facing both east and west. The farm buildings and pastures stretched far to the east on level ground, and in a dip south of the farmyard and beyond the school buildings, a pond reflected the golden Colorado sun. Linn stood at the top of the gentle hill and watched children below playing outside.

She knew she mustn't linger. The day was so like those she had lived in the tent city—relentlessly sunny and hot with storm clouds gathering in the west. She was oddly comforted. She would walk back across the bridge and find her tent and her father. He would be well. She needn't go to the druggist's after all.

Maimonides Mountain Hospital for Consumptives

11

MAIMONIDES MOUNTAIN HOSPITAL CARRIED A TUNE OF ITS OWN
invention. It might be a march: awake at 7:00 a.m., take temperature,
wash, drink milk; 8:00 a.m., eat breakfast; 9:00 a.m., out onto the
sunporches; 10:30 a.m., drink eggnog; noon, eat dinner; 1:00 p.m.,
back outside or to the crafts room or on a walk around the grounds;
3:30 p.m., an afternoon snack, perhaps milk toast; 4:00 p.m., exercise if prescribed; 6:00 p.m., supper; 7:00 p.m., back outside on
fine days; 8:00 p.m., take temperature, drink milk; 9:00 p.m., wash,
bedtime. Consumptive patients came and went, two, three, four.
Recovered patients stayed on to work in the laundry or kitchen
or dairy or horse barn. They marched from the infirmary to the
wards, from the wards to the cottages, from the cottages to home
in Chicago or New York or Philadelphia or to a new life in Denver.

At the same time, the hospital played a second rhythm: breathe-
two-three, in-two-three, out-two-three, in-two-three, out-two-three.
It was the ebb and flow of a waltz sometimes interrupted by the jig
of a cough, the staccato of strangling on sputum, or the sixteenth
notes of gurgling blood. The physicians wanted no Haydn surprises,
no Schumann-esque highs and lows, no feverish Bach inventions,
no Stephen Foster nonsense—no banjos on knees—only the in-
two-three, out-two-three of breath.

There were no debutantes here. No bankers' sons, no bankers'
fading wives. There were no dances and midnight suppers. No telltale
streaks on coyly held silk handkerchiefs. No Violettas, but more than
one struggling Mimi. No pale young men rode horseback across the

133

vast prairie or enjoyed gentlemen's camping trips, nor did they take sea voyages to someplace like Samoa. Fishing, tennis, golf, carriage rides, picnics, dinner parties—none were allowed. No sympathetic friends flounced in for tea in the afternoons bringing little gifts of cut flowers or a jar of honey or jam or pickles for the housekeeper to tuck away. Huddled masses yearning to breathe freely took on a different meaning at Maimonides. Here the word was *rest*. Eat your eggs and drink your milk. Rest. Be the best patient you can be.

Do not be misled. It was not a lovely vacation to lie on your bed on the sunporch and contemplate the blue sky and the bulk of the Rockies, though it was better than lying indoors where the expanse of pale-green walls was broken only by tall double-hung windows that were kept open on all but the coldest nights. On the other hand, if one had come from a New York tenement, then Maimonides provided space, fresh air, good food, and discipline. It did not supply love or personal warmth. The doctors were there to cure you. You were their project. The nurses had a schedule to keep. Now and then a nurse had to be reminded that just because her patients were on charity didn't mean they weren't still deserving of her respect, and if she would rather go to one of the other hospitals in town where well-to-do patients might nettle the staff with airs and demands, where the shoe of respect was not going to be on *her* foot anymore, then perhaps she should change her ways.

Give us your children, Maimonides Mountain Hospital said. We will house them, we will feed and clothe them, exercise them, and discipline them. We will teach them. If they are little children, we will keep them busy and safe. We will watch over them. The new teacher, the widow Mrs. Walcott, has taken them on because other applicants wanted older children, not the irrationality of two-, three-, and four-year-olds who couldn't be made to understand that Mama was too ill and Daddy had to work twelve-hour days. Mrs. Walcott seems a bit too sure of herself, but Dr. Dixon Merrell himself hired her. He manages everything, including the school, when one would think the patients kept him occupied enough. He does not mind, or does not know, that she's full of ideas and makes too much of these children, makes toys. She herself did not make them, but it was one of her ideas to have the carpenters make blocks and blocks and blocks from scraps: square, rectangular, triangular. She painted alphabet letters on the sides of the square ones. She asked for round ones with holes in the center, like doughnuts, and a wooden peg to stack them on. She wants slates, paper, chalk, and a blackboard even for these little ones. She wants modeling clay so the little hands can roll rope worms and mold balls into bunnies and cats.

She takes the children outdoors even more frequently than prescribed. They take walks with her dog to look for flowers, trees, leaves, insects, worms, birds. They go to the pond and look for tadpoles and frogs, and sometimes see ducks and maybe the fox family and raccoons. They catch bugs and butterflies but set them free. They cut cattails before winter ruins them. She has taught all of them their colors, and now they look for red, blue, and green dragonflies. Back in the schoolroom, Mrs. Walcott has made a large-print list on her blackboard of what they have seen. There are columns for each day and checkmarks for each sighting each day. She has made bird sightings more complex. Is it blue? Is it black? Is it making noise?

They go to the farm every day. They look at the milk cows and watch Mary Big Hawk and her son Grant separate cream or make butter. They see farther away the stocky white-faced red cows, and this teacher does not divulge their fate to the children. Their tiny hands plunge into the sheep's wool and search for an egg or two from the chicken house. They back away from the nosy goats. With Argo they look for barn cats and kittens and watch men harnessing and unharnessing the giant-footed workhorses.

Though there are no pigs here, most other tenets of Jewish dietary law are disregarded. Drink your milk and eat this beef, chicken, or lamb, or your recovery may be delayed and may not happen at all. Yes, we have a chapel. Yes, the doctor may have to touch you for your own good. Perhaps someday we may have a female doctor, but you don't want to wait that long. Alma Beckstein, the head teacher, knows just enough Yiddish to settle some of the children into this new world they did not make. Yes, the children have *shabbas* dinner every Friday, even the ones who aren't Jewish. She lights the candles, and the older children recite the prayer, and then the children eat their non-kosher meal.

Linn preferred teaching arithmetic, history, geography, and reading, but she needed work, and this position came with a furnished, postage-stamp-sized cottage in lieu of a full salary. She was allowed to keep Argo there on the basis that he had saved her life and was not any longer a roamer. He herded his little children on their daily excursions. Soon he had worked his way into the classroom and was content to lie quietly observing or sleeping.

Linn's cottage was last in line. Some thorny shrubs had been planted between each cottage to give a sense of privacy. Several other employees lived here, including Miss Beckstein, who managed the school; the head nurse of each shift; and the chief of maintenance, whose staff must repair everything from balky bed-cranks to livestock fences. Locks were not a problem. Hardly anything was locked except the narcotics safe and the children's sleeping quarters, and the latter only at night.

The classrooms and dormitories sat southeast of the hospital building, whose rooftop was barely visible from the low ground the children lived on. Unless she went into town, Linn never had to see the mountains, and she was so busy it was easy to think about only the tasks at hand.

She had previously experienced only a late spring and summer in Denver, and she had to adjust to the vagaries of the fall weather's changeable, short snowstorms in late September, heat in October; and wind, clouds, and snow in November. She cursed whoever designed the school. To and from her cottage, she had to walk through the breezeway that separated the younger children's quarters from those of the older children, and the northwest wind blew right through the opening. It carried snow to the other side of each building and left it under the windows. It blew snow into her face or down her neck.

Farther east, at the low point in the property, a summer-trickling creek had been dammed to make a winter pond for skating.

Linn received abundant advice from Miss Beckstein, who taught and supervised the older children and was Linn's superior. Miss Beckstein was full of don'ts. Don't coddle, spoil, or spare the rod. Don't be weak, permissive, or sympathetic. Linn knew that Miss Beckstein watched her. First, she disapproved of Argo. Linn felt rather than saw her eyes as Miss Beckstein watched. Linn's tactic, then, was to take the children outside. They tried to catch the big ball Linn borrowed from the older children. Round and round the circle, Linn saw her ten charges' coordination grow. She kept them busy, read stories, began counting and ABCs. A is for Apple. B is for Blythe. C is for...no. She resisted going farther down that path. When the evening attendant came on duty, Linn took Argo for long walks to exhaust herself and ward off unwelcome thoughts.

'Chrosite stayed in its place until the Saturday morning in mid-November when Linn went to the undertaker's to arrange with closely held savings for a stone marker for Peter's grave. The streets were as muddy as ever with melting snow. Linn let the children play ball and make snowmen and play in the snow forts the older children had made. She constructed a similar structure in her mind against any incursions of Blythe Walcott, 'Chrosite, Maudie, medical practice, the white mountain world of winter, the struggling spring and its wild streams, summer wildflowers, and the shimmering gold facets of aspen leaves and the watchful eyes on their trunks. Memories leaked nevertheless. Linn avoided the streets she had walked those ten years before. She never passed the drug store. Brick Victorian bungalows had begun to replace the tent encampment. The school and her cottage, the playground and the ball fields all sat in a bowl such that her new world was blind to the mountains.

It was a splurge, but Linn stopped in the news agent's and bought a *Harper's Magazine*, then chided herself. Blythe and *Harper's*. As they walked near the railway station, Argo bounded forward and barked once at a girl who was standing against a store doorway as if to absorb some warmth. She was ill-clothed for the sunny but cold day. As Linn drew closer, she saw that the girl was trying but failing to attract the attention of the men who passed by. When she saw Argo and Linn, Flora Hunt turned away and hid her face with her hands. Someone came out the door, and Linn grasped Flora's shoulders and moved her aside. When she turned Flora around, the girl was crying. Her cheeks were pink with the cold, and she wore a poke sunbonnet that her straight, ash-blond, and not very clean hair hung below. Linn didn't know whether to hug her or scold her or both, but she couldn't walk away and leave her. Some man quite probably would come along and want her, even in her bedraggled condition. How had she come to this? They continued to stare at each other until Linn said something inadequate while Flora continued to sniffle and did not answer.

They moved away from the door, and Linn demanded to know what she was doing, though it was quite obvious. Why was she in Denver? Where was her mother?

"Doc sent me," Flora strangled out.

Linn was speechless. "Doc?" she finally managed. "Why?"

"Can we go somewhere warm?"

Linn put an arm around Flora and led her to a lunch counter near the station, where her appearance would be less remarkable. After a bowl of soup and bread and butter, Flora told Linn how she came to be in Denver.

"Daddy made me have a baby and Doc took it away and told Daddy he'd kill him if he touched me again, but he did, and Doc put me on the train and sent me to stay with a druggist, and he was nice, but his wife was awful, and I left. I don't know whether he killed Daddy."

Linn tried to keep calm and measured, but it was difficult. She wanted to scream, *You had a baby? I've been gone only four months.*

She wanted to gasp, *Where did Doc take it?* She put her hand on Flora's and said, "How are you now?"

"Scared, still."

"Tell me slowly everything that happened."

"Daddy did things to me and made me do things—not the big thing. You know what I mean"—Flora dropped her eyes—"until last summer. I got a baby, and Doc said that was against the law and talked really nasty to Daddy. Doc got the baby out when he and Mama said it was just a speck, but she was crying and mad, and Daddy left home for a while. He came back last month and did it again, the big thing, and Doc sent me away before he made another—you know."

Guilt wracked Linn. She had suspected for years that Floyd Hunt had been molesting his daughter. It hadn't had to be "the big thing" to give Flora her otherworldly face.

"And you found the druggist, but you ran away."

"He was nice, but his wife said I couldn't stay there. She said I was trying to entice—that was the word—her husband. He gave me some money and told me to go back to 'Chrosite, but I just couldn't."

Linn wanted to ask more questions, but first she took Flora back to the cottage. Before they reached it, she had her story firmly set. This is my niece, Flora. My sister in Illinois is a widow—yes, both of us. It is too bad. Flora has been having a difficult time in school, and she and my sister's intended and his children do not get along very well, and my sister thought a change of scene would be good for Flora, and she's old enough to look after herself, and we'll do some schooling every day after my school. It will all work out for the best. Yes, she does need some warmer clothes. She brought so little with her. My sister is a bit, well, what can I say.

I hope I can stop telling lies sometime, Linn thought.

Strict isolation kept the children from visiting their consumptive parents, nor could the parents visit them. Linn saw quickly which children's lives were being devastated by this rule and which were either bewildered but too young to understand or old enough and stoic enough to accept it. She learned that the doctors wanted to temporarily break the bond so the parent could concentrate wholly on his or her own health—two, three, four. The children who acted up most were the most insecure, the most angry. Before sanitarium treatment became available, they might have been sent to Grandma's house or shuffled off to Aunt Alice, who already had too many children and made it known that she was a martyr. At the Maimonides Children's Home, these children were the most frequently and severely disciplined, which only firmed their resolve to make life as miserable for their caretakers as it was for them. In her first weekly meeting with Miss Beckstein, Linn questioned the rule.

"These children need to know their parents still care for them," she pleaded on their behalf.

Miss Beckstein was adamant that parents must concentrate on their own well-being, not on their children's. "The children will get used to it," she said.

Linnie Ann Adams Walcott was not accustomed to being told what to do. Depending on the judge, 'Chrosite, Colorado, had made her either a leader or a troublemaker.

First Linn asked the children to draw pictures of the absent parent, and she made a thumbtacked display of them. For the smallest, those who could barely hold a pencil, she asked what Mama or Papa looked like and drew, in her own unschooled way, some sort of likeness, perhaps only to the hair color, but she always added a big smile. This was not enough for the angry, disruptive children. Linn took one aside and asked whether he would like to be able to send some of his drawings to his parent.

"Who cares?" was the response, but Linn saw a tiny spark of hope in the eyes. She began saving papers and scribbles. Naturally, Miss Beckstein saw this as negative and a waste of time. "Stick to keeping them busy, if you please." Linn had another idea and went to the appointment she had made with Dixon Merrell, risking a firestorm from Miss Beckstein.

Merrell was formidable and tall with a voice no one wanted to but occasionally did hear raised in rage and frustration at humbling staff. Otherwise he was affable, warm, dedicated, and the secret passion of half the nurses as well as lonely women patients. Linn stood tall and shook his hand. She kept reminding herself she could stitch up a wound at least as well as he could. She had rehearsed her opening argument and put it forth without formality.

"I was hired to teach these more or less orphaned children, as you recall. How can a parent get well when he or she worries about the welfare of the absent child? Can they not have some contact? Would it be possible for the children's little drawings and things to be sent over to the parents? Perhaps the parents could send little notes back that I could read to them? I could transcribe little notes back. We could keep a connection between parent and child for each one's benefit."

"You are going over your superior's head, I suppose," Merrell answered.

Linn nodded. "She thinks it's a waste of time."

"Tell me, why do you think you know what helps or doesn't help a consumptive?" Merrell wasn't frowning or looking superior, just asking. Linn was back on solid ground.

"I nursed my father through the last stage, though that doesn't have anything to do with why I'm here today. Some of these children, well, they're just lost without their parents. It depends on the parent, I imagine. I'm not saying this just to make my own position as teacher easier. I hope I'll still have that position when I leave this room." She smiled at him. He shrugged and smiled back. "They need that contact, that security that Mama or Papa is over there in the big building thinking of them. That everything will be OK eventually. That when the parent goes to a cottage, perhaps there can be visits. Belief that Mama and Papa will come home someday."

"But sometimes Mama or Papa dies. How does that figure into your plan?"

"What happens now when Mama or Papa dies? I expect it's 'Boom, Mama or Papa died. You're going to live with Auntie Alice now. Say goodbye to your friends. You're leaving tomorrow.'"

Merrell was silent for a minute. Linn was encouraged that he wasn't standing up and escorting her out of his office and perhaps out of the institution. He sighed and told her he appreciated her concern, but he couldn't approve her idea. It might upset the parents as well as the children. "I've heard you run those little ones ragged."

Linn was about to protest, but he waved her off and continued.

"Just keep them that busy and too tired at night to be upset about anything. No more ideas, all right? Just go along with Miss Beckstein. Do what you were hired to do."

Linn did do what she was hired to do, with her own stamp on the job. Often she pulled Flora into the outdoor activities and then little by little into the classroom. All ran smoothly until a smaller child told his older sibling that he had heard his teacher and Flora talking about sending drawings to Mama. Miss Beckstein demanded an explanation. Linn gave it, watching Miss Beckstein's face swell and her mouth pucker like a lopsided balloon. Linn hoped the woman wouldn't burst.

Miss Beckstein stormed and paced. "What made you think you could get away with something without asking me?"

"I wasn't trying to get away with anything. I was hoping to do what I thought would help my children."

"They are all *my* children, and I say what they may or may not do. I am going to talk to Dr. Merrell about this. I don't think this is quite the place for you. Or your niece. Or your *dog*." She seemed to shudder at the word.

Linn withheld the news from Flora, who was experiencing one of her homesick spells and wanting her mother. At the same time, Linn had seen her wandering over to the stable with increasing frequency. One evening after supper, Flora said she was going for a walk on a remarkably warm December evening. Later, when Linn walked out with Argo, she went in that direction and saw Flora, clothes askew, with one of the farmhands.

"Flora," Linn called. "It is time to go home. Come with me."

Flora lingered in the shadows of one of the smaller stable doors. A stable hand stood behind her, only slightly visible. Linn strode to the door as Flora faded back, but Linn called again in a voice she had not used since a row with Blythe. Flora crept forward, and Linn took her by the arm. "You are coming home now." She propelled Flora back to the cottage and sat her down.

"Your clothes and hair are a mess," she said. "I'm not going to accuse you of anything, but here's what I have to say. Maybe you like that young man, and maybe you don't. You suffered through the unwanted attention of your father for so long that I wonder whether you think there's any other way of being with men. Letting them play with you and your body may only get you into trouble again."

"I wasn't..." Flora began, but Linn waved her away.

"Even if you weren't, spending time alone in the dark is not the proper way to meet nice young men. And you do want to meet nice ones and not sneak around with one who may think you have an easy virtue or may force you while you're out there all alone."

Flora began to cry, but Linn wasn't finished.

"What your father did to you in 'Chrosite was terrible and wrong, and I blame myself and Doc for being suspicious but thinking it couldn't be happening. So please." Linn stood Flora up and wrapped her in her arms. "Don't seek that kind of attention from men. It's not the only kind. Do you understand what I'm trying to say?"

Flora sniffled and nodded, and from then on, Linn began to keep a better watch over her movements.

Linn put aside thoughts of the future and plodded through day by day. Neither Alma nor Dr. Merrell had told her to pack and leave the school. One frozen Sunday afternoon near Christmas, when the ice on the pond was deemed safe, the older children were allowed to skate. Soon one came screaming up to Linn's cottage to come quick. There had been a crash on the ice, and there was blood everywhere. Linn moved as fast as she could and found one of the older girls lying on the ice bleeding and panting, too shocked to scream or move. Another lay nearby crying.

"Bring them to shore," Linn commanded a couple of bigger boys. Linn saw that the bleeding girl had worn only a thin jacket over a long-sleeved shirt. In the collision and fall, the second girl's blade had run a deep, long cut through the fabrics and along the inside of her arm. Linn made a tourniquet of a boy's belt while she sent another off to get sleds from some of the children playing nearby. The boys lifted the injured girl onto the sleds and pulled her toward the school building.

Miss Beckstein had come running, shouting, "Take her into the hospital."

"Too far," Linn told her and kept the children working. One retrieved the medical kit, one brought a sheet. Linn unlocked the morphine. The injured girl was laid on a table. All the while Miss Beckstein circled the scene and objected.

"Didn't I tell you we ought to have morphine with this kit? Now see why," Linn said.

"You can't give morphine to a child." Miss Beckstein fluttered and almost levitated.

"Do you want to hold her down while I stitch this up?"

Miss Beckstein's agitation increased tenfold. "You? No, no, stop." She tried to push Linn away by grabbing her arm. Linn turned the syringe and needle straight at Miss Beckstein and said some words the children repeated, giggling, time and time again after the fact. Linn went back to work. She examined the wound and found it to be clean. When she began stitching, most of the children faded away. One of the younger girls stayed right beside her. "Are you a doctor too?" she asked.

"Right now I am," Linn replied. "You can help me by bringing me the brown paper packages there in the kit."

Linn kept on stitching even when she heard several pairs of running feet coming toward her. A young man hovered and moved his hands toward hers.

"Here," he said, "I'll finish this."

"I have it well in hand," she replied and turned a warning elbow in his direction.

"You don't know what you're doing," he said and tried once again to take the needle.

She turned to him and said low and fiercely, "Don't make me say more words the children shouldn't hear. Now leave me to my work. You can admire it later."

He did back away. "Where did you learn to do that?" he asked. Linn ignored him while she explained to the curious child, who had not moved, what she was doing. She sprayed the wound, wrapped it in sterile bandages, and told the child that the word *sterile* meant that the bandages were as clean as they could get.

The young doctor wanted to move the girl into the hospital building.

"You should know that's not safe," Linn told him. "I will take her to my cottage. I will monitor her temperature and change her dressings."

"Dr. Merrell will hear about this."

"I'm sure he will," Linn said. "And I defy him to find fault with what I've done."

All Dixon Merrell said on Monday morning was, "You again." He did not find fault with her stitching or the cleanliness of the wound. He told Miss Beckstein to requisition replacement supplies for the school medical kit, and when she had left Linn's cottage, he invited himself to stay and have a talk.

"Where did you learn to do that?"

"Funny, that's what one of your young doctors asked me after I refused to let him take over."

"And you said…"

"After I told him to go away?"

"Yes."

"I didn't tell him. If I tell you, will you promise not to tell anyone?"

"Why does that make a difference?"

"Because I'm a teacher here. All the rest is in the past."

"It will be between just the two of us if you wish."

"Thank you." Linn stopped and thought about where to begin or how much to admit. "My husband was a doctor in a mining town. He had a contract with a mine and mill. He trained me to do more and more with the people in town when he was away. After a while I could do many things, but not surgery."

"Give me some examples."

"Stitching up wounds, as you saw. We had lots of those. Gunshots, knives, saws. Equipment would rip into miners and mill workers. Kids were always getting hurt, or having bellyaches, or septic throats, or vitamin deficiency. I can do an uncomplicated delivery. I've set bones. I compounded medicines, I made salves and solutions. I treated miner's con and altitude sickness, and mercury poisoning, and, well, the typical Saturday night diseases." *No modesty.* But she had to practice some with this man.

"And now you're teaching school."

"Yes, well, I am qualified, even though I didn't tell you the truth when you hired me. I never did teach in the mountains." Linn hesitated and lied. "My husband died." *Quickly, think of how, if Merrell asks.*

"Why couldn't you carry on?"

The scene at Opal Faye's flashed through her mind. "People liked me, it's true. But they didn't trust me without my husband to back me up. Another doctor in town helped spread that fear. It was better to move on."

"Do you miss doctoring?"

"Yes, I do. My husband thought I might try medical school, but that would have meant leaving the town and him, and I didn't want to."

"And now?"

"I have to work. Much is provided here except much actual money. And my days are full."

"May I ask you an intensely personal question?"

"I suppose so, but…" She trailed off, not imagining what they had to be personal about.

"Have you been too busy to look in the mirror or to listen to your body telling you that you are expecting a baby?"

She could only breathe out a long "no."

"No, you haven't been too busy, or no, you haven't any idea?"

"It can't be. I'm nearly thirty-five. I can't be having a baby."

"Never mind age. Perhaps your husband never taught you the symptom called the black mask of pregnancy, but if you looked at yourself you would see the brown stain going from your cheeks up and over your nose."

Instinctively, she put her hands over her face. "No," she said again.

"If I figure correctly, you will have this baby in just a few months. When did your husband die? Let's say May or June. Then it took a little while for you to settle things and move down to Denver. So let's say February or March. And here's my question: How could you have possibly had the gall—the wonderful Yiddish word *chutz-pah*—to take a teaching position when you knew you were expecting, and how can you deny knowing it?" He strode as far as one wall of her small sitting room would let him then circled back and sat down again and leaned over close to her. "I'm trying hard to believe there actually was a husband. This puts the whole school in a bad light, a bad way. A teacher expecting a baby, getting large among all the children? Then again, we can't very well throw you out in the snow. As I understand it, you have a niece living here. Awkward. Awkward."

She barely heard him. She did not want to explain how her body did not tell her what most women's did, or that the baby hadn't been conceived until late July with a man who was not dead, but a man she would never go back to. All those years, so much passion, and then on the last night, when she blotted out everything but wanting him, he had given her a child.

She could scarcely accept Merrell's diagnosis until only a few days later when she felt the first stirring of life within her. She covered it with her heavy coat and took the children outdoors more and more frequently. She wrapped herself in scarves indoors and said she was just chilly all the time.

She had never appreciated her height until she tucked the baby in by standing tall. She finally had to confess one night when she saw Flora watching her undress. Flora looked up at her face, knowingly.

"You think I'm getting fat?" Linn asked while she put on her nightgown.

"Not really fat, more like…"

"Like what?"

"Like Mama gets. Used to get. You know."

"I do know. That's what I'm getting."

"But you don't have a husband. At least not here. At least not for a while."

"I had one in 'Chrosite. You probably wonder why I didn't stay with him or why I didn't go back. Doc and I, um, well, I just had to leave town and not come back. I didn't know about this baby until just before Christmas."

"Maudie was so upset after you left. So was he."

"I wrote to Maudie once. I told her I was going back to Illinois. I didn't want to tell her the truth and have Doc coming down here looking for me."

"Maybe he wouldn't have come."

"Maybe not." Why did this thought hurt her pride?

"He scared me even when he was helping me," Flora said. "Not like Daddy scared me, swinging out at whoever was in the way. Doc looked like he was holding his breath, like he was waiting for something awful to happen."

"He scared me too. That was one of the reasons I had to leave."

"But he wasn't so much like that before you left. He changed. I wish you hadn't left. Let's go back after the baby comes. Doc would like it. He'd like the baby. Can we?"

Going back became Flora's refrain after Linn had told her the baby was coming. Doc was lonely, he missed her, he would love the baby. Rebekah might need both of them. Mama would be worrying. Linn suggested Flora write to her mother, but Flora cajoled Linn into writing the letter. It merely said that Flora was safe. There was no return address.

The storms are called upslopes. The one in April covered Denver with feet and feet and feet of snow. It shut down the city and brought Victoria Barbara Walcott into the world.

The heavy, wet flakes began falling in late afternoon, but supper was delivered and the nighttime caretaker arrived as usual. By mid-afternoon Linn knew the baby was coming and willed herself not to call Flora over to finish the children's messy painting project. By the time she was able to leave the school building, she had to fight her way to her cottage against the raking southeast wind and the first foot of snow. She had already told Flora what her role would be when the baby arrived. This snowstorm was both a blessing and a curse. No one would be out, but going for help would be slow if not impossible. Linn had never believed she would have anything but a normal childbirth, but now doubts crept in. She knew too much.

She was restless, and she fussed that there was not enough wood for the stove. She tried lying down but could not relax. She paced the small cottage. She unfolded and refolded the baby blankets and clothes she had accumulated. She felt guilty as Flora struggled in with a fourth load of wood. They laughingly prepared to boil water.

The city, the hospital, and the school hardly moved for three or four days after the storm. As if the farmworkers hadn't enough to do, they were expected to forge a path from the hospital kitchen to the school. The children could neither sit nor stand still, and Miss Beckstein expected Linn to entertain her group. Flora volunteered. She kept Miss Beckstein on the doorstep of the cottage and promised she would be right out and ready to take bundled little ones outside to run up and down the shoveled paths that made tunnels and corners to hide around. They were mazes that no one managed to get lost in.

When the snow finally melted and Linn had to go back to her charges, she arranged with Flora to spell her off every three hours.

—Flora, I'm going to need more of your help in the schoolroom.
—And with Victoria.
—We'll be a relay team.
—What's that?
—Well, there are more than two in a real sports contest. One runs a certain distance and then hands a baton—a bar—to the runner waiting to run the next phase. Does that make sense?
—Victoria is the baton.
—Exactly.

Linn would run back to her cottage, feed and diaper Victoria Barbara—shortened by Flora to Vicky—put her in her dresser drawer cradle, and run back to the classroom. She still wore her big shawl or a scarf to cover herself in the event she felt her milk let down and leak onto her clothes. And Flora loved the children. She was better than Linn at settling a scuffle over shared toys and soothing a skinned knee or a head cold.

—May I take the alarm clock to the schoolroom?
—What on earth for?
—To try to make them understand sharing. In settling wanting the same toy, one child can have it for a certain amount of time. I'll set the alarm, and when it goes off, the other child can have the toy.
—And they can learn to trust you.
—Oh, I think they already do.

Dixon Merrell stopped into the classrooms now and then. One day Flora happened to be working with the children when he came in. He watched her for a while and questioned Linn about her when she came back.

"She doesn't have any credentials," Merrell pointed out. "How old is she?"

"Seventeen. She has little brothers and sisters and took a lot of responsibility for them. At the same time, she used to visit me and help me in the clinic."

"How did she end up here?"

"I found her on the street downtown. She had been sent away from a home she thought would be safe. She left our mountain town because her father, um, was not a nice man."

"How's her book learning?"

"Her mother made her leave school after eighth grade. I kept after her to read as much as she could."

"And you—are you well? Is the baby doing well? Of course you haven't been to a doctor."

"I can tell that we're doing fine. She's an angel, really."

"Good. I'll be over to see her one of these days."

12

Linn had been up too many hours with Vicky and Flora making steam and saltwater and tea for their head colds. The sound of contentious voices coming from her schoolroom even before the children arrived sapped the energy she was trying to save for them. She looked through the small window in the door. A man sat, all shoulders and arms with the rest of him folded into a child-sized chair beside a little girl who shared his curly hair and round face. Linn suspected from the half-Yiddish, half-English exchange that the father and Alma Beckstein were arguing about food. Linn could distinguish Yiddish from Russian now, though mostly through rhythm and tone rather than actual words. Some of these new people spoke both. Alma had lately complained to Linn about their poor English, their increasing presence, and their religious scruples.

The little girl was clutching her father's hand, and her eyes were like those of cornered prey when Linn said hello. Alma began to explain Sonia's situation, but Solomon Chernigov waved her off from his seat.

"I will tell," he began. "My wife is sick in the hospital. I work at the farm. Sonia cannot live with me. She must live here and have school. I will come for supper."

Alma fluttered and was ready to tell Chernigov he could not come for supper, but Linn intercepted her with a hand on her arm.

"Sit with her, yes?" Linn clarified. "Before *shluffen*."

Chernigov seemed surprised that she used the word. "You speak Yiddish?"

"A few words," she said. "I'm best at English." She produced a weak smile.

"You help me learn."

Linn wanted to flare and say, *No, no, no, I will not teach you English. I have enough to do already,* but she softened to, "Sonia will learn fast. She can teach you."

The other children began coming into the room. Sonia was even more alarmed at their chatter and noise. Chernigov turned to her and spoke to her quietly and at length. She began to cry. He stood up and picked her up. She locked her arms around his neck and buried her face. "Papa," she sobbed, "no."

Chernigov talked to her again. "*Mama vet verren besser. Ich vel zein bei dein belt ven du gaist shluffen.*" Linn heard, "Mrs. Walcott," the *w* sounding like a *v*, before he stepped to her, pried Sonia loose from his chest, and transferred her, struggling, into Linn's arms. He kissed Sonia's wet cheeks and promised, "*Ich hub der lieb. Ich vel kummen yeden nacht.*"

Linn, not happy with this extra burden, appealed to Alma for some words of comfort for the little girl.

"Say '*Alt vet zein gut*' and pat her."

Linn sighed and carried Sonia around the schoolroom showing her drawings the other children had made, the toys and blocks, and how to make marks on the blackboard. When she placed Sonia at one of the children's tables, the little girl looked around in alarm and continued sobbing. Again Linn spoke the Yiddish words to her, "*Gib a Kuk. Die kinder lachen und zingen und spielen,*" and repeated that all would be well before she had to attend to the whole class.

When the children went on their usual walk, Sonia at first clung to Linn's hand as if she had never been outdoors in her life. Luckily the pond was alive with ducks, and Linn was able to distract Sonia with the mix of colors and the quack of the mallards, until she seemed to be a little happier.

Chernigov kept his promise to Sonia. Every evening he sat with her at supper, frowning at the lack of kosher food, and kissed her goodnight at bedtime before traveling to the boarding house where he lived. His tasks at the farm seemed mainly to be working the horses in the fields. Whenever Linn took the children to the farm, they could see him in a far field plowing, harrowing, and clearing weeds. One day when the children were walking near the barn, he was removing harness from the two workhorses, one as black as the sharps and flats, the other as white as the ivories.

"Papa," Sonia screeched and ran toward him. Before Linn could stop them, the rest of the children ran forward. Chernigov swooped up Sonia and placed her astride the black horse.

"Hold his mane," he told her.

"Me, me," shouted some of the other children. Without asking Linn, he picked up one after another and placed him or her on the horse, each child with its arms around the waist of the child in front. When five were on the black horse, he placed the other willing children on the white. Some children hung back. The horses stood eighteen hands. The children sat as if on a mountaintop.

Some of the boys began kicking the horses' sides, signaling giddyup, but Chernigov became stern and told them no, no, no.

"Horses are tied." He showed them the lead ropes secured to iron rings. "Horses cannot go. Do not..." He seemed to be searching for a word.

"Confuse them," Linn offered.

"What is *confuse*? What is this word?" Chernigov turned to her.

"The horses know they must stay still, but the children ask them to go. The horses are being asked to break the rules."

Chernigov still looked puzzled, and so Linn tried again, holding out one hand. "Over here, stay." She held out the other. "Over here go. This is *confusing*."

"You mean they do not know what to do."

"But you have trained them—taught them—so well, they would not really try to go."

Linn suggested it was time to let Mr. Chernigov do his work. Sonia tipped forward and clutched at the black horse's neck, not because she was falling but because she didn't want to dismount. Chernigov lifted each child from the horses, and when only Sonia was left, he spoke to her and kissed her cheek and lifted her off without a struggle.

One evening after the children's bedtime, Flora sat on the davenport reading while Linn mended stockings. A knock called Linn to the door. Solomon Chernigov took off his hat and held it in his two hands like some sort of mendicant about to ask for a handout. Linn asked him to come in.

"Please, Mrs. Valcott"—he still mixed up the letters—"I ask you to help to write a letter."

"Oh, well, I suppose. In English, yes?"

"Yes, of course."

"What shall I write on? I don't have nice writing paper."

"Doesn't need to be too nice, maybe plain white."

"I can ask Miss Beckstein."

"But don't tell her why, yes?"

Their eyes met and Linn frowned. "It's not something, hmm, wrong, or bad or…"

"No, no." Now Chernigov frowned. "But I want trust you."

"Tell me what this is about then."

"You ever see the big green plants in children's garden? They are mine."

"I suppose we've seen them. I thought Miss Beckstein's children grew them. What are they?"

"Sugar beets."

Linn was surprised. She never considered where sugar came from. Maple syrup and candies—a Christmas treat—yes; molasses, maybe. "Sugar in beets? Surely not the beets we eat."

"No, no to eat. Big beets." He held his hands apart to show how big. "Not the same red. I worked in Russia. Many fields, took to mill to make sugar. I try to grow now."

"You want to write to someone about sugar beets?"

"Sure. The college where they grow plants, study plants. I want to know, will they help me with my beets? I have a book, but I do not understand it very much."

They sat down at the table, and Linn wrote on school paper to his dictation, telling him how it would sound better and be more clear to a botanist at the agricultural college in Fort Collins. Chernigov wanted advice about seeds and planting time, fertilizer (Linn had to teach him that English word and others), and the usual harvest time in Colorado. He wanted to send or bring in this year's beets for analysis.

Linn was impressed with Chernigov's knowledge and determination. She asked questions.

"I want a farm," he said. "This land, this, what you call? Rain, snow, sun." He made a huffing and puffing sound.

"Weather? Climate?"

"Maybe. What are these words?"

"Weather. Well, it's the rain or snow. Or the summer heat. What happens day by day. Understand? Climate is more like weather all over. For example—do you know what *example* is?"

"Maybe," he said tentatively. "Something like something."

"Yes, I suppose," she said. "The climate east, on this side, that is, of the Rocky Mountains is dry, sunny, and has snowstorms. Storms. Snow comes, snow goes. Rain in the summer." *And the climate in the Rocky Mountains is dry, sunny, and has even more snow,* she thought, but she didn't say it so as not to confuse him with her unwanted memory.

"I understand. This weather, this climate, is good for sugar beets. I have a plan in mind, but I need money and land, but first to ask college to help me."

"When your wife is well, you want to do this?"

"She will not be well. I tell Sonia different, but I know."

"But how do you know?"

"She doesn't want. She is happy to die." His voice held a trace of scorn.

Linn just stared at him. She had never heard a husband or wife speak so harshly of the other. To each other, oh yes. She had done it herself until she wore out. Perhaps a physical illness could create the same effect.

"Did the doctors tell you that?"

"No. They would not, but I know. She is tired, she is weak in body, weak in…" He made gestures with his hands as if bouncing a ball upward.

"Spirit? Outlook? It is hard to just lie in the hospital."

"What is this outlook? Looking outside?"

"Hmm," Linn said, "something like looking outside yourself, looking on the sunny side."

"The sunny side. Good American words. We have a hard time to look on sunny side where we come from."

"Why is that?"

He scoffed. "Not sunny to have laws saying you must to live only here, you cannot to live there, you must leave your school, you must leave your village, you must not to live in the large city, Kiev, and when we want to scare you, no, much worse than scare…"

"Frighten?"

"Worse than that."

"Terrorize?"

"Maybe. I do not know this word, but they ruin our work and beat us and kill some, and run through the town like *meshugena*, worse than *meshugena*, like very bad people. They catch these things from one another, like disease."

"And so you and your wife and Sonia came to America." She reached for his hand where it rested in front of him on the table. "You know, you do not have to be afraid here."

"Maybe not," he said. He took his hand away and a pointed a finger at her. "But," he continued, "your army killed many Indians near here. Just like in Russia."

"I don't know about it."

"Yes," he said. "I heard from dairy people. Just ask them."

She didn't know what to say. She imagined for the first time that her own ancestors had probably been terrorized out of somewhere. She didn't know the stories; it was too long ago, and no one remembered. She had never considered that some of her ancestors had probably killed Indians or at least driven them away. No one remembered that either.

"I will," she said to Chernigov.

He leaned farther across the table. "So, you will get paper and make a nice letter from this." He tapped the school-ruled paper she had written on. "When?"

"Come back on Thursday. And I will ask for an envelope. You bring the address—the street name—you understand? And the person's name. Can you sign in English letters?"

Chernigov nodded then placed a hand on hers. It was large and rough and reminded her of the hands of her uncles and cousins in Illinois. She seldom thought of them. "You teach English to me? So I can understand the book—and more." He had the same hat-in-hand look she had seen at the door, but he was uncannily persuasive. She felt in the roughness of his hand the kind of struggles she had never known or known about. He was an exotic, and she felt the pull of the unknown.

"Yes," she said.

For the first lesson, Solomon Chernigov and Linn met in the classroom after the children had finished supper and gone to bed. She wrote the alphabet on the blackboard, which was all very well until she began pronunciation of each letter.

—A: ay as in late, ahh as in arm, broad as in cat, hat, sat.
—But how do you know?
—You just have to learn.
—Oy.
—Speaking English helps. You are doing well at that.
—Not so well. How can I know all this?

—But Yiddish has the same letters, doesn't it?
—I don't know. I know only by talking.

By the third lesson he threw up his hands. He stood up and came to the blackboard. "Look," he said, picking up a piece of chalk. He began with *A*, but from there, most of the letters were unknown to her. One looked like a spider, one an inverted *V*, a backward *N*, the *P* was *R*, and the *R* was backward. Another was a circle with a vertical line through the middle and another half an *H* with an *O* attached.

—This one is pronounced V.
—But it's a B.
—Ah, but not in Russian. It is Russian I learned in school.
—Why not Yiddish in school?
—Not same school. Remember the word confusing you taught me?
Too confusing.
—Why have two kinds of school?
—Why have the Czar? Why have the Pale of Settlement? Why have
Russians, why have Jews?

"Look at this Russian letter—this one has two marks up, and you see the little…" He made a sort of comma shape in the air. "This one has three marks up but no little…"

"Tail," Linn supplied.

"Tail, very small. Not like a cat," he said. He went on to show her another letter, like the second but with a tail. "Ts, sh, shch. Repeat," he said.

"Tsh."

"No. Try again. Ts, sh, shch."

She made notations in small letters under his large ones. "I will show this to the children tomorrow. We shall all learn the Russian alphabet."

"Oh, you think it is easy for little children. You make fun of me. Not nice for a teacher." He crossed his arms and stared at her.

She stared back, not wanting to back down, but also because she hadn't noticed before that his eyes were darkest blue, shading into a still deeper blue at the periphery of the iris. Perhaps a deep ocean blue, Linn considered, having never been anywhere near an ocean. She would have liked asking him if the ocean he crossed matched his eyes. Maybe when she knew him better.

The stare continued until he began to laugh. "You have not said 'shch.'"

Linn kept trying but could not do it, and she broke out in giggles. In no time, Miss Beckstein opened the schoolroom door. "What is going on here?" she asked with a frown.

"We've having an English lesson, but Mr. Chernigov thinks I should learn the Russian alphabet. It made us laugh."

Alma did not think the Russian letters were amusing. She pursed her lips, turned away, and closed the door behind her.

The next afternoon Dixon Merrell arrived at Linn's cottage just before supper. Linn had not seen him for months. He made much of Vicky, but he frowned as he looked at Linn.

"I understand," he said, "that you are teaching English to one of the parents."

Spy, Linn thought. *She would like to get me out of here. Since Flora, Vicky, and Argo didn't do the trick, she wants teaching English to Mr. Chernigov to be a mortal sin.*

"Yes," she said aloud. "He's quite eager, but we just began, as I'm sure Alma told you." She hoped he caught the knowing edge in her voice.

"Have you had experience in doing this?"

"Heavens no. Really, I'm doing him a favor. He can speak tolerably well. He can't write or read it, though, and that's what he wants, badly."

"Do you really want to do this?"

"Dr. Merrell, I can't have what I really want. Teaching is rewarding, and teaching Mr. Chernigov will be a nice antidote to spending my day with little ones."

"What do you really want?"

Supper arrived with a clatter of trays before Linn could answer. She rose and carried Vicky to her highchair at the kitchen table. Flora followed with the food, and she and Vicky began quiet negotiations on what Vicky would and wouldn't eat.

Linn sat back down and said, "I really want to work in medicine, but I won't be a nurse. I can't be a nurse with these family obligations. Even if the medical school would have me, I don't see how I could have it."

"You've said what I hoped to hear, because I think we can make an arrangement."

"No. I don't make arrangements, or whatever you care to call it."

He smiled. "I'm sorry. I put that badly. I have a quid pro quo for you, but it's strictly professional." He rose and took a few strides this way and that through the small room. Noise from the kitchen distracted Linn's attention from Merrell, and she at first didn't think she heard him correctly. "I can probably get you into medical school."

Those words took her breath away, she was so quickly crushed by the weight of her life and her need to make a living for the three of them. "It's not possible. I have no choices."

"Then let's make some. Here's what I've been thinking today after, yes indeed, Alma told me. You know, you must be careful. You are such an attractive woman, and Chernigov is probably lonely. You two alone."

"Alone in the classroom where Alma can pop in any moment? And he's a married man. I'm sure you know his wife."

"I know his wife, and I know human nature."

Linn sighed audibly. "I had what I wanted in a rowdy mountain town, and the minute I came down here to supposed civilization, the suspicion of a woman alone was everywhere. I am not looking for a client or a husband or a lover or even an admirer. I don't have time."

"You have me for an admirer, and before you throw me out of your house, let me finish."

She sighed again, but at least she had had her say. "You may."

He sat down and pulled his chair closer to hers. "See what you think of this." He clasped his hands as if praying she would approve. "Alma tells me," he coughed lightly, "that your niece is quite good with the children." Linn nodded. "If—and this is a big if—she were willing to get a degree from the Denver University teachers' college, she would be expected to take over your work with the little ones while you attend medical school."

If only, if only. Linn's thoughts swam. Could it be possible? Would Flora do it? Would the medical school admit her? *Don't get your hopes up,* she told herself. *But if only.*

"Well?" Merrell asked.

She outlined all the problems. He had answers for them.

"Flora gets herself ready for college, and you can help her. We would continue to pay the same small salary, maybe a bit more, plus your costs at medical school. Here's what I expect from you." He leaned even closer to her, picked up her hands, which had been resting on her knees, and held them in his. "Your appearing on my doorstep, so to speak, with your background and your frustrated ambition was a miracle it took me a long time to see."

She saw it too. "After medical school I stay here?"

"I need you so much, you have no idea. Some of the women patients don't want male physicians touching them, especially bare skin, and listening to their breathing. I want you to head the women's section of the hospital. You won't have a crisis an hour, as you had in the mountains, and you won't have to make house calls miles away."

"Not very exciting."

"Do you want exciting?"

"To tell the truth, it doesn't have as much appeal now that I have Vicky." On cue, Vicky toddled into the room, and Linn scooped her up and put her on her lap. Merrell pulled off one of Vicky's socks and played "This Little Piggy" until Vicky laughed and screeched. When she calmed down, Merrell addressed Linn with one more task he wished her to undertake.

"To avoid any appearance of impropriety, I suggest you take on several other employees of the hospital who need to improve their English. Have a group class. They all speak a certain amount of English, so no need to start with 'I am,' 'you are,' 'he is,' et cetera. You and your Mr. Chernigov will have plenty of chaperones."

"He is not my Mr. Chernigov," she bristled. "He is his daughter's Mr. Chernigov. He's devoted to her."

"No, I'm sure he's not yours," Merrell said as he got ready to depart. "Nevertheless, under all the field dust and horse sweat, he's quite an appealing fellow."

As soon as Vicky was put to bed, Linn sat down with Flora and told her what Dr. Merrell wanted from both of them.

"I can't," was Flora's first reaction.

"Yes, you can. You are so good with the children. Better than I am, I must admit. We'll find out what the requirements are for admission to the teachers' program. Your reading is perfect. We'll work on writing. We'll find someone to tutor you in mathematics. When I went to normal school, all I needed was some algebra. You know your multiplication tables, fractions, and long division. You learned that in 'Chrosite. Two years of college and you can teach."

Linn resisted battering Flora with guilt: I took care of you in 'Chrosite; I took you in in Denver and saved you from a miserable existence; I have fed and clothed you. You owe me this. And perhaps Flora felt it, because she climbed mountains in the writing assignments Linn gave her.

When Linn learned from Solomon that he had studied mathematics in *gymnasium* in Kiev, she established yet another quid pro quo. She taught him and five other employees of the hospital English, and he tutored Flora.

"I do not know after geometry," he said.

"She needs only algebra and geometry, luckily," Linn told him. So after English lessons, Linn went home to Vicky and Flora went to the classroom, which seemed innocent enough for Alma and Merrell. Linn was not happy at first, given Flora's history, and the first several sessions she herself spied on them. But it appeared that Linn's constant praise, their bonds of friendship, and Flora's goals had dampened her interest in male attention.

The reality of Merrell's offer didn't settle into Linn's mind for a few weeks, even though she knew it was true. She saw Flora working toward college. Flora was on her path, but Linn had to wait, and waiting for more than two years dampened the anticipation.

She had not told Solomon anything about her past. She had seen him glance at the cheap ring she wore, but he had never asked about a husband. One evening, Flora returned to the cottage after her mathematics lesson and told Linn that Mr. Chernigov wanted to see her in the classroom. He needed help with a letter.

He was sitting on one of the children's tables. "Too much time in little chairs," he said.

He held out a letter. "Would you read please from a professor at the college?"

Linn read the letter word for word and, glancing up, saw Chernigov smile. He rubbed his hands together.

"My dream," he said, "may be start."

"A start," Linn corrected. "What is it?"

"At harvest time the professor said—you read it—that I can send my beets for that word I don't know, but I understand the idea. He will test. This is my dream, Mrs. Valcott. Not plowing hospital fields with hospital horses, not living in a boarding house."

"I understand perfectly. Dr. Merrell is going to help me have my dream. He wants me to go to medical school."

"You?" As if it were impossible.

"Yes, me. A woman. It's not so impossible."

"How can a teacher be a doctor? No, no."

"Yes, yes. I can. When I lived in the mountains"—she swept her hand westward, where the sun had left pillows of glowing cloud-coals—"my husband, a doctor, taught me many things. I want to do them again."

"You go to the mountains? After?" He looked concerned. "To this husband?"

"No. I don't know where he is now. I will be here at the hospital for the women patients. Many want a woman doctor." She realized she had slipped up and told him the truth about Blythe, but who was there for Chernigov to tell?

Linn watched him absorb what she had told him. He still looked concerned. *I've said too much, and he is wondering what kind of woman I am and should I be amongst little children. Was there really a husband and if my child is…*

"But where is the husband? You have to know where he is if there is something wrong with your child and you need help." He seemed like a big brother, not a judgmental stranger. Nevertheless he was a stranger, and Linn had said enough.

"Mr. Chernigov, I cannot discuss my personal life with you."

"Two words, please tell me. *Discuss* and *personal*."

Linn wanted to tell him to go home, but she also wanted to laugh. The conversation was turning into another English lesson.

"*Discuss* means to talk about something with someone or several people. *Personal* means something is for me alone, not for you to know. You have personal things I should not know about. And personal things should not be asked about."

"I will not ask about the husband."

"Thank you."

"It is better to say, then, we both have our dream. We keep on day by day for long time until then."

Halfway through Flora's year of studying, Solomon arrived one day glowing.

"I have such good news. Dr. Merrell wants me to be head of the farm," he announced. "I will have the cottage next to the horse barn, and Sonia will live with me. No more cold rides on the streetcar."

"You will be able to baby your sugar beets now," Linn said.

"What is this *baby*?"

"Take special care. Watch over—no, you will have time every day to see that they are good. *Baby*—a word in English for taking good care of something."

"Words in English again. Words you show us but don't spell the same. Achh. Red, read, sale, sail, two, too, to. Too many words, one thing for another," he said.

"You might learn some of them. Americans use them all the time."

"Americans might learn some in Yiddish. They can be funny."

"And in Russian?"

"Not for me. Russian jokes are not nice for us."

Vicky was two years old when Flora began her teachers' training. Flora struggled, even with Linn's tutoring. Linn felt as if she were dealing with two two-year-olds instead of one. She had to reason with Vicky when she tore on ahead of her and Argo or broke into screams when she wanted someone else's toy or balked at food she liked yesterday. And she had to remind Flora that rereading Louisa May Alcott was not part of her college requirements but keeping up on mathematics was, and that she would eventually make friends.

"You don't have any friends after all this time," Flora tossed back. "Don't tell me to be patient." Flora dropped her eyes. "I'm sorry."

"You should be. That was very unkind," Linn reprimanded. She sometimes talked with Mary Big Hawk after English lessons. Mary spoke both Arapahoe and English and was eager to learn to read, but her early-morning duties at the dairy and her shyness made the conversations short. In truth, Solomon had become Linn's best friend, and sometimes he stayed after the class, though now that he lived on the hospital grounds he brought Sonia along to sit in the classroom and keep busy with a book or paper dolls. At the same time, spending the day with little children, giving lessons to adults, and coaching and propping up Flora exhausted Linn. She determined a cutoff point in her adult class when a participant could sign his name, write a passable letter, and read with understanding most of the newspaper.

Solomon wanted more. He wanted to understand better the letters that flew between him and the plant scientists at the agricultural college. The scientists did not dilute their language. Solomon and Linn dissected the densely written results of the college research. In the spring, Solomon planted rows of sugar beets using the seeds and suggestions from the scientists for improving his harvest.

In the fall, a professor invited Solomon to bring the beets to Fort Collins in person. They wanted to meet him and to show him how they sliced, chopped, mashed, and cooked up his beets in preparation to test them for sugar content.

He went on the train and stayed overnight, and Sonia came to Linn's cottage. On the Sunday morning, Dixon Merrell knocked on Linn's door looking for Chernigov.

"Please don't think that I thought he would be here," Merrell said. He drew her out onto her porch.

"Thank you for realizing that we don't have room for *my* Mr. Chernigov."

"This is serious. His wife died early this morning. He didn't answer at his cottage. I couldn't find him working around the farm anywhere."

"Oh no," Linn said, a hand to her face. "He will be crushed he wasn't here. He went to the agricultural college for the weekend. His daughter is staying with me."

"When he gets back, have him see me. And what is he doing at the college? Is he going to improve our farming practices?"

"He can tell you about that, but please let me tell him about his wife. I know him well enough to know that he would try to put up too brave a front with you. To be manly, you understand? I know what time his train arrives. I can meet him at the trolley stop. I will tell him while we walk through the grounds, steer him off somewhere quiet. Then I will send him to see you."

Merrell looked at her skeptically. "I appreciate that you have taken him on as a project, but..."

Linn stopped him short. "I've taken them all on, all those who wanted to learn to read."

"I think you know what I mean," he said.

"Perfectly," she said.

Linn hugged herself in tension at the trolley stop. She had never had to tell such wrenching news to someone she cared about so much. In 'Chrosite it had been Blythe's responsibility to declare someone dead, to notify the family or the coworkers and the company. Once she had been summoned to the bedside of a little child, but before she arrived he had died, and so Linn gave comfort to the parents but not the shocking news. But then the fire, oh God, the fire, where she had seen men die while others helped her identify them.

When Solomon stepped down from the trolley, he was surprised to see her. She took his arm. She had never done that before, and he looked uncomfortable. She steered them onto a path where she knew she would find a bench. It faced the Front Range, and she might have to look in that direction, but her own feelings were nothing compared to what she had to tell Solomon. She wanted to keep up a light conversation until they sat down. "Sonia and Vicky were up rather late last night. You know how they are together. They were taking a nap when I left my cottage. Now, tell me about the college. What happened?" Linn wanted to hear the good news before she told the bad. "What will happen next?"

"One professor was nice. He liked my beets. He said they were, a new word for me, robust. I like this word. He wants me to try another kind too. Next year we will test both." He turned to her. His eyes sparkled with anticipation and pride, and Linn was so happy for him and so sad at the same time. "This professor said there is land for a whole farm, but how can I buy? I have no money, and a bank would say no to someone like me. And I cannot leave here because of Elka."

Linn reached for his hands, and he let her take them. "Solomon," she said, "I am so, so sorry to tell you." She released one hand and put hers up to turn his face toward her, to meet his eyes. "Elka died this morning."

He continued to stare into her eyes, then he closed his and dropped his head into his hands. "And I was not here," he said quietly. "I was not here. I was doing my own plan."

"It was for all of you, for the future. Do not blame yourself."

"Yes," he said. "I must blame. It was for me and Sonia. I knew Elka would not live, but I never told her I was sorry for making her unhappy, for coming to America, for leaving family, for her illness, that not having sons was all right, even though I would be telling a lie. I say to myself there is time one day to tell her and make her feel better. Or maybe not. But I was afraid that she would"—here he waved his hand—"brush my sorry away. Not care for it. Too late sorry, she would say."

The next day Solomon, Sonia, and Linn stood together at Elka's grave site at the eastern edge of the hospital property, the only mourners at the burial. Solomon helped Sonia scoop and drop a shovelful of soil onto the plain pine box in the bottom of the grave, then he did the same. They brought Sonia back to the classroom dry-eyed and ready to join in. Solomon told Linn he thought Sonia was too young to understand what happened to her mother. Besides, Elka had been out of Sonia's life for too long. Solomon himself looked sorrowful, but Linn knew him well enough to believe he still felt shock and guilt more than anything.

Solomon asked to suspend his English lessons. He had to write letters, he said, and she didn't see him for weeks. A month after Elka died, he brought the letters to the schoolroom one late afternoon for Linn to look over. She gave two of them back to him.

"Russian," she said.

"You must learn," he said with the trace of a smile, and Linn felt his response held the promise of the Solomon she knew.

Dixon Merrell found more employees for Linn to teach English. She felt as if he was trying to test her energy. At the same time, she helped Solomon design recording sheets for his beet project. She still helped him understand some of the letters as well as the scientific papers the professors sent. Sometimes she went to his cottage rather than have him bring sheaves of paper and pencils and pens to her crowded cottage or her schoolroom, which was already brimming with toys, papers, clay, easels, drawings, and chalk.

One evening when she was leaving his cottage, he held her shawl and left his hands on her shoulders while she fastened it in front.

"I like you very much," he said.

She could have walked out from under his hands; she could have turned and stepped back while saying goodnight. "I like you very much too," she replied. She wanted to take a step forward, closer, into his arms, and raise her head for a kiss. But his like and hers might not be the same, and she couldn't risk pushing him into something he did not mean. She raised only her eyes, and when they caught his, he bent and kissed her—not a Blythe Walcott kiss, but gently, not long, a naïve kiss as if he had scarcely done it before in his life.

"We are not hurting anyone now," he said.

"No, not anyone anymore." She coaxed longer kisses, put her arms around his neck, and pressed against him.

Every time they met, they ended this way. Sonia was asleep, the blinds were closed. Standing near the door was safe. Sitting on Solomon's secondhand davenport reached a danger zone they dared not cross. There was no safe crossing until one Sunday afternoon soon after Christmas. Sonia did not celebrate Christmas, so had no novelties to play with while Solomon compared seed catalogs with suggestions by the college agriculture professor and Linn took the part of translator of some of the flowery booster claims in the catalog.

Flora and Vicky came calling to ask whether Sonia could come to their cottage to play with Vicky's new doll clothes. As soon as the door closed, Solomon took Linn in his arms. "We have both been married," he said. "We both know what we have been wanting."

It was over almost before it began, leaving her disappointed and frustrated. They had not wanted the same thing, it appeared.

She tried but failed to keep tears from spilling onto the pillow. She had expected to find Blythe Walcott, but instead she was looking at the round face, the unruly hair, and the deep blue eyes of Solomon and feeling the bulky half-dressed, half-undressed body against hers. She never imagined that all the wanting would end this way. Yet she liked him so much and admired his ambition and his gentle nature. Extricating herself from his arms felt wrong, but so did staying there unless she was honest. *Honesty, not modesty.*

"Solomon," she said, "women want to have the same feelings as you."

"Yes, but…"

"Yes, surely."

"Not Elka. She wanted only for babies."

"Do you know that for certain?"

"She didn't love me. I knew. I knew how she thought in bed."

"Why didn't she love you? You are quite lovable."

"She loved someone else, but our parents decided she and I must marry."

"And was that all right with you? Did you love someone else too?"

"Not then." He wiped the trace of tears from her face with the sheet that covered them. "Do you love me?"

"Do I love you?" she said, questioning herself. "Yes, I love you, but I am not in love with you. Does that make any sense to you?"

He had that impatient look again on finding another barrier in English. "What is this *in love?*"

"*In love* means to think about you all the time and want to be with you all the time and cannot live without you and have bubbles in your head and probably want to get married."

"I can't marry you. I must have a Jewish wife and have sons."

"I know that."

"I have no bubbles in my head."

"I'm sure you haven't. You aren't the bubble type."

"Type. What is *type?*"

"The kind, the sort, think of a type of beet, the kind of beet."

She almost laughed but settled herself. "The one who would have bubbles."

"But do you love me? You said I am lovable. What type of love is this?"

She couldn't say some of the things she wanted to—for instance, that he was lovable like a large shaggy creature one wanted to put one's arms about. He was lovable because he was eager to be an American yet was so stubbornly resistant to some of its ways. She was able to say, "You are lovable because you are a fine man, a good father, you can be very funny, and you can laugh at yourself. And you are nice to kiss." She moved her lips closer to his. She thought, *I'm missing the best part, and I have to teach him.* She brushed her fingers over his hip, his thigh, his inner thigh, and more.

"She never touched me there," he whispered.

"Do you mind if I do?"

"No, please."

She touched, she talked, she suggested, she led, she followed. And not in vain.

Nor again for a long time. When she walked next into his cottage to help him with letters and papers, she felt that the current between them would have swept her into his arms if not for Sonia playing with her doll on the davenport.

"I'm going to teach you a new word tonight," she said. "Privacy. We don't have any."

"What is this privacy?" He had trouble with the *V*.

"When you have privacy you are alone, or with someone else, or maybe in a meeting of revolutionaries, but no one is there who doesn't belong or whom you don't want to be there."

"What revolutionaries?" He frowned.

"Just an example of people who might want privacy. You don't tell or share. Kind of like having a secret."

He said quietly, "We have a secret, but not privacy."

"Yes. Quite right. And there's another word, *private*. Private, privacy. It's a word that modifies, describes, makes clear another word, like a private talk, a private letter, a private room. It's sort of like secret but not exactly. Hard to explain. I just wanted you to know."

He reached across the table to lace fingers with hers. He kept his voice low. "Children, Flora, Alma, my workers. No privacy for being together again. I would like." They gazed at each other across the table. "Would you?"

She gripped his fingers to stay grounded while she melted into his eyes, blue into blue. "Yes," she whispered.

13

LINNIE ANN ADAMS WALCOTT CAME EARLY TO HER FIRST CLASS IN
medical school: anatomy and physiology. She sat in the center of
the student seats and reread the course information she had been
sent. She and a skeleton were the only people in the room, but as
the other students arrived, Linn became an island in a sea of males
who left two or three seats between her and themselves. When the
professor walked in, all the students rose in respect then settled back
down for his words. He told them they were undertaking a rigorous
course of study that required dedication and seriousness. He went
on in this way for some time before he began to lecture on the actual
subject of anatomy. He had pull-down charts that reminded Linn
of the maps in her Illinois schoolroom, but instead of the world
or the United States, these showed the organization of the human
body. There was one with musculature, one with the circulatory
system, one with the nerve network, and one with internal organs.
He showed them what they would be learning, memorizing, and
burning into their brains forever.

"These parts of the body could not exist without the skeleton,
or we would be wriggling on the ground with the worms," he said
and paused to let that concept be absorbed. A few of the students
guffawed. "We wouldn't need arms or legs. Let us first be grateful
to the skeleton, and second make it our companion." He walked to
the dangling skeleton and began at the top.

Everyone made notes as they watched the professor, their
heads bobbing up and down like feeding livestock. *That's what*

we are, Linn thought, *taking in, digesting, then.* . . . She smiled. She hadn't had an exam for twenty years. Blythe had trusted her without grilling her. He used gentle reminders. He was gentle in every way, until he wasn't. *No, no, no.* She came back to the reality of skull sutures.

By the next class period, she had memorized the skeleton from skull to distal phalange. She passed the exam, and she still sat next to empty chairs.

"Today," the professor said, "we will form groups and be assigned a cadaver. You will watch a preceptor dissect, you will follow along in your books, you will take notes, and then you may use the instruments yourself to very carefully explore the topic of the day. Mark yourself off in fours, beginning with this corner." He pointed to a student on the end of the first row. "One," he said.

The next student said two, and so it went until Linn's turn. Before she could say, "Four," the student in the third chair to her left said, "Four." Before the student next to him said, "One," Linn spoke up. "Four," she said clearly.

"Four," the student said again.

"Mr. Stevens," the professor drawled, "it appears you would like to be in the same group as Mrs. Walcott. I admit she would be an attractive cadaver mate, but under my system you must be a one and start a new group."

Mr. Stevens turned scarlet while the rest of the men laughed. He did not look at Linn, and she did not look at him, though she would have liked to.

"One, Mr. Stevens," the professor said.

"One," he said defiantly.

"Two," and so on until all students were sorted.

Mr. Stevens remained dismissive of Mrs. Walcott. When he learned she had passed a test exempting her from taking pharmacology, he tried undermining her. He made comments about women sneaking into a man's world and insinuations about what she might have done to get there, about how she had probably seduced the pharmacology professor, about whether she was cheating on the exams. He never spoke to her.

Linn's anatomy-mates were not warm at first but were at least decent, and finally they accepted her. They even admired the deft touch she had with dissections and how well she retained the relationship of skin, muscle, tendon, and nerve. Because she had the schoolroom to herself in the evenings, she brought the three other students in her group in for study sessions—without approval from Alma. Denny Henderson accepted Linn from the outset. He and Stevens had known each other at the university in Boulder and were never friendly. He liked seeing Stevens made a fool of. Sam Tubbs had come down from Leadville. Linn froze when she first heard, but Sam never hinted that he knew anything about doctors in 'Chrosite. Ruben Silver had lived in Denver all his life. His parents had a store and had been lucky enough to stake miners who prospered. His mother had been one of the concerned citizens who had worked for the establishment of Maimonides to keep consumptives off the streets of Denver.

Ruben didn't warm to Linn until he saw the buildings, the layout, and the children's section. He was determined to specialize in pulmonary studies and cure the world of consumption. He was an enthusiast. When he studied medical microbiology the next year, he fancied himself becoming the American Louis Pasteur.

The study group grew to six to learn names and symptoms of the infectious organisms. Cures were not so easily done, they also learned. Linn did not blush when they discussed venereal diseases, nor had her classmates expected it after watching her pick through the intimacies of the male and female reproductive systems. "No modesty," she told them. "It doesn't belong in medicine." The words came out as naturally as if she had made them up herself. In so many ways, she knew she would never be quit of Blythe Walcott.

Denny finally wrung her background out of her. He lingered one evening after the study group had been exchanging first experiences with real patients. Linn had been assigned a casualty clinic. She felt a rush of excitement when the first patient was a child who had cut his arm on a broken window. She knew exactly what to do. She wanted to get her hands on the child and stitch him up to enable him to stop crying. She wanted to tell the physician in charge that he did not have to explain every step to her. She clenched her fists to keep from reaching out to the needles, the sutures, the carbolic, the bandages, the child's rumpled hair. Medical school sometimes felt like a descent of the Florentine, and she tried to remain that undemanding plant living on a cliff face, but it wasn't always that simple.

"Yes, yes," she kept saying while she nodded and silently critiqued her teacher's technique. When the child and his mother left, she could not stop herself from asking the physician why he had not used a different suture. He frowned and asked roughly what she could possibly know about that. When she told him he said, "You still have a lot to learn," and walked away. He told another physician what this mere student, a woman at that, had said. He had taken it as a challenge.

Word went around, and Denny questioned her about her past.

"You already knew about wound dressing. And you could skip pharmacology. You knew it already. Do you know what Stevens said? Oh, I shouldn't have said that. It just slipped out."

"I'd been away from potions and poultices for a few years, but I guess nothing in pharmacology has changed since Hippocrates. And never mind about Stevens. He will never have anything good to say about me."

"You must have delivered babies. You were able to skip the basic class, short as it was."

"Yes."

"Set broken bones?"

"Simple fractures, yes."

"Taken out tumors?"

"No. I don't really know what goes on in a living, breathing interior. I've seen, but he wouldn't let me do anything else."

Linn's tutoring Solomon had succeeded too well, she thought. He was engrossed in his beets and the college. He understood its correspondence and rarely asked for help. They hardly had time alone but found little excuses for moments together: time for a few kisses; a longer time for a deep embrace; time, once, to fall to the urgency pent up in both of them. Linn was not ashamed but rather bemused to recognize that the hay barn had given her the same excitement at the danger of discovery that aspen meadows had when she was with Blythe at the hot springs.

Solomon did not express any opinion about her meeting with her classmates in the schoolroom where she and he had first become friends. *He can't be jealous of twenty-three-year-olds any more than I can be jealous of sugar beets,* she thought.

On the day she sought him out to tell him about her humiliation at the casualty clinic and to feel comfort in his arms if for only half a minute, he held her even longer and said he wished he did not have to tell her his news that same day, but he must. The college had offered him a job—not just a job but a position as the manager of its beet test farm.

"Oh," she said, holding him even closer. "I'm so happy for you, but so sorry for me. I will miss you very much."

"And I will miss you every day."

"But you must go. It is your dream." She smiled up at him.

"Yes. Both of our dreams are coming true. But Linn, here is good news too. They will let me have the house that is on the property. Not a beautiful house, but good enough for Sonia and me right now. You will visit."

"You will not have to ask me twice."

"Ask twice? What is this? I already asked."

She hugged him again. "Just some silly English. I accept your invitation."

Everyone expected her to faint or at least leave the room during the first practical in surgery. She didn't expect to do either, nor did she.

A few of the men turned away when the knife first cut skin. Others blanched at the insertion and tension of rib spreaders. They anticipated Linn's turning scarlet when a woman's lower abdomen and pubic area lay bare for a hysterectomy. She didn't. She learned how to treat compound fractures, a skill she had always left to Blythe even in his blackest depths. She learned that most of the men students disliked the idea of putting a hand inside a woman's body for any reason from pregnancy to cancer. The professors failed to stress treatment of women's problems, as they were best left, the men taught, to other women. Linn boiled silently, having learned by this time to stay quiet. *Someday I will teach medicine a different way,* she thought.

She had been making a weekly progress report to Dixon Merrell. "Well," he said one snowy March afternoon, "your Mr. Chernigov is causing me a great deal of trouble in telling me he is leaving here for work in Fort Collins. He liked so much to be in charge of everything that he has no natural successor among the other men out on the farm."

"I suppose that is one of my flaws as well," Linn said. "It's a miracle Alma and I got on as well as we did. She's happier with Flora, who is more pliable. And by the way, he is not enough of *my* Mr. Chernigov that I would go with him. He wouldn't marry me—couldn't marry me in terms of his faith."

Merrell asked her from time to time whether she had fallen in love with some other aspect of medicine, and when she told him how the coursework dismissed women and their unique medical needs, he promised she would be allowed to treat "the whole woman," as he phrased it. He admitted that his own medical education had glossed over not only women but also children. He apologized for shooing her away when she had wanted to keep the parent-and-child connection fresh.

"Honestly, you frightened me that day. You are probably frightening your classmates and professors."

"I've learned to keep my head down finally, but when I get back here with my diploma..."

"The great Maimonides whirlwind will have arrived."

"You have sown the wind, Doctor."

"I welcome the reaping."

Merrell drove Alma, Flora, and Vicky to Linn's graduation ceremony himself, along with his wife, who seemed uncomfortable with this unorthodox family. Solomon and Sonia sent a card of congratulations on which Solomon had penciled, "I look forward to a doctor's visit."

Linn sat among her classmates, Denny on one side and Ruben on the other, but her thoughts drifted away from the several speakers to one, two, three mountain ranges away. She paged through that chapter of her life, from the first morning with Blythe and the bottles and jars, through childbirth, wounds, measles, chicken pox, mine accidents. She lingered over some of the pages, riffled through others, skipped some: the twins, the fire. A great emptiness welled up, shook her core, and ended this celebration of past accomplishments. She locked the memories into her mental box and came back to the beginning of a new chapter.

The nurses knew what was coming. They were not smiling at their first meeting with Linn on the first day she wore the white coat with her name embroidered on the pocket above *Maimonides Mountain Hospital for Consumptives*. Merrell had slipped it on her and kissed her cheek. She promised not to turn the well-ordered world of the women's ward upside down and then told them what she wanted. She made it sound as if she were going to do all the new work. She appealed to their sense of solidarity—women healing women. The younger ones left the meeting with their jaws less set than the older ones did.

Linn read the charts of every one of the women in the wards. She interviewed each patient and took notes. She asked them what other needs they had, were they happy, whether they felt well in spite of being consumptive, whether they cheated on the treatment program.

—Happy! No one ever asked me that before.

—I hate eggnog.

—My baby died, and the doctors said I had to come here and get well or the next baby, and the next, and the next would get it and die.

—I'm so bored.

—Someone stole my underwear. Why can't you keep out crazy people?

—All we have to read around here is the Old Testament and silly inspirational books. Can you get us some novels?

— The minute I get up out of bed, I have to, well, umm, make water really urgently. I'm so embarrassed.

— You taught my children? I've seen them only out of the window since I came here.

Daily, Linn made rounds on the men's ward with Merrell and other male colleagues. She heard from her female patients that one of the men always leered at them. She heard complaints from the male patients that some of the women were bothersome flirts. The men were also more openly restless and bored than the women. Linn suspected that many of them felt ashamed they had had to give in to what they had tried to dismiss as a cold, a little cough, hay fever acting up. Several times Merrell had required her at the bedside of a bad bleed, and she learned what Blythe had warned her about there in the shade of the Cherry Creek cottonwoods. *Turn his head over and down so gravity takes care of the flow.* She pushed Blythe back into the box in her mind.

The growing Vicky moved Linn to save as much as she could of what seemed to be a gold mine of salary. She bought a home near the streetcar line. She loved the oval glass in the house's front door. The smooth-rolling pocket doors closed off the living room and dining room from the hall that connected to the kitchen and small back bedroom that would be Flora's if she wanted to leave the cottage. The indoor plumbing was a miracle, and they had their own telephone. She sent for the piano she had stored with her cousin near Normal. The two had corresponded fitfully over the years: when Peter died, when she was in 'Chrosite, when she taught school at Maimonides, at Christmas. *Some women,* Linn thought, *imagine their lives are over as soon as they're forty years old. Mine has begun. Again.*

Until she went to public school, Vicky had never expressed an interest in fathers. The children at Maimonides were temporary orphans, but at James Madison School, everyone had a father except her. Linn didn't want to lie and tell Vicky her father was dead. Flora knew he wasn't, and Linn had warned her from the subject if it ever came up.

Linn, for reasons she hated to examine, had packed a photograph of Blythe when she left 'Chrosite. Its presence in her life had been put away in a real box, but now she brought it out and showed it to Vicky. She had the same dark-brown, thick hair and the same face shape, but she had inherited Linn's blue eyes, a mercy to Linn, who did not want another pair of beautiful light-brown eyes with the green flecks looking at her every day.

Telling lies again, now to my child. Linn cringed inside but went ahead. "Your father was very sick and went away to get well and never came back." She alerted Flora to this fabrication.

"Will he come back someday?" Vicky asked.

"He doesn't know where we live now, honey, so probably not."

"Why didn't you stay where he knew where you were? Why didn't you go with him?"

Quickly, a half-truth: "Well, I was up in the mountains, and I got too cold and there was no work, so I came down to Denver."

"What did you do up there? Can we go sometime?"

Linn kept the mental box closed on what she did. "Maybe we can take a train trip up there. Maybe not to the exact place. I don't know where the trains run anymore."

"Let's go next summer when school's out."

"We'll see." Wasn't that what all parents said when they really meant no?

After supper on a visit to Solomon's farmhouse, and after Vicky and Sonia had gone upstairs to play, he carried tea from the kitchen.

"Let's sit and be comfortable. We must talk about something." The thing Linn had been steeled for. "Elka's cousin and that cousin's cousin are coming to visit me."

"Ah," Linn replied. "A cousin's cousin who is not married?" She smiled at him, but her heart hurt.

"Yes, both. Elka's cousin's husband died last year."

"And if the cousin's cousin is plain and has an unpleasant voice and cannot cook, you will feel obligated to marry her because she came all this way in hopes of finding a husband."

"No."

"And if she has curly hair and beautiful eyes and a soft voice and she likes you..."

"Of course not, but that would be better."

Linn tried to keep smiling. "Promise me you will marry not from guilt or because of a pretty face. Marry a woman you love and who loves you. Remember, you are lovable. You deserve love."

"I will not take mine away from you, no matter what happens."

She twined her fingers with his. "And I will keep warm with it and return it. But someday you will have that other person to love best. Remember what you said about not hurting anyone."

He picked up her other hand and held both of hers in his. "I understand you," he said. They were quiet, then he said, "You and me. If I were not Jewish."

"If I were."

"If you wanted more children."

"If I wanted to be a farm wife."

"If you didn't already have work you love."

"If I didn't have a husband somewhere in the world."

"I will tell you a naughty saying about 'if.'"

"I can't believe you would tell anything naughty."

"Oh yes, I will. If my *bubie* had *batzim*, she would be my *zaidy*. You can imagine what *batzim* are."

Linn laughed, surprised at this aspect of him she had never known before. "You are naughty," she said.

"There are very bad words in every language. You think I didn't learn them in English at the farm?"

"I'm sure you did. May I tell you something?"

"Something naughty?"

"I want to tell you a secret and not-nice wish of mine."

"I will never tell your secret."

"You might not like it. But at any rate, I sometimes wish my husband, wherever he is, could see me in your bed."

Solomon frowned and caught her eye. "No," he said. "You should not wish that. It is bad for both of us. For you it is revenge. Remember you taught me that word? Better think about forgiving."

"I told you what happened that last day."

"And you left him."

"I'm sorry I told you my secret. Let's not talk about him anymore."

"Yes, we must. He was not in his right mind or he would not have done such a terrible thing to you. And it is not nice for me to think of you thinking of him watching us. I want only you in my bed."

"Just my revenge, as you say, but only in my mind, obviously."

"And I say, no revenge." He drew her to him. "How many will be in my bed tonight?"

"Only one if the girls don't go to sleep soon."

The girls did finally go to sleep. As they had done on other visits, Linn and Solomon had made up a bed for her on the davenport for appearance's sake. After he was in bed, she changed into her nightgown. She quietly went into his room and turned the key in the lock. He raised the covers, and she slipped under and into his arms. She felt safe there. She never wanted to leave them and pretended, through the long night of goodbye, that she would never have to.

"If only," he whispered.

"If only," she replied.

"Mama," Vicky asked when the train pulled out of the Fort Collins depot, "are you going to marry Mr. Chernigov?"

Linn, sleepy but at the same time savoring the quite publicly passionate kiss she had exchanged with Solomon at the station, had thought, *I'll never see any of these people again.*

"No, no. What made you ask that?"

"Well, you kissed him before we left, and Sonia said she saw you kissing one other time, and that when people kiss, it means they're going to get married. And what about my father?"

"No, I'm not going to marry him." Linn hoped to steer Vicky's thoughts away from her father.

"Why did you kiss him then?"

"Sometimes good friends kiss goodbye." Was that going to be enough of an answer?

"I'm glad you aren't, then."

Linn wondered how long Vicky had been troubled about her and Solomon. "Wouldn't you like that?"

"No, because we would have to move up here and live on that dusty road, and it would be a such long walk to school, and would Flora come, or what?"

"And what about Sonia? You could be sisters."

"I like her, but I like having my own room. Let's just visit."

Linn imagined Solomon's wife learning that the little friend's mother had stayed overnight when they visited. "Perhaps she can come to us instead," she suggested to Vicky. *And no awkward questions that way.*

14

THE FIRST HINT OF THE STORM CAME ON A GUST OF WIND THAT blew some of the papers from Linn's desk onto the floor. She retrieved them and turned back to face the west window. Gray rain columns supported darker gray clouds in the southwest, and black smudges—more brushstrokes than clouds—moved east, coalescing as they came. She closed her window and continued to watch the metamorphosis of a beautiful day. Lightning flashed at the far edge of the darkest clouds. "One thousand one, one thousand two," Linn began a count that reached five before she heard thunder.

It was almost time to go home, but there was no point trying to outrun this storm. She would not reach the tram line before it hit, so she stood and watched. She loved lightning. She loved the hours-long chain lightning flashes in the mountainous summer thunderheads above the plains east of town. Once she saw a green bolt but never again, in spite of watching and watching. Sometimes a bolt wasn't seen, but the light hid in the clouds—on, off, on, off, like a sputtering lamp. Linn never lost her awe of the power.

The rain came pouring and almost blotted out the buildings across the courtyard. It pounded the roof and pelted her windows. One thousand one, one thousand *crash*—the lightning was two miles away. In no time there was a flash, and a cracking, deafening explosion of sound right overhead. Linn cringed, much as it excited her. Yet again, a flash and boom preceded a prolonged rolling growl like boulders in 'Chrosite tumbling on and on downhill after a powder blast. She expected that like most Denver storms, this one would blow over quickly, so she settled back down at the desk to try to review a chart. She heard a hurried tread on the stairs, and then a nurse stood in the doorway.

"Please, Doctor," she panted, "there's a new patient in the infirmary causing a fuss. Can you come?"

"Isn't Dr. Merrell here?"

"No, ma'am, he's not back from the health department."

Linn generally didn't see the male patients, but she sighed and rose from her chair. "All right. Infirmary?"

"Yes."

The infirmary was a six-bed men's ward where new patients stayed until the extent and course of their illness were estimated. Linn gathered current charts and dropped them at the nurses' station on her way. Three patients were in their beds; two were out of the room. She knew the men because she did go on men's ward rounds with the other physicians, so bed three must hold the new man, who was now quiet with his eyes closed. He was thin and flushed. His unkempt hair and beard were streaked with gray. Linn stood at the end of the bed.

"Hello," she said, looking for the patient's name on the clipboard she held. "I'm Doctor…"

The name she was about to say and the name she read were the same. The world rocked, and she grasped the foot of the bed for support.

Blythe Walcott opened his eyes wearily, then they fastened upon her. "What the hell," he said and tried to sit up. He fell back coughing.

Linn could not put a coherent thought together, much less speak. Blythe regained his breath and began to swear.

"Jesus Christ, this must be a bad dream." He pushed the sheet back and attempted to move his legs off the bed, but hospital corners trapped him. He kicked. "Goddamn it, what are you staring at? Get away from me." He fell back again. "Lying bitch," he croaked. "And what are you looking at?" He waved an arm at the other patients.

Linn, still stunned and mute, looked at the clipboard in her confusion, but the name jumped out again. She couldn't absorb any of the other information.

"I want the doctor. Get out of here. What the hell are you doing here, for God's sake? I never want to see you again. Got to get out of here." He struggled again. "Where's Ivy? Where's the doctor?"

Now Linn met his eyes, the only thing she recognized in the wreck before her. In another life those eyes could draw hers from across a room, make her smile, and melt not just her heart but her whole body. Fate had not broken their ties after all.

—I fell in love with you the first time I saw you.
—Stay with me tonight and marry me tomorrow.
—It's the glue that holds two people together.
—I felt like a train off the track.
—You've done all you can do.

She finally regained her voice if not her equilibrium. "I'm the doctor."

"Bloody hell you are. You're a piece of trash I picked out of the gutter." His voice rose, and the other patients looked on with interest at the most diverting thing that had happened since their arrival. They also called Blythe down.

"Simmer down," one of them yelled back. "She's the doc."

"Watch your language," warned another. "You're talking to a lady."

Blythe made a scoffing sound. "She's a lying bitch, is what she is. Ran away with my money, killed my practice, killed me." He was fighting the sheets and nearly succeeded this time in getting out of bed. Linn stepped around to prevent it.

"Get the hell out of my way," he yelled and swung an arm at her. She intercepted it and hung on while pushing him back down. He wasn't strong. His body smelled unwashed. His breath smelled of alcohol.

"Leave her alone!" and "Stop!" came from the other patients.
"Stay in bed," she commanded.

"I will if you'll hop in," he said to her in a leeringly low voice.
"You liked it, didn't you, in bed. Whose are you in now?"

"Stop it," she shouted, tossing his arm away.

There were footfalls in the corridor, and then Dixon Merrell's large frame filled the doorway. Like naughty children, five pair of guilty eyes turned to him.

"Thank you, Dr. Walcott," he said calmly while he advanced into the room. "I'll see this patient."

Linn handed him the clipboard as they passed without looking at each other. She was walking through rushing water. Maybe the rain had poured inside. The going was heavy, as in those dreams of running with tons-heavy legs. If she could only reach the stairway and grasp the railing, she could pull herself out of the flood. She couldn't drown in the corridor with the nurses watching, but one of them stopped her. Why wasn't she wet?

"That new patient, his wife wants to speak to a doctor. She's been pestering whoever she can find, and Dr. Merrell was about to when…" After the nurse said the words "his wife," the water roared in Linn's ears, and she heard nothing else. She tried to keep her head up.

"Are you all right?" the nurse asked and put a hand on Linn's arm.

Linn came up for air and said, "Tell me that again. Sorry."

"She's on the west porch. That new patient's wife. She wants to talk to a doctor, and now Dr. Merrell is busy, so…"

"Certainly," Linn responded. She thought, *Certainly I will see Blythe Walcott's wife. It's my fate to see his women, but I don't care. I'm free. A divorcée. God, I hope the neighbors don't find out.*

She fished a handkerchief from her dress and arranged it in the breast pocket of her white coat so it lapped over her embroidered name. *Two Walcotts are bad company,* she thought. *Three are un-thinkable, but let's see what she's like. Perhaps, after all, it's that girl, what's her name? Blythe helped her out once. I wonder whether it was his child even back then. Damn him.*

Linn found a damp figure who hopped up expectantly from the porch railing then faded. She was small and dark, thin and pale, and not the girl from 'Chrosite. Her secondhand dress needed laundering, and springy curls escaped her secondhand hat. Had she made Blythe's life neat and tidy? She herself needed a good deal of tidying up.

"Oh, I was hoping to see the doctor."

"I'm a doctor," Linn said neutrally. "What can I do for you?"

"Oh. Oh. Well." The woman was flustered but carried on. "It's about my, well, my husband. I brought him here. My aunt helped raise money to start this place, so I knew about it and thought they could help him, but he hasn't come out. Can you get him?" The woman spoke quickly as her agitation increased.

"I believe he is going to stay here. Can you go on home now and come back tomorrow? He's in the infirmary. That means he's pretty ill and needs to stay." Now that her curiosity was satisfied, Linn just wanted her to go away.

The woman became more agitated. "I need him to come with me. I can't...I don't..."

"What?"

The woman's words poured out. "They turned us out of the boarding house. We—I mean, he—was coughing, and you know what that means around here. And we had no more money, and we've been sleeping out, sleeping rough. I can't do it alone. He was working for a while. He's a doctor, you know, and he was taking care of anyone who needed help, and he hoped they could pay a little. He's just too kind." Linn continued to listen, unmoved by this last. "But then he started drinking again, and I'm no help, sorry to say. But I didn't think they'd keep him here. He just needs a bit of medicine."

We, I mean he... echoed in Linn's mind. *She's got it too.* She was pulled two ways. She wanted the woman to leave, most particularly because the shock of seeing Blythe was still running through her and she wanted to go home where she could catch her breath. But she recalled her own uneasiness staying alone in the tent all those years ago. She had had a roof over her head, at least. Furthermore, this woman should not be out on the streets and staying with groups of people most likely debilitated by drink and malnutrition. At this hour it was against schedule rules, but Linn took this wet, flushed, wisp of a woman into the hospital and into an examination room. Hers were the worst lungs Linn had ever listened to. Or rather not listened to, for there were minimal breath sounds on the right side, and the left upper and middle lobes were involved as well.

"Tell me the truth now," Linn said. "The two of you both have tuberculosis, and you must have known that."

The woman nodded. "I suppose," she said, her large brown eyes cast down, "but I've been feeling good lately. I have to have him healthy. I brought him so you would just give him some medicine and he'd be back with me."

"Maybe he can keep you safe on the streets, but neither of you will get well there. You can't cure this disease with just a little medicine. You need to be here just like he does. I can arrange for a bed if you want to be treated. It's a bit irregular at this time of day, but I'll deal with the nurses." Linn went on to explain the treatment regimen: breathe, two, three; out, two, three. Let's get rid of that Scott Joplin syncopation I hear inside you. Follow the rules, two, three, four. "We'll get you into something dry and into bed."

The woman nodded, and Linn went to the nurses' desk for admission papers. The nurses scowled.

When Linn returned she said, "I don't know your name. I apologize." *But I was drowning,* she continued to herself. *Now that I'm breathing again, I'm running on pure irony.*

"Oh, it's all right. My name is Ivy Caro...Well, Ivy Caro Walcott, that is." No address, no next of kin except the husband-patient. The aunt didn't seem to count. She had few belongings to check in, only the small valise she had been protective of. "It has a change of clothes for both of us and a couple of books."

A Tale of Two Wives, Linn thought. She almost smiled at the absurdity of the situation, and when one of the nurses who was protesting adding a patient to her ward in such an unscheduled manner called Linn "Doctor Walcott" within Ivy's hearing, Linn crossed her fingers and prepared to tell a lie when Ivy joked that perhaps they were related.

"Yes, it is a coincidence, isn't it, having three Walcotts in the same hospital? Perhaps it's like that birthday rule. Do you know it? For every something-like-twenty-six-people, two have the same birthday." She was babbling but couldn't stop her attempt to deflect. "We should ask around here. I'll bet we could prove it. All right, now, you can go with Miss Cutler, and she will get you all settled."

Linn's emotional effort imploded as she watched the two women walk away. She wanted home. She wanted Vicky and normalcy and to forget that while planting three trees, or tulips, or roses created visual interest, planting two other Walcotts in her garden could create an endless bramble.

Dix is going to hear about this, and maybe there will be only two after tomorrow, she said to herself as she headed for her office.

She wasn't wrong. When she arrived at the hospital the next morning, there was a note from Dr. Merrell pinned to her office door: *See me as soon as you get in.* On the way, she tried to prepare herself for being let go. There was no evading what she had done.

"Three things happened yesterday," Merrell said when she was seated across the desk from him. "Tell me the connection between them. First you raised your voice to a patient named Walcott. Not just raised, shouted. Second, you admitted a woman named Walcott to the women's ward after hours and without any consultation with me. Third—well, this didn't happen yesterday—but your name is Walcott."

Linn took a deep breath and plunged in. "He's my daughter's father, and yesterday I learned he is now my former husband. I remember I told you I was a widow. I also told you how difficult it is to be a woman alone, so you're right, I didn't tell you the truth. It's not a pretty story." She looked Dix straight in the eye. *Just get it over with and tell me to leave,* she thought.

"And the wife?" He seemed focused only on the medical.

Linn shrugged. "I don't know anything about her except she has the worst chest I ever listened to."

"You know we don't take patients like that. This smacks of some sort of favoritism behind my back, and I don't like it."

"Why would I favor a woman I didn't even know my long-lost husband was married to? He might have looked for me in those nearly ten years, and to let me know we weren't married anymore. I almost sent her away, but I just knew. You know how sometimes you just know? And they were living on the street. She was afraid. She's just a very ill woman, and I'm a doctor who can help her. And what do I care about him anymore?"

"You can help her to die," he said. "I saw her this morning, and I doubt there will be any miraculous recoveries. I should send you off or demote you to the laundry, but I need you. One demand, though: stay away from him. When we do rounds in his ward, you drop out."

"So you had this pretty well figured out already?"

"I just wanted to be sure."

"I'm sorry to have upset everything. I never expected a day like yesterday. I went home and collapsed on the davenport. Vicky thought I was sick, so I played along, and she brought me a nice cup of tea. I couldn't tell her I was just trying to pull myself together because her father had come back to life."

Ivy Caro Walcott brightened the women's hospital immediately. Once she learned Blythe had agreed to stay on, she adapted to the schedule, drank her milk, ate her eggs, monitored her temperature, and rested on the sunporch. She nudged recalcitrant patients. She chatted with those who responded; she said hello every day to those who were morose, lonely, jealous, or haughty. She elicited stories from those missing their children. She looked at photographs of them and of beaus pined for.

"Are you married? Do you have any children?" she asked Linn.
"No," Linn lied. "You patients are my children, I suppose."
"Well, you need someone besides us. Do you have a sweetheart?"
Linn didn't lie this time. "No."
"Do you live alone, then?"
Before she could stop herself, she said no again.
"That's good. Is it your sister or mother?"
"My niece," Linn told her. "She is a teacher."
Ivy brightened. "Oh, that's good," she said. "It's hard being alone, but then sometimes it is better. My parents wanted me to marry someone I didn't like very well. That's when I left and went to San Francisco, and there I met Doc—well, Blythe—my husband. Have you met him there on the men's ward? We're a pair, aren't we?" She laughed, saving Linn from answering. Ivy continued on as long as Linn would listen. In spite of herself, Linn liked her.

In the mornings there was no mixing of the sexes. The doctors made rounds. The patients bathed. The able washed their clothes, and the bedridden darned stockings and mended. Ivy could not sew a stitch, so, propped up on the sunporch, she bartered hairdressing. Soon braids and ribbons overflowed her account. Her curling iron stayed hot in a lamp chimney. She exchanged harmless gossip and refused the spiteful and malicious. She seemed not to have heard about the row between her husband and her doctor.

In the afternoons, in all weather, patients rested on the sun-porches. Here the men and women could be together, though staff squelched questionable relationships immediately. At least on the porches they were in plain sight. While there was little privacy anywhere, romances did develop but generally failed. Affairs, even chaste, were not considered good companions to the regimen of rest and tranquility, and one nurse was assigned to ferreting out attachments. Gently at first but with increasing intrusion, she discouraged, then forbade smitten pairs any contact. Other nurses who hadn't the skill or patience were happy to take on her duties when she was on a mission, as they termed it.

Once Blythe was released from the infirmary to a general men's ward, he and Ivy were never found in dark hallways or empty rooms together. Blythe spent every afternoon with Ivy on the sunporch, he in a wicker chair beside her bed. She usually slept for more than an hour. He catnapped and stared for long, silent periods at the mountains.

Linn avoided the women's west sunporch in the afternoon. Rarely she passed Blythe in the hall on his way to sit with Ivy. Neither acknowledged the other, but it was a fully conscious disregard, their eyes following lines on the floor. Linn's hand always gripped harder anything she was carrying. One afternoon she was obliged to be on the sunporch talking with a homesick, tearful young patient who spoke little English.

Another Elka, she thought, *and Sarah and Mary Margaret and Natasha and Katerina and plain Yankee Mary Smith, whom we are trying to fit into one world at Maimonides. And at least the Maja Stinas and Kaysas can feel comfortable at Swedish Sanitarium now.*

Linn took her patient's hand, as she had taken so many reluctant hands, and started cajoling gently when Blythe's voice carried down the porch.

"Linn. Help me." How that voice mobilized her, and how she hated admitting it. She rushed to Blythe as he was trying to quiet Ivy's struggling for air and thrashing against the blood that poured out of her mouth.

"Crank down the bed," Blythe commanded, and Linn did it. "Turn her."

A nurse came running with towels and a basin. Linn held Ivy on one side while Blythe on the other side of the bed held the basin and towels close to Ivy's mouth.

"Cough, spit, come on, spit it out, then you'll get a breath." He was as cool as if she were a stranger.

Linn held fast and pinned the arm that Ivy flailed to scatter the demons suffocating her. Blythe kept talking, urging, wiping. His shirtsleeves were bloody. A nurse took away the stained towels and brought a large pail to collect more. Linn forgot where she was. It might have been the 'Chrosite clinic or at a mine accident. It might have been Daph Hunt's bedside littered with bloody sheets and towels. They were together again: his urgent voice, their capable hands close, suddenly touching, burning, so that they both darted back.

Ivy drew some ragged breaths, ceased struggling, and relaxed a bit. "Easy, babe," Blythe said while he stroked Ivy's damp curls. The nurses took away more soiled towels and the basin and brought fresh ones. Linn, back in the present, listened to Ivy's breath sounds and heartbeat, and looked at her eyes and fingernails.

"Not too bad," she said to Blythe. She brought the head of the bed back up, and they turned Ivy onto her back. Her breathing was regular now, but her eyes were enormous. She picked absently at the covers with one hand and gripped Linn's hand with the other. Linn said, "Just lie here, just rest. Is there anything you want?"

Ivy shook her head. She searched Linn's eyes then turned to Blythe's. A light flickered in her own momentarily before her gaze turned inward. If she ever solved for the dimensions of the triangle she was in, she never revealed the answer.

Ivy had not lost so much blood that it alone brought on her decline. She burst with energy one minute then spent the rest of the day in bed. Soon she lost her appetite and interest in the people she had first reached out to. The once-clear areas of her lungs, isolated as they may have been, lost their normal sounds. She resisted the dining hall. Her temperature was elevated and stayed that way. She was terrified of another public bleeding episode, so she was moved to a private room with a sleeping porch. Blythe was allowed to stay with her the majority of the day. He urged her to eat. He gave her bed baths. He read to her and promised to be there when she woke from naps. Such breach of protocol was barely countenanced by the older nurses, and they were resentful. They whispered among themselves that Ivy and Blythe received special treatment because they were Linn's brother or maybe sister or at least cousin. Three people at Maimonides knew the truth, and they held it close. For Linn, the arrangement meant she and Blythe crossed paths more often. He never spoke to her. She was Ivy's physician, but somehow Ivy had slipped away from her care to Merrell's through Blythe.

Linn would have admired any other husband who gave the care Blythe gave Ivy. *Is he doing it to spite me?* Linn wondered. *Or is he saying he isn't so bad after all, after 'Chrosite?* She chided herself for assigning him motives involving herself and for even taking the time to wonder. She called herself mad for flares of unbidden, unwanted jealousy.

For four months Ivy struggled through the days until she changed to merely floating. Blythe helped her to the toilet now. He washed and brushed her hair. He stroked lotion onto her face and body. He was her nurse and sole companion. Linn crept into her room sometimes when Blythe stepped out. Ivy had the look of death about her. Her cheekbones became prominent. Her fingers were bony.

At nearly noon on a warm sunny day in June, Linn was talking with the nurses when Blythe left Ivy's room and came toward them.

"It's all over," he said, his eyes blank and his mouth slack.

Linn stood and said, "I'm so sorry. She was a fine woman."

Blythe stiffened and glared. "Damn fine," he spat at her. "And you and your condolences can go to hell."

He strode away while Linn fought for breath. Her face flamed, and heat rose up her back and scalded her. The nurses stared. Linn grasped the desktop as an anchor and a self-imposed tether to keep from running after him screaming out the anger and pain she had locked away for all these years. *Someday,* she thought, *I'm going to do it, even if it's on your deathbed.* Instead, she pulled out Ivy's chart and walked slowly toward her room to write the final notes on her life.

15

DIXON MERRELL AND LINN WERE THE ONLY TWO LEFT IN THE
staff dining room. "I've been thinking about having a talk with
you about my favorite patient," Dix began.

Linn made a scoffing sound.

"Listen." He laid a hand on her arm for emphasis. "As I've
told you before, his disease is localized, but I'm concerned that
if he doesn't start taking more interest in his recovery—and
I think he can recover—he probably won't. He's extraordinarily
bright, Linn."

She nodded. At least they could agree on that.

Dix went on. "We have stimulating discussions. He's interested
in microbiology, has some insights in laboratory diagnosis, and, as
you know, Trudeau himself is self-schooled in microbiology now.
We have to keep up. I want to interest Blythe in working with Jean-
Marc in research. I want a brain of his caliber with new ideas that
are testable in the lab, and we've got one right here killing himself.
I want you to stop him."

Working right here every day? she wanted to protest. *Where
I have to see him?* But aloud she said, "You know he won't even
talk to me."

"While I don't want to meddle in family affairs, will he talk to
your daughter? Letters, I mean. You don't have to be involved at all.
He needs something to live for."

Linn raised an eyebrow, and Dix grinned in understanding. He
remembered.

Linn was about to speak when several nurses came into the room and sat nearby. "Let's go to your office," she said. "It's more complicated than that." She would have to tell him the truth, and he would truly get into family affairs. Seated in Dix's office, she sighed deeply. He cocked his head quizzically.

"If you kept your promise not to tell him about Vicky," Linn said, and Dix nodded, "then neither knows the other exists. Of course Vicky knows she had a father." Linn made a wry face. "I've always told her I didn't know what happened to him, and until his wife brought him here, I wasn't lying. Now call it a sin of omission. What should I have told her?" Linn threw her arms wide. "Vicky, I found your father. He's a derelict who may die of either tuberculosis or alcoholism."

Dix continued to look at her as if she were untying a fascinating knot. His gaze willed her to continue.

"I never tried to contact Blythe after you told me I was expecting. Our last several years together in 'Chrosite were miserable. I won't go into it, but I had to leave. There was no question of going back to him—crawling back, it seemed to me. That's why I asked you not to mention Vicky. I didn't want him as a part of my life again. It's bad enough just to run into him now and then in the hallways."

"Knowing he has a child, someone to live for, mightn't that bring him out of his black depths? Look, think of this as a physician. Wouldn't you do anything you could to help one of your patients begin to heal?"

"Of course, but this is so..." She couldn't find the words.

"I appreciate that what I'm asking is difficult for you, and painful. It brings up old memories."

"You have no idea. I try to keep them locked away." She could make this admission to Dixon Merrell.

"I know you do." He got up, came around behind her chair, and put his hands on her shoulders to rub them tenderly and therapeutically. No woman ever mistook his warmth for an advance.

"You are a remarkable woman. You're strong, you're compassionate. Use those two traits to bring Blythe Walcott back to life."

"Oh, God," she said and put her hands on Dix's.

Two days later, after losing sleep and rehearsing her lines, Linn went home early and sat down with Vicky ostensibly to play double solitaire after piano practice. During the second game, Linn, barely beaten by Vicky's slapped-down two of hearts on its ace, slowed her play and said casually, "Honey, I have some news for you."

"What?" Vicky was still playing furiously.

"Let's stop the game a minute while I tell you."

Vicky looked up. "What news?"

"Your father came to our hospital."

They had not mentioned him for some time. Vicky looked stunned, then she rallied and became excited. "Is he still sick? Can I see him, Mama? Did you talk to him? What's he like?"

Linn told her calmly that he was at the hospital as a patient. He was very sick, and Vicky couldn't visit him, but she could write to him. It might make him feel better to know he had a daughter.

Vicky's face began to crumple. "Will he die?" She knew people died there. She put down her cards and came around to Linn.

Linn hugged her and said honestly, "I don't know."

Vicky was quiet for a while, then said, "What should I write?"

"The same things you write to Sally or Ellen." They were Vicky's friends from hospital days who had moved away with their healed parents. "You can write even more because he doesn't know you. Tell him about yourself, what you look like, about school, what you're reading. Tell him about Argo and what a good friend he was and how you miss him. Tell him Flora lives with us and is a teacher." *That would be a surprise for Blythe,* Linn thought.

"Will you help me?" Vicky asked.

"Maybe a little, but this is private and special just between the two of you."

Blythe's room door was open two inches. Linn could see him sitting up in bed with a cup of coffee. A rejected breakfast tray sat on his side table. She knocked and heard a gruff, "Who is it?"

"It's Linn, Blythe."

"For God's sake, go away."

"Please," she said. "It's important." She tried to put on a pleasant face and pushed the door open a few more inches. She hated standing here in the hall where others might see or hear. He told her again to go away.

"Doctor's orders," she said, walking in and leaving the door slightly ajar as it had been.

"You're not my doctor," he reminded her in the roughest tone.

She plunged straight on. "Dix is worried about you. You aren't eating. We're all concerned you're killing yourself. I want you to know you have something to live for."

"What do you care?" he scoffed. "What should I live for?"

"There's something you should know. Someone you'll want to know. Something to live for."

"And what could that possibly be?" he threw back at her.

"This." She approached him and held out a photograph of Vicky. He looked at it and grabbed it away.

"Where did you get this?" His voice was intense and loud. He shook the photograph at her. "Did you steal this from me like you did my money?"

Linn did not understand. Blythe was becoming more agitated.

"You want me to get better, then you give me this?" He waved the photo at her. He said again more forcefully, "Where did you get this?"

"I had it taken here in Denver. Look at the back."

"The hell you did. This is a picture of my sister, and you're a hell of a fine healer to remind me of her now."

"Your sister?" Linn gasped. "You never told me you had a sister."

"I never told you a lot of things," he said bitterly. He slammed the photo face down on his bed and closed his eyes in a pained face. Linn was thrown off balance now, her aim misdirected. She was trying to force the sister out of her sights.

"Leave now," Blythe demanded, pointing at the door.

"No," she said, and he said, "Yes," over her as she went on. "That is a photograph of your daughter. Our daughter."

He opened his eyes and gave her an ugly stare. "Not possible. You expect me to perk up and open my arms to your bastard child." He laughed an ugly laugh. "Oh, I see. When I die you think your child will come in for an inheritance? A plantation in the Piedmont?" He made a scoffing sound that was equally ugly. "Sorry, dear. Nothing to carry back from old Virginny."

"Stop," she said. Last time she said that to him, she was shouting.

"You stop," he threw back. "I never would have pegged you for a gold digger." He gave another bitter laugh. "Except you did steal my money, didn't you?"

She forced herself to stay calm. She held out an envelope. "She wrote to you. She enclosed blank paper from her school tablet, a pencil, and envelopes. She went to the post office and bought you some stamps with her own money." Linn laid the envelope on the bed. "In the letter she tells you how old she is and when her birthday is." She locked onto his eyes as she backed out of the room. "You're good at mathematics." She fled to her office before she exploded.

"Damn, damn," she repeated a hundred times as she paced her office, too upset for tears. She should never have agreed to this absurd idea. Of course Blythe would reject anything from her. She had told Dix as much before she crumbled. "Compassion. No, I'm just a fool."

She stopped and stared out her window into the bulk of the mountains, into their invulnerability and solid immobility. *Just like him, just like him,* she thought. She wondered whether her gaze one, two, three ranges away was centered on 'Chrosite, like a reverse periscope. What would she see? Had the roof fallen in on that house where Vicky was conceived in mindless passion, as if she were willing two halves to create her whole and overwhelming her mother, who was being driven by need rather than love? Had Vicky been striving to exist as relentlessly as an avalanche, an earthquake, a flood to carry Linn into Blythe's arms one last time? Jesus, born to save mankind; Vicky, born to save her father. But if he wouldn't be saved, if he never wrote back, Linn would be responsible for Vicky's devastating disappointment. Linn would have to heal her beautiful child's pain, both acute and chronic. Vicky, a little Charlotte Brontë to Blythe's M. Heger.

"Oh God," Linn wailed.

Linn had flagellated herself understandably but needlessly. Vicky ran out to meet her as she was coming home two days later, waving a letter. After that, a letter always came a few days after Vicky's return to Blythe. Linn allowed Vicky to read the first one out loud. She had that much curiosity. Subsequently she suggested the letters were private—just between her and her father—as she had said before, but Vicky was always excited and wanted to share. Linn allowed her to tell her things now and then. Over time Linn heard about Scotland, Germany, and San Francisco.

Vicky made herself a wallpapered shoebox and inside, tied with a ribbon, she kept Blythe's letters. She made one for him and sent it along with Linn, who slipped it into his room when she knew he wasn't there. He was just coming back down the hall from the shower room and saw her.

"Doctor Walcott," he called out. "I have an appointment with you. Now." The last word was loud and compelling. Linn stopped and turned around slowly, trying to wish away the knife going through her. She had not seen this face since the night in 'Chrosite when he found her napping on his bed. "Step into my room, or we're going to have a scene in the hall."

"What on earth about?" She didn't carry off the superior, condescending tone she wanted.

"You know damn well what about," Blythe hissed. Linn was

afraid if she turned her back on him he would push her right into his room, so she backed in feeling trapped and angry.

After he closed the door, he turned on her. "You didn't bring my child back to me. I will never forgive you for this. You didn't come back to 'Chrosite even after you knew you were going to have her. You denied me my daughter for nine years. Nine years of her life." Linn closed her eyes and let his fire rage on. When he stopped she had nothing to say.

"Well?" he said at last. They stared at each other.

Finally she said, "I couldn't."

"Why in hell not?" His voice began rising again.

"I don't care to revisit all the reasons."

"Goddamn it. It would have made all the difference."

Here we go again, she thought. She shook her head. "No, it wouldn't."

"You don't know that. You don't know what went on in my mind. How I would have changed."

"Of course not. You never told me what went on in your mind. Don't let's start that. I'm finished with it. I'm finished with 'Chrosite and with you. I like my new life. I don't want to revisit the old."

"And another thing. Why didn't you tell me Floyd Hunt threatened you?"

She was unnerved at the change of subject and by the subject itself. She had almost forgotten Floyd Hunt. But the answer came out the same.

"And what would you have done? Asked him nicely to leave your wife alone because she's too busy taking on all the work of the medical practice to have to be frightened by a bully like you? You weren't being a husband or a protector in any way. Why should I have expected it of you?"

"You've said it all, haven't you."

"No, I haven't. I have a lot more locked away. Don't tempt me."

"Perhaps I will someday. It might be good for you." He almost smiled, but it was just a ghost.

Linn took a deep breath and wrapped herself in her arms to keep from flying apart. "And who told you about Floyd? I suppose it was he himself after I left. So proud of himself."

"No, it was Maudie. When I couldn't find you, I imagined what he might have done. I confronted him, and he laughed. *Laughed.* And you told Maudie but not me. I will never forgive you for that either."

"Then we will be equal in never forgiving things." He was silent, she was exhausted. "Look," she said, picking up the decorated box from the foot of his bed. "This is from Vicky. Try to be happy you have her now." She pushed the box into his hands, turned, and escaped.

—Mama, Daddy said there are so many ships in San Francisco. I wonder whether I'll ever see a ship or the ocean.

—I hope so.

— Mama, Daddy has been in castles.

—Mmm. Prince Charming.

—Mama, Daddy sent me a whole page of fraction problems. Will you help me?

—Only if you get stuck.

—Mama, Daddy had a horse that was related to President Jefferson's mare named Silver Tail. I would like to learn to ride a horse.

— That's a good idea.

—Mama, Daddy drew a map of the town he lived in up in the mountains and where everything is there.

Linn fumed silently, *The nerve.*

Linn was giving her standard talk to a new patient. We will take care of you in every way. Your job is to relax and let in the idea of healing. Drink your milk, eat everything you are given. Soak up the sun, the views of the mountains, the gardens, the pond. Rest when it's time to rest, and exercise in a few weeks or a month or whenever we determine it's good for you to begin. Everything will be all right, but it is up to you to keep a positive attitude. Attitude, that's the key. Yes, we have our schedule…two, three four. Yes, we have our rules…two, three, four. You may not like them at first, but they are what's best. Just relax and breathe…two, three; out, two, three. Here is a form. Record your temperature every morning and evening. Make checkmarks in the little squares when you have milk or eggnog, meat, vegetables, sweets. Write down how long your naps are and how many hours you sleep at night. Be honest.

A nurse from the men's ward came into the room. Her lips were pursed; she was not relaxed, nor did she have a positive attitude. "Doctor Walcott, the *other* Doctor Walcott wants to see you as soon as possible. Actually that's not quite how he put it," she said, shooting Linn a look as if Linn were responsible for Blythe's behavior.

Linn could not mask her annoyance with a cool professional nod. "Oh, my," escaped her.

The nurse whispered back, shaking her head, "He's impossible again."

Linn whispered back, "In a minute," while her internal voice set up a protest: *Damn, damn, damn.*

On her way down the hall, her heart began to pick up its pace, and she felt little fear prickles in her stomach. What could have come over him now? Everything had been going so well—meaning she hadn't spoken to him since their confrontation half a year before.

He was leaning against his doorframe and might as well have been tapping his foot in impatience. When he caught sight of Linn, he raised an arm and waved it toward his room. *Like Custer urging his troops forward,* Linn thought, *and must I be one of them?* Anger washed over her. He was commanding her in demanding this interview. The nerve, the gall. She didn't care that her face was set and her eyes hostile when she walked in. He didn't say hello or thank you for coming. *There are so many things he never said,* she thought.

He waved a piece of paper at her—a letter from Vicky. "She has the measles. Why didn't you tell me?" His voice low and explosive, but at least he wasn't shouting.

"She's telling you. And by the way, I don't read either of your letters."

"I don't care what you do. I want to know more about her. How is she? Is she feverish? Is she lucid? Is she—this can be terrible. It can be…" He trailed off, turned, and went to his sunporch door to stare out.

"She's fine. Just normal. It's been going around school. You know those springtime epidemics. Last year it was chicken pox."

He turned back to her and seemed to swell and burst. "Just normal!"

They stared at each other—her eyes hooded and hard, his wide and accusing. Then his chest heaved, and Linn saw a film of tears just before he turned away again. She did not understand, so she tried on him something that encouraged her own patients when she felt they were holding back. "What more would you like to tell me?" Asking outright whether there was anything more always brought forth an immediate no.

He was silent, then in a raspy voice said, "My sister."

"Vicky looks like her."

He nodded. "She died." His voice was flat. "Of measles. He said it was my fault. I brought it home from school. If Vicky has the same course, if she…there would be no life for me."

"Why didn't you ever tell me? Blythe, it wasn't your fault. And who is 'he'?"

"My father. My doctor father. I got sick, then she did. I got well, she didn't. He never forgave me. His little girl. Now I understand."

Emotion welled up in Linn. She took a few steps toward him, yet she could not comfort him, her *bête noire*, except through words, and probably not through those either, but she tried. "Truly, it wasn't your fault. Please don't worry about Vicky."

He turned her way again, and the past dissolved for a heartbeat, perhaps two.

"If she turns…" He trailed off.

"Of course."

"Would you allow me to see her if…"

"Certainly."
"Thank you."
She nodded. She took no joy in her having everything and his having two letters a week to cling to.

The measles passed.

—*Mama, Daddy says we can go to baseball games. Is he getting better?*
—*Yes, a little.*

—*Mama, Daddy sent me a list of books to read.*
—*That's very nice.*
—*He agrees I should learn to ride horses.*
—*Good.*

And so the pattern went for two years. Little by little Blythe gained weight and optimism. He ate the prescribed diet, and he sat in the sun. His temperature returned to normal. He read, and he wrote to Vicky. Dix bragged about him to Linn, and she made the appropriate responses. She caught rare glimpses of Blythe before he melted away. One day they could not avoid each other, and though they didn't speak, she saw something new in his eyes. Perhaps he wanted to say, "You saved my life," and wouldn't. She dreaded what his return to health meant: in a number of months, Blythe Walcott would be released from Maimonides and come knocking on her door.

Dix was ebullient the day Blythe transferred from the main hospital to one of the cottages. The inevitable was about to occur.

Linn liked to have time to herself first thing in the morning to sit at her desk reviewing each of her patients: her progress, her setbacks, her needs both physical and emotional. Most of the physicians on staff looked askance when Linn brought up a patient's mental state unless she was about to go psychotic and hurt someone. Linn ignored her colleagues because she knew she was right.

While she turned the pages of her personal patients' notebook, she sensed a shadow at her door, which she never closed. No one ever just wandered into this corner of the second floor. She stifled a startle when she realized Blythe Walcott stood in the doorway, but she was afraid her face showed exactly what she felt. She knew why he was here and dreaded it. She had tried not to think about it ever since she started seeing him going to and coming from the laboratory building and not from the direction of the patients' cottages. He was no longer under hospital care.

Linn waited for him to ask to come in; she did not invite him.

"May I have a few minutes?" he asked softly.

"Yes, you may."

He came in and looked around. He eyed her overloaded bookshelves, the big bouquet of homegrown tulips, the pile of charts on the floor keeping company with a stack of journals. She didn't care what he thought. She waited a few more seconds and then suggested he sit down. There was some color in his face, whether from the sun or the effort this visit made. His hair was grayer.

"Now that I'm well and respectable"—a pause—"again, I'd like to meet my daughter." He was looking straight at her. "I have a job with Jean-Marc. I'm not living here anymore."

Linn could think of nothing in reply. She looked idly at her desk while her emotions roiled. She couldn't deny him, but she didn't want to make it easy for the man who had not been there for birthing, feeding, diapering, and nursing through an illness. Never mind he hadn't the opportunity.

"May I come this Saturday afternoon?"

Oh, no, not so soon, and yet like an angry wound, it must be seen to. "All right. What time?"

"Two."

She didn't want to chaperone at her own house.

He read her mind. "I'll take her to the park or something."

"She has some library books due. You can take her there as well."

"Is ice cream OK?"

"Yes, but listen, she might ask you for something special that I've said no to, though she's really not that kind of girl. She wants a puppy. Don't come home with one."

"No more Argos?"

Linn flared immediately—she was that close to the limit of control. "He was a wonderful dog. He was Vicky's nanny. He loved her."

Blythe pursed his lips and shook his head in mock dismay.

"He did." She hated herself for overreacting but could not stop. "He saved my life."

"He did not. He provoked that cat, and you know it. And it was probably actually a bobcat, in spite of what you believe."

"You never liked him."

Blythe stood up. "We were in love with the same woman, and he won." Absorbing her stunned expression, he took a stride to her desk, rapped it as if to call this session to an end, said, "Two on Saturday," and walked out.

16

VICKY AND BLYTHE. BLYTHE AND VICKY. VICKY AND CHINESE noo-
dles. It was love at first sight. After school was out for the summer,
he began coming for her more often. He took her to the boarding
house common room and taught her to play gin rummy, Russian
Bank, and poker. They began going to Bears baseball games, where
he taught her the strategy of the bunt, the intentional walk, and the
well-placed single as opposed to swinging for the fences. She got
a crush on the catcher and read the game summaries every morning
in the *Rocky Mountain News*. He began teaching her mathematics
somewhat above her grade level and bragged about her to Jean-Marc,
who was not impressed and saw no reason for females to have this
knowledge and said so.

When Linn first heard about their going to Chinatown, she
followed Blythe out onto the front porch and demanded to know,
in a quiet hiss, why he had taken Vicky to such a dangerous place.
All he said was that he had friends there. Linn complained about
the boarding house.

"What kind of people? People who use salty language."

"Your own language wasn't always so pure. And two of the res-
idents at my place were your patients."

"That doesn't make them angels," Linn said. "And poker!
A barroom game. This is the limit."

"She's learning a lot," he said. "Are you going to forbid it?"

Linn just shook her head, but she felt keenly her position was
being threatened. She was simply jealous and could not help it.

Vicky was blossoming as never before. How could Linn isolate her from Blythe now? But she demanded he not call Vicky on the telephone. She did not want her party line to know more than they already suspected.

She forbade one place: Blythe's laboratory. Vicky would see the cages of rabbits and guinea pigs and be upset—not to mention the number of live cultures he must have there. So he brought a microscope and light source to the boarding house. They looked at City Park pond water, and they made fingerprint impressions on plain agar to see what would grow.

One day Vicky came home with the news that a former officer in the Confederate Army had moved into the boarding house, and he and Blythe had talked about the war and hospitals and wounds.

"It sounded horrible, Mama."

Linn said little, but this piece of news stuck in her mind. She could not reconcile it with what she knew.

In August Vicky and Blythe took a picnic to City Park and lay on a blanket after dark to watch the Perseids meteor shower. They checked out a book on the stars and found Sagittarius in the southern summer sky. When he showed her how the Big Dipper rotated around the Pole Star, Vicky told him she already knew that. "Mama and I always look for the Big Dipper."

One of Blythe's friends at the boarding house could recite Edward Lear, and Vicky loved "The Owl and the Pussycat." One day, Vicky brought home a box. Inside was a brown tabby kitten with a big purr and such comical white face markings Linn couldn't say no. Vicky named her Louisa May.

"Louisa May Walcott, get it, Mama?"

When baseball season was over and the days were shorter and colder, Blythe brought an infernal jigsaw puzzle. He and Vicky set up a card table in the corner of the living room and agonized over colors, shapes, and Louisa May's knocking pieces onto the floor. Linn never quite remembered how it came about that he was spending more time in her house. Gradually and insidiously, Blythe's presence invaded her life and her mind. She stayed out of their way to the extent that she didn't feel like a prisoner in her own home. Sometimes she floated in and out of their concentration. She had good eyes, though she was not fond of puzzles. The first several times she saw the place for a piece and put it in, Vicky moaned, but one evening when Linn picked a piece from the floor and found its home, Vicky said, "Mama, if Daddy lived here, we could all work on this more often." In the silence that followed, Blythe seemed to think he saw more pieces on the floor.

17

It had been a ninety-plus-degree day again with no thunderstorms to give relief. In spite of taking off her corset and petticoat and putting on a loose cotton dress, Linn was sweaty and cranky. The red brick house had been absorbing heat for three days, and no breezes had come in the windows. These spells put the patients in a foul mood as well, and Linn had had to be particularly careful not to exacerbate their edginess with her own. She wished she could be like Louisa May and spend daytimes in the cellar and evenings under a shrub.

Linn was working at the dining room table when Vicky burst in and danced over to her. Linn felt even warmer just to look at her.

"Bears won! Bears won! Carl Block hit two home runs." She took a batting stance and swung. At least the antics provided a little air movement.

"And you're too excited to think about bed."

Vicky nodded, dancing on her toes.

"Well, it's too hot anyway. Maybe Daddy and you can read to each other. Take the kerosene lantern out to the porch. It's cooler there."

"Eeew, no," Vicky protested. "Millers."

"I haven't seen one for weeks, honey. They've gone to the mountains."

Vicky stood her ground.

"All right," Linn said. "Bed at one hundred degrees upstairs or a book on the porch."

"OK," Vicky drawled out. "I'll get my nightie on." She sauntered upstairs.

Blythe, who had been hanging back at the front door, came to the opposite side of the table and looked upside-down at the papers spread out in front of Linn.

"Dix has you working at home as well?"

She sighed. "I shouldn't in this heat. It just makes me grouchy, but there's so much data." She swept a hand over the papers and record books. "Dix wants to correlate time to recovery—or not—with all kinds of symptoms: age, weight, length of time from diagnosis, you name it." Linn sighed again.

Blythe came around to her side of the table and leaned over to look at her work.

"In some patients it's straightforward," she said, "Then there's, well, you for example, falling off my charts." She turned toward him. His face was closer than she expected, and their eyes caught and stayed.

"That's because you saved my life," he said quietly and brushed her cheek with his fingertips.

Vicky came rocketing down the stairs and broke the spell. Blythe straightened up to greet her. Linn put on a big smile, but she was lost. She watched the two of them go into the kitchen for the lamp then out the front door. She dropped her head into her arms. She did not want to be drawn to him. The box was closed, but his eyes had been right outside it, and his lips inches away.

She pushed back from the table, her mind too disordered for statistics, and went into the kitchen for more ice water. She leaned against the drainboard trying to settle her feelings. That touch. It had been eleven years, and against old tears and anger, she struggled to make her mind a blank.

Eventually, Vicky broke the reverie for a goodnight kiss. Blythe tarried, kissed Vicky, and sent her upstairs. Linn stared at the floor. She hoped he would just leave, but he didn't. He came into the kitchen. Linn kept her eyes down.

"Forgive me. I stepped over the line."

Heat rose up her spine. Not the heat of fear she had felt on the Florentine or in front of the mountain lion; this was a fuse burning up to the black powder she saw explode in her head and burst the box. Her head came up.

"Then don't ever, ever, ever do it again," she spat. "You will never change. I will never change." She brought her clenched hands to her breast. "You care, you love me, you'll change, you make love to me, you leave, up, down, here, there, sorry, sorry, sorry. Drunk, sober, in bed for days abandoning everything to your perversity." Her voice was rising and it alarmed her, but she couldn't stop. "And you've done it again. To me, maybe that's one thing." She glared at him. "But I swear if you ever break Vicky's heart, promising and failing, loving and leaving, I will stab you through your heart. And you know I know how to find the right spot."

She was wringing her hands now, clasping and unclasping them on her arms. Anger, frustration, years of silence—nothing could make the jack go away now that he was out of the box. She needed to scream at him, punish, and wound Blythe as he had her.

"You left me standing in some whore's bedroom. You went right from my bed to that, that—creature. You walked away and closed the door." She nearly broke down, but she had to finish. "A blue door. And I closed the door on you. Why did you have to come back?" Her voice was nearly a scream by now, which brought Vicky downstairs and Flora in from the back porch where she had been talking with her beau. The four of them stood in the kitchen, all frightened. Vicky's wide eyes stared at Linn. Linn walked to Flora and sent her back outside. Blythe knew what to do with Vicky. He always did.

"Don't worry, kiddo," he said while he put an arm around her and turned her away, back into the dining room. "Mama got upset about something I did a long, long time ago. It's not about anything you did. You weren't even born then." He walked her back to the stairway. "I'm going to talk to Mama and try to make her feel better."

You can never do that, Linn wanted to holler after him.

"Wait," Blythe said to Vicky. He went outside, plucked Louisa May from a porch chair, and brought her back into Vicky's arms.

"Too hot for cats, Daddy," she protested.

"Take her. Give her some pets and let her stretch out on your bed. You'll feel better."

Vicky went up the stairs reluctantly.

"It's OK, it's OK," Blythe repeated, the way he would have soothed a spooked horse.

He came back into the kitchen.

"I don't want to hear it," Linn said, holding her palms out toward him. "Just go."

"We can't just drop this. We've both misbehaved. Let's sort it out."

"I haven't misbehaved." She took a step toward him. "I've held this in for years."

"But you frightened your child. It's my fault ultimately, and now it's time to hear me out."

"What could you possibly say—"

"A lot. Please. I had a long time to do nothing but think. I need to tell you."

She followed as he led her outside, but still she was on her guard against the same avowals and excuses he had made in 'Chrosite. They sat, each in a chair on either side of the lantern. It did not flicker. It put him into a glowing profile. She did not want to think how many times she had thrilled to the same sight.

He began by saying how wrong he had been never to have told the truth from the first.

He had not been sent abroad before the war started. He had been at home in Charlottesville and going to the university. When he was nineteen, his father, a doctor who had volunteered for the Confederate Army after the first shot was fired and a man intent on his only son's future as a physician, began taking him out to field hospitals well behind the lines. He knew Blythe would never acquire in a lecture hall knowledge like this: anatomy lessons on the living, pain relief such as it was, wound dressing, wound inflammation, wound suppuration, gangrene, amputation, saws, knives, needles, tinctures, salves, bone, brain, gut, blood, death.

"He thought I could take it. And I could. Until one day." They were southwest of the fighting, down the Orange Plank Road, when General Longstreet was brought in wounded, and everyone ran to him, remembering Stonewall Jackson being injured just one year ago. Amidst much fuss and flurry, Longstreet was sent off farther behind the lines. Blythe was helping dress wounds in a tent at the east end of the hospital encampment when a trickle and then a flood of patients in unspeakable condition poured in, screaming or in shock or dying. All burned. Blythe was among the first to confront this disaster. He froze—not only because he had no idea what to do, but because he was terrified by their pain. They might have been medieval torture victims who would not renounce their religion. The faces, the eyes, red and black, cloth both Union blue and Confederate gray stuck to tissue; buttons and buckles were seared into skin. He turned away in horror. In spite of everything he had already seen and done, he could not look at or help them. He ran, vomited, and hid.

His father was furious at not being able to find him. Here was an opportunity to learn about the most dreadful of injuries—and lots of them. Blythe hid out in a barn until hunger drove him back to camp. Word spread, and his father came roaring down on him. The punishment was that Blythe was to nurse the survivors. He began to cry—all this in front of a gathering, silent crowd. His father began berating him again and reminding him that boys younger than he was were out in the trenches fighting for their country.

Blythe sealed his fate by blurting out, "This isn't necessarily my country." The two Walcotts stared at each other for ever so long.

"By God then, you'll get out of my sight. Go home to your mother, you two Yankee lovers."

Eyes in the crowd hardened. Blythe wasted no time liberating a horse, and he was off, still dressed as a hospital orderly. When he met anyone, his purported mission was to catch up with Longstreet's party to hand over some misplaced medicine, but he veered off to Charlottesville. His mother hid him for the next eleven months. Once or twice his father came home and barely acknowledged him. When the war was over, Blythe was sent almost immediately to Edinburgh to university and medical training—excellent training.

Here Blythe stopped talking, but he did not turn to look at Linn. She dared not speak. After a long silence he began again. "All right," he said, "here's another story not told." He pressed his lips together as if that would keep the truth within him, but in the end it needed telling.

He didn't go home for nine years. He was a qualified physician. He liked Scotland and planned to stay. America had torn itself apart and him with it.

"But I came home because my wife and child died."

This was the last thing Linn expected, and a kind of empty, dizzy feeling passed through her. "Oh, Blythe. No," escaped her. She turned to look at him, but he still stared straight ahead. "Why didn't you ever tell me?" She put a hand on his arm. He seemed to be lost in memory. She pressed his arm again. "I'm so sorry," she said.

The baby had come early—placenta first, stillborn. It was a girl. The mother died shortly after. Blood was everywhere. "Now you understand what I said when you..."

He was alone with them, a physician, but he couldn't save them. Linn stifled the tears and a pain in her throat because this was Blythe's confession, not hers to dramatize.

He couldn't stay in Edinburgh, and he couldn't go home. He studied awhile longer in Europe before he went to the Colorado mines, where he could follow a seam to a whole new life. "I found you. You reminded me of her in many ways. In looks, from the first. But you were"—he looked for the right word—"strong. It didn't take long for me to realize you were yourself, not some recreated ideal. And she wasn't an ideal, in truth. She was a little older, more experienced in life. Perhaps I recognized some—I don't know how to put it—some infecundity in you. Is that a word? I didn't want any children."

Linn might have challenged him on that point but under the circumstances let it go.

At the St. Agnes, the fire and the burns turned him back into that boy. The horror and inadequacy settled onto him and would not rise. He heard his father's voice minute by hour by day reminding him he was a failure. Black moods sent him to bed or to drink or to that girl at Opal Faye's. At last he turned to Linn with a seriousness born of his years of self-examination and a confidence that he finally understood himself. The lantern lit him as it would a soliloquist, and his tone might have been saying, "Tomorrow and tomorrow and tomorrow leads this petty pace..."

He rarely slept with that girl; rather, he needed to be with someone who didn't judge him. She was soothing, empty headed, and loquacious. She expected nothing from him. At the same time, in his mind Linn assumed the role of the senior Walcott. What Linn felt now was too familiar, and she let out an audible breath. She thought she knew where this conversation was going, but she was wrong.

"No, no. Please let me get to the point. The more frantic you were, the worse I became because I despised myself and wanted you to despise me more. At the same time I was angry with you, and when you left I was furious. Now I really had something to hate you for. I buried your ring and said a curse over it."

Linn dropped her eyes to her clasped hands. "I took all I could take. I had to save my own life."

"You were right. No one could change me. I had to confront my own crazy thinking. I had to want to badly enough, and for a long time I didn't. Right now I want to apologize for cursing at you when Ivy died. I walked out of her room knowing I had nothing. And there you were, so admired, so accomplished, and I hope you won't get angry again if I say that you looked so beautiful. I didn't have you, and I didn't have her. I blamed everything I did on the fact I was a cowardly failure, and then..."

"Apology accepted. Then what?"

"Vicky. I thought I had lost everything and was about to lose my life, nor did I care. Then you told me about Vicky. Out of the blue I did have a reason to live, but not the way I had before, God forbid, on the off chance I would live to know her. So I thought that if I had no control over healing my body, I could try to heal my mind or somehow examine how it had been…hmm…leading me astray, betraying me. As I say, I had—surprisingly, given my failing body—a long time to think. I don't expect you to forget anything or to forgive me," he said, rising. "Just to try to understand."

"Yes," she said, "I will try."

"Can't ask for more than that." He gave a faint smile. She rose as well and stepped behind her chair, partly to let him pass to the porch steps and half-unconsciously as a defense against the Blythe Walcott who had just led her through his heart's dark secrets and out into the light.

Back in the house, Linn fell heavily into the big chair in the living room. Blythe's words bounced in her mind like an errant ball. *Fire. War. Wife. Blood and baby. Fire and father. War and wife. No. No. Wife had nothing to do with the war, except that it drove him away and to her. Warm slippery morphine. He'd had that with her. Had he coached her into it too? She was experienced. She taught him. So naïve. Had she heard the war stories? War. Fire. Screaming. I will never forget it. He hadn't either. He lived under the covers. He buried it and thought it was dead. He buried my ring and treated me as dead. The ring. Was it actually the Scottish woman's? A secondhand ring that had once flashed in the sunshine thousands of miles away. Secondhand Ivy. How many women he has lost: the baby; the wife; me; Ivy; his sister; probably his mother. He never talked about her. Losing Vicky would kill him. I told him not to or I would kill him. Burned soldiers, burned miners. Wouldn't explain, wouldn't say I'm sorry. In bed. I pounded on his back. What else did I do? It wasn't my fault. I wasn't the father who called him down in front of other people.*

No one could change me.

You reminded me of her in many ways. In looks, from the first. So I was just a substitute for poor dead Scottish woman. If I hadn't looked like her, I wouldn't be who and where I am today. I might have married my third cousin back in Normal and be the mother of ten. Thank you, Blythe, for pushing me off a cliff at the bottom of which I landed on my feet. The second cliff.

Was he having bad dreams about the war on those restless nights? How is it that I never really knew him? Did he ever really know me? While I was just being myself, he wanted me to be whatever-her-name-was, so he pushed me away after I picked up the pieces of the fire? Damn him for not knowing what he wanted. All that love, all that passion—was it really for me? He didn't say, did he? I want the good times to have had value, and there I go, sounding soft already. How can I forget the blue door?

The rhythm of circling thoughts lulled Linn to sleep until first light woke her, and she forced herself out of the chair and up to bed.

Ever since Blythe had begun working at the hospital, Linn had arranged her lunchtime in the staff dining room to avoid his. He went early, so in spite of sometimes being particularly hungry, she waited until near to closing. Now and then she would be surprised to find him still deep in a discussion with Jean-Marc or Dix or both. Jean-Marc always cornered the conversations, wagging a finger to indicate that any view other than his own deserved no credit at all. He was brilliant, but Linn usually tried to avoid him—more than ever after he took on Blythe.

Slowly, almost without her realizing a change, Linn began to feel softness around the edges of life. Perhaps her shoulders relaxed a bit, perhaps a smile came more easily, perhaps the locked box in her mind opened a little and made room for some light. She wouldn't say "I forgive you" to Blythe, because she hadn't. There was hardly an opportunity to speak about anything. He had stopped lingering at the house. Sometimes when he came for Vicky, she said, "Bye, Mama, Daddy's here," and was out the door before Linn could react.

Besides, Vicky was twelve years old and could strike off on her own to meet her father.

Linn, without analyzing it, wanted to signal to Blythe not a peace offering and certainly not to talk to him about anything personal but perhaps to say, "I'm trying to understand." She chose nothing more than to come to the dining room at random. The first time she sat down with Dr. Jerome and some interns, she resisted sweeping the room for him and was pleased with herself. A few weeks passed during which their eyes met momentarily several times from a table or two away. One day when she was almost too late to get food, there was only one group of diners left: Blythe, Dix, and Jean-Marc. She could not very well sit at the other end of the room. Blythe stood and pulled out a chair for her. The others continued talking, and she wondered whether Blythe felt the same slight thaw of the glacier that rested between them. At any rate, neither added much to the conversation. When the men stood up to leave and said their goodbyes, Blythe looked at her across the treacherous ice. "Nice to have lunch with you," he said with the slightest suggestion of a smile so like the ones he gave those first months in 'Chrosite.

One hot evening in late August, Vicky and Blythe invited Linn to go with them to the ice-cream store up on Colfax Avenue. Vicky and Blythe kept up a conversation about whether Flora and her beau might get married. Linn added little, but on the walk home Vicky went on ahead, engrossed in her double scoop.

"May I ask you something?" Blythe said.

"About…?"

"Vicky used to mention a Mr. Chernigov and Sonia in letters, but I haven't heard the name lately. Is Sonia his daughter?"

"Yes."

"And they live in Fort Collins, and you sometimes visited."

"Yes. We were friends from hospital days." *No*, she thought. *Do not offer information.*

"But not anymore?"

"He remarried."

"Oh." A long, drawn-out, knowing oh.

Linn forced herself not to respond.

"Before that you two were close friends."

"What do you mean by 'close'?" This was her chance to let Blythe see her in Solomon's bed, but she wasn't sure she wanted to anymore.

They had slowed their pace. He turned his head toward her, and she turned toward him with a trace of a wicked smile nevertheless.

He said, "I mean what you're telling me with that expression. I hope he made you happy. Enough said."

"He did. My turn," she said. "You said that nothing could have changed you, yet you also said that my being so hard on you made me even more a father figure and drove you farther away. I was rather in a bind, wasn't I?"

"You could have screamed at me every day or gone on your knees to me every day. It wouldn't have, couldn't have changed anything. It was all in me, but it was easier to burden everyone else. I was making you a villain, and I was completely wrong. "

"I've tried to understand," she said.

He acknowledged it. They walked on in silence, then Linn asked something else. "What was her name?"

He told her. "Elspeth."

"She's more real that way."

"The first time I saw you, I thought she was real again. But it was you who were real. I didn't know that at first. I still needed to save her by saving you."

"I wish you had told me. Couldn't I have been of some comfort about her and the baby?"

He ran a hand across her back to her shoulder and pressed it. "You were. You just didn't know it."

She resisted moving closer to him. She needed to keep talking to keep from feeling too much. "Will you tell me something? It may seem silly, but I can't help wondering."

"About what?"

"Did you keep her ring? Was my ring her ring?"

"God, no. Her ring was a family ring. They wanted it back. Yours was a virgin ring."

Linn felt her eyes sliding toward his as his did toward her.

"What made you ask that?"

"I got to thinking what a short time between, well"—she was going into deep water and hadn't seen the sign—"when you asked and the"—looking for a neutral word—"wedding."

"The week after the twins were born, I went over to Breckenridge and saw to its making."

"Oh. But you hadn't…we didn't…" Getting deeper.

"I had touched your skin; you drank in mine. You dropped the sheet you had wrapped up in. I'd been too afraid of frightening you before that. I thought the caring went all one way. I felt a change."

Memories of that time flooded out of the box and swam before her eyes. All she could say was "oh" again.

Vicky was waiting on the porch steps. Linn said a quick goodbye to Blythe, feeling as if she were almost running into the house. She opened the box lid just enough to push back the escaped sun, moon, and stars that he had been to her, once.

18

In the middle of October on a Friday evening, Blythe and Vicky worked late in her room on a school project, while Linn in the living room concentrated on a manuscript she was revising. The crack of a broken and falling tree branch and the whomp of its landing sent Louisa May off her lap and Linn to a window. A fast-moving autumn snow had quietly piled up on the leaves and limbs. Up and down the street, and all over the city, the limbs sagged in defeat at the hands of the inexplicable Colorado weather. Just now a wind picked up and brought large wet flakes slanting against the windows. Across the street another branch broke.

Blythe came downstairs and picked up his coat. It was lightweight, and he had no hat or gloves. The storm had come out of nowhere, but that could happen any autumn.

"Vicky sends you a goodnight kiss," he said.

"You can't go out that way," Linn said. "The snow is too wet, and the wind will cut right through your coat."

He protested he would be fine.

"You don't have enough body fat to keep a flea warm," she told him. "Stay here. You can sleep on the davenport or in the spare room."

He wouldn't stay. He would go.

"Limbs are falling."

They went a few more rounds of "yes" and "no" while she stood with her back firmly against the front door. With his hands on her shoulders, he tried to move her sideways. He was stronger than she expected. She tried to push him away amidst more "just stays" and "nos" and pushing back, but their stars said that when they stood this close, their arms must go around each other. Their lips brushed, questioned, clung softly at first then deeply and perhaps a little awkwardly before settling into the familiar: *I remember you. Where were you when I needed you? I remember all of you.* They put paid to a dozen years of kisses owed, and when he was sure they were in the black, Blythe said, "Now you see why I can't stay here? I don't want to sleep on your davenport or in the spare room, and where I want to sleep, well, it may be legal, but it's not right."

"I don't care." She pressed against him.

"Yes, you do. And keep these to yourself." He took her hands away from their running up and down his neck and across his shoulders, kissed them, and tucked them under his chin.

Yes, she did care. Suppose she lured him—and she thought she could—to the davenport or her bedroom. Too much lay between them to lie down together now. They would rise ashamed and embarrassed, unable to meet each other's eyes. He would leave, and next time they met, they would be cool and impersonal— perhaps forever.

"I know you're right, but we're both free. Is that what you mean about legal?"

He frowned quizzically. "Would you prefer to be free?"

It was her turn to be confused. "I didn't have a choice, did I?"

He looked at her silently, then a light came into his eyes and he smiled. "You believed Ivy, then?"

"About what?"

"She wanted to be respectable. Have you ever seen her gravestone?"

"I never go over there."

"It doesn't say Walcott."

They stared at each other. When Linn understood, all she could say was "oh." She took her hands from his and put them up to her face. "Oh, no."

"Oh yes," Blythe said. "For better or worse, for richer or poorer, in sickness and in health." He grimaced. "I guess we've punched those tickets."

One ticket was left, and she knew in a flash, in the warmth of his presence, the glow of his kisses, and the love he showered on their child, that she alone held this ticket. She wanted to use it now.

"Come," she said, drawing him into the living room. She seated him in the big armchair and herself on the davenport at right angles to it. In her haste and passion, she began wrong footed, circuitously, and fell right into trouble.

"Blythe, you know Vicky loves you best in the world, and you love her more than anyone, and…"

He held up a hand. "There is someone I love more than I love Vicky."

Linn had been looking at the floor in front of her, not at him, because she was afraid of what she was saying. He still had warm, soft eyes, but she heard only the words and was devastated, furious.

She leapt up and spat at him, "Then you can just go out into the snow to her." She pointed at the door she had just been defending.

He rose from the chair, lowered her arm, and holding onto it, said, "She's not out in the snow." He allowed her to take her arm back. "Who do you think I love best in the world?"

She dared not suggest Elspeth. "How should I know?"

"Who do you *imagine* I love more than anyone?" They stared at each other.

"Me?" she tendered in a whisper.

"Didn't I tell you once I fell in love with you almost at first sight? I loved you for someone you weren't and then loved you for who you really were. I loved you when I was making you miserable at my worst in 'Chrosite. I loved you when I was cursing you in the hospital. When there was Ivy, it was you, even while you dripped ice over me for ever so long when I came to see Vicky."

"And I," she said, still afraid but plunging on, "have been fighting falling back in love with—just imagine—my own husband."

231

He leaned his forehead against hers. "Do you know when I had the first hope of that, or at least that you had a bit of feeling left?"

She rubbed her head no against his.

"That night you let loose on me and said 'I will never change,' speaking of yourself."

"I so loved the person you were. I can't forget that. And I've come to love the person you are now because of Vicky. How you are with her. How happy she is. There's just that middle part."

"And you know I can't come to live here, if I understand what you were suggesting, and just ignore what happened then. The past is the past, sitting like a crouching tiger, no matter how we are in bed. We don't have just a rough patch anymore. Linn, do you forgive me?"

"I've been working toward it, trying to understand, and I haven't forgotten yet—especially that morning at Opal Faye's."

"Good, because I haven't forgiven myself, and if you had forgiven me, I would think less of you. I'd believe that you were emotionally shallow, that you don't care much about me even if you say you love me."

"Honestly, I don't know whether I cared about you when I left 'Chrosite, but I cared about us. There wasn't such a thing anymore."

"We will never know whether there could have been if you had come back. That thought haunts me. That you didn't want to try."

"I still say I never would have, and you're still carrying that anger. We have a lot to talk about. Let's sit down." She put her hand on the arm of his chair. He covered it with his.

"Where do you want to begin?" he asked.

"At the beginning. At the fire. Do you remember what I did and what you did?"

"Tell me your version first."

And so she did, because it had been burned into her memory just as the Wilderness Fire had been burned into his. They talked until after midnight.

Eventually Linn said, "I just need a little sleep," as she rested her head on the arm of the davenport.

She woke to a golden-pink light working softly through the living room window and along the fireplace wall. She looked for Blythe, but the chair was empty. She raised her head to look at the chairs in the corner and the piano stool. A sick feeling coursed through her. After all the talk and promises, he was gone. She wanted to cry. She called herself a fool. She would never, never trust him again in spite of his declarations of love.

Almost at first sight.

When I was making you miserable.

Yes, she thought, *you certainly do that.* She clenched her teeth and got up from the davenport. The pink light glowed, and the bit of sky she could see was rose gold. The pocket door to the front hall was closed. *Well, that was nice of him before he left.* She walked into the hall from the rear living room door and nearly screamed. The pink coming through the oval front-door window silhouetted the figure of a man. She steadied herself on the hall wall and caught her breath, her heart going sixty miles an hour. It was Blythe looking out. He heard her and turned. She walked toward him and relaxed. He kissed her, and they turned to look outside. The ground was littered with downed limbs, branches, and six inches of snow. Leaves had been beaten and blown by the wind on top of it, but it was beautiful as the sun rose through its horizon and painted the snow pink and pinker. The whole sky was pink.

"I thought you had left."

"I don't do those kinds of things anymore. Will you trust me?"

"I'll try."

"Come," he said and led her to the kitchen. "Where do you keep the mistrust?"

"Keep it?"

"In your head, your heart, the tips of your fingers?" He raised her hands to his mouth and kissed each fingertip. "Let's do an unorthodox medical procedure." He cupped his hands and held them to her head. "Let it all flow."

She began to laugh, and he said, "This is serious," but he was smiling. After about a minute, he moved his hands to the sink and washed and dried them.

"Gone," he said. "Where else? In your heart?" He cupped his hands between her breasts.

"Are you doing this so you can touch me there?"

"Of course," he said. He washed and dried his hands again. "That should do it for now. Let me know if we need to repeat."

"I feel better already."

"Here's something I don't feel very good about."

"Tell me."

"So suppose we talk out the past and have learned to live with it, but there's a present that wounds my masculine pride, my status as the breadwinner, my patriarchal prerogative."

"Your *what*?" She couldn't help laughing.

"All right, I'm joking about that last bit. But seriously, you own this nice house, you make a good salary, you go to money-raising dinners for the hospital, your photograph is in the newspaper. My salary is not big enough for me even to have a dinner-going suit. I would be here at your discretion."

"Did I live with you in 'Chrosite at your discretion? Would you have turned me out when the list of my sins reached a certain threshold?"

"Didn't have any sins."

"Until…" They were silent, as if they had reached a dead end. Finally she said, "The next airing out and more washing out should be about trust and mistrust, and that you think I might want you to leave. I remember so many times when you did leave for days. And you can't forget that I did leave."

"Are we in earnest together about this?"

"Absolutely. Especially for Vicky. How terrible she would feel if we began raging about the past when she expected a happy present and future. Not just expected—we would be promising her."

"Promise."

"Yes."

He looked at the floor. She fired up the stove to make coffee. When she turned back to him, he said, "I have something of yours. It's time to give it back." He reached into his watch pocket, brought out the watch, and detached something from the chain. He picked up her left hand and placed her wedding ring in her palm.

Linn's eyes grew wide. "Oh, Blythe." She was breathless. "You said you buried it." She picked up the ring and turned it around and around in her fingers, watching it sparkle in the morning light coming in the kitchen window. She had loved it. She had almost gone back for it as she went out the front door of the house in 'Chrosite, but she wanted it to leave the message that she was gone. Not on a call or an errand. Not over to Maudie's. She was gone. From him. And so she had left it.

"I dug it up before I left 'Chrosite. I've been carrying it ever since."

"Oh, Blythe," she said again and clenched the ring hard in her palm. "Take the curse off. We'll have enough to contend with without that. "

"I did, but just in case…" He laughed and recited in his best Scottish lines that were remarkably like those once written to a mouse. They smiled into each other's eyes. "It's been blessed and it's been cursed, but now it's my pledge that whether it takes a hundred years, whether we have to stay awake until midnight every Friday night to talk it out, I'm not going to give up on you and me."

Linn took her own watch out of its pocket, opened the clasp, and slipped the ring onto the chain with the rhodochrosite inclusions. "Two things you gave me in 'Chrosite." She held them up.

"Don't forget the third. The most valuable."

She smiled at him. Talking together like this could be easy and agreeable, the old life not threatening the new life.

"You know, if it takes a hundred years, you won't ever have lived with Vicky and watched her grow up day by day and made breakfast for her on Sundays."

"We need to speed it up then," Blythe said.

"If little by little we lowered the anger, softened the resentment, fogged the memory, studied forgiveness…"

"Sounds like something out of a book."

"One of those Europeans."

"You read them?"

"To put myself to sleep."

"I can do better than that."

"No fair," she said moving across the room. "Tell me what you did the day I left."

"You tell too."

"I promise," she said.

Acknowledgments

The glimmer of this book began in the mid-1960s, when part of my job in the microbiology laboratory at Saint Joseph Hospital in Denver, Colorado, was to look at "TB smears." These were glass slides covered with samples of sputum specimens and stained to make the mycobacteria (the causative agent of tuberculosis is *Mycobacterium tuberculosis*) stand out. My mind wandered during the three-times-across-each-slide examination. This story had its genesis in that tedium. I should be grateful that my supervisor, the late Sara Wilde Andersen, assigned me that task.

It was a serendipitous day that the late J. Kenneth McClatchy, PhD, hired me to work in the Mycobacteriology Laboratory at National Jewish Hospital (now National Jewish Health). Mycobacteriology was no longer dull (I didn't have to look at the smears). There were highly drug-resistant cultures all around me, and I learned to have respect for this ancient enemy of mankind.

In that laboratory I worked with many dedicated people who knew what they were doing, liked it, and stayed on the job for years. In the mid-1980s, the late Leonid Heifets, MD, PhD, asked me to work on a research project in the same lab. I was lucky to have him as a mentor, and we went on to write a number of scientific, peer-reviewed papers on antimicrobial action on mycobacteria. Dr. Heifets's friendship and generosity meant so much to me. The saying to the effect that it is a blessing to be at one with your work applied to my years at National Jewish.

Thanks to National Jewish physician Michael D. Iseman, MD, who lent me insightful books about physician scientists.

This story could not have taken shape without the Western History Collection at the Denver Public Library; a reader cannot regret losing a whole day in its books. Thanks as well to the Multnomah County Library in Portland, Oregon, and the Reeves Medical Library at Cottage Hospital in Santa Barbara, California.

My editor, Kristen Hall-Geisler of Indigo Editing & Publications, the master of commas, was kind and smart in her suggestions for making my story come together in the best possible way. Thanks to other Indigo staff—Susan DeFreitas, Ali McCart, and Vinnie Kinsella—who assisted from start to finish.

Jenny Jo Graham and Natalie Roesch read early chapters and planted some excellent ideas—who knew that Oscar Wilde went to Leadville!

Without Tom Bissell's class at Portland State University, this story would not be what it is. Tom said to give writing everything you have. I hope I have. Thanks for letting me in your class. Natan Meir, PhD, professor of Judaic Studies at Portland State, helped me with the creation of Solomon Chernigov. Meir's book, *Kiev*, was invaluable.

Judith Trutt, friend and neighbor, gave me the Yiddish. *A sheynem dank*.

Isabella Bird, I wanted you in the story. Maybe I found you in Linn, though she could only look at Long's Peak, not climb it in a skirt.

Thanks to my family for encouragement, and especially to my husband, Larry Levy, for reading the manuscript and understanding all the times I disappeared into my computer.

About the Author

Pamela Lindholm-Levy, a native Oregonian, lived and worked in Denver, Colorado, for forty years. While working and raising two children, she received a master's degree in biology from the University of Colorado. Her job in the "TB Lab" at National Jewish in Denver provided the real-life education behind *Count the Mountains*, while deeply felt and well-remembered seasons in Colorado painted the backdrop for it.

She lives in Portland, Oregon, with her husband, Larry Levy.

CPSIA information can be obtained
at www.ICGtesting.com
Printed in the USA
FSOW02n1536111215
14032FS